GEARED FOR LOVE

KACI LANE

Copyright © 2023 by Kaci Lane

All rights reserved.

This is a work of fiction. Names, characters, organizations, places, events and incidents are either products of the author's imagination or are used fictitiously. Any resemblance to actual persons, living or dead, or actual events is purely coincidental.

No part of this work may be reproduced, or stored in a retrieval system, or transmitted in any form by any means without written permission from the author.

*For my friend, Brittany, who always has
a story to share.*

GEARED FOR LOVE

CHAPTER ONE

Daisy

"You're one goat away from never getting married."

I chug my Gatorade to try and combat the bitter taste created by Adrianne's comment. The beauty about our friendship is that we can speak freely and tell one another the honest truth. But sometimes, the truth can be ugly.

My silence speaks volumes as our other friends exchange awkward looks. With impeccable timing, Mullet saunters up to me and nudges my knee.

Adrianne reads the room and tries to retract her statement. "All I meant by that is you don't want to get a reputation of being a crazy goat lady. That's all."

I nod and half smile. If it were just the two of us, I'd make some sarcastic jab about how she met and married her husband. But Bianca, Carolina, Hannah, and Ashley are here. Plus, it's more fun to play the victim and watch her grovel.

Before Adrianne can dig her grave any deeper, all eyes cut toward the front door. I follow my friends' gazes to none other than our county sheriff standing in my doorway.

"Is it hot in here?" Bradley fans his face with his signature tan cowboy hat.

"Sorry about that. The AC isn't working right. I've got a guy coming tomorrow," I say.

He doesn't respond with words, but rather pulls out his phone and turns on music. Everyone but me starts laughing when he moves his hand toward his belt. I'm so used to him posing with his hands on his hips that I don't realize what's coming until his shirt hits me in the face.

It slides into my lap as I blink. That few seconds is all the time Bradley needs to cross the room to me. Everyone laughs and smiles as he sets his cowboy hat on my head and winks.

"Happy birthday, Miss Daisy Mae."

Adrianne cackles beside me. When she calms down enough to speak, she elbows me and announces, "Gotcha!"

Bradley turns and shakes his butt in my face. I pull his hat over my eyes, causing everyone to laugh harder. My face heats up, as I'm mortified beyond measure.

I massage people for a living. I massage people for a living. All kinds of people—old, heavyset, and old heavyset people—and they're all shirtless. But none of them shake their tush in my face.

Perhaps I should count my blessings that it's only Bradley.

Wait, is he twerking? Never mind.

I stand in an attempt to abandon my position, but my short stature does me no favors. He spins around, and I bump into his chest. My friends giggle as Bradley jiggles his upper body. I wince when his pecs pop in and out like they have their own pulse.

There's no way out, so I sit down and grit my teeth until

he backs away. He takes his hat from my head and fans it around in what I assume he would call a seductive dance. I'm so used to goats butting stuff around and roosters puffing up their feathers that it will take much more to impress me.

Ashley, on the other hand, seems captivated by his performance.

She and I are the only single women left in the room. At least, I think she's single. She and Samuel are on a break so often that I've taken a break from keeping up with their status.

Bradley does a little two-step toward the door and bows. Everyone claps, including me—mainly out of relief it's over.

He takes his shirt from where it fell and tips his hat toward me. "Miss Daisy, happy birthday."

"Thanks," I muster through heated cheeks.

He disappears through my front door, and I let out a sigh of relief. Now that he's renting Adrianne's old house down the road, I can think of an easy revenge. Something to do with chicken poop.

Adrianne's voice near my ear cuts through everyone's chatter. "Sorry about the whole goat thing. I had to find a way to distract you to keep you in one place."

I narrow my eyes. "Just when I thought my birthday gathering was a ruse for a goat intervention, the intervention was a ruse for a sheriff striptease."

Adrianne giggles. "Daisy, you're so funny."

Too bad I didn't find the goat comment funny, or the striptease. Thank God, he stopped at his shirt.

"And sorry about Bradley. I could tell that embarrassed you."

"I'm not used to men ripping off their shirts and shaking their butts in my face."

Adrianne cocks a smile. "Well, just wait until you're married."

I snort. Is that what marriage is like? I'm so behind when it comes to men. I've never even had a *real* kiss. Unless you count the time Mullet licked my face when my mouth was open, which I don't.

In high school, I had a crush on all the same guys other girls did. Except those guys dated girls like Adrianne, not girls with pink hair and bell bottoms. That left me debating whether to turn down the few oddballs asking me out or sit in the corner and pine away over the athletes.

Now that my hair is a color God intended for human hair and bell bottoms are coming back in style, I've thought more and more about finding someone.

"Happy birthday to you," Ashley starts singing in an opera tone as she wheels a cake in on one of my massage carts.

My nerves tighten as I stare at the cake and everyone joins her in singing. Two candles sparkle in the center of a delicious strawberry cake. One is a 2 and the other an 8. Twenty-eight. I've known this day was coming all my life, but seeing it literally flash before my eyes sets my wheels in motion.

That's only two years until my thirties. Before I know it, the numbers will be flipped, and I'll be eighty-two.

I suck in a breath to try and calm my worries. Just in time for Ashley to shove the cake under my nose so I can exhale and blow out the candles. The girls clap and cheer.

As Ashley moves the cake, I scan the room, smiling at each of my friends. Also noting that four out of five have diamonds on their ring fingers. If Ashley would quit wasting her time with Samuel, she could settle down too. That would leave me with a bunch of goats, chickens, and candles.

Maybe there's more truth to Adrianne's distraction statement than I care to admit? Am I really one goat away from never getting married?

"Here." Carolina sets a plate of cake in my lap. "Birthday girl gets the first piece."

"Thanks." I dig the pink plastic fork into the cake and savor the first bite.

My eyes roll back in my head as strawberry cream tickles my tongue. Maybe staying single isn't so bad. I can't imagine a kiss being any better than this cake.

The others get their cake and start chatting as we eat.

"I wish Mrs. Mary would give someone this recipe," Hannah comments.

Carolina shakes her head. "She'll take it to her grave. I've already tried. So have Jonah and Jack. Once Jack watched her make a cake start to finish at the lodge. She doesn't measure anything, so it's impossible to copy it."

"I hope she at least writes it down someplace. It'd be a shame for something like this to die with her." Adrianne licks her fork and stares at the cake mournfully.

Mullet bleats, and I turn toward the kitchen. He's sitting in his usual seat at the table. "I'll be right back, y'all."

I go and cut him a piece of cake and set a bowl of water beside him. When I return to the living room, Ashley is staring at him with amazement.

"He sits there and eats like a kid?"

"Well, technically he is a kid." I giggle, then snort.

Nobody else laughs at my odd sense of humor.

I clear my throat. "But yeah, he eats every meal like that."

Ashley cocks her head. "That's impressive. You should train other people's goats."

I shrug. "I've offered a time or two, but there's not much demand for housebroken goats."

"I guess not." Ashley smiles, then takes the tiniest bite of her tiny piece of cake.

"Is that all you're eating?" Bianca asks.

Ashley nods.

"You didn't eat much Mexican either," Hannah adds.

Ashley shrinks back and slumps her shoulders. "I'm just watching my figure is all."

Everyone exchanges looks, but nobody says a word. For someone so pretty, she's incredibly self-conscious. I decide to lighten the mood.

"So who's idea was it to have Bradley entertain us tonight?" I narrow my eyes at every woman in the room until someone fesses up.

Adrianne smirks. "I went by the house to get some furniture I'd left there and mentioned your birthday. He offered."

"Well, how sweet of him." I roll my eyes.

"That's why I'm keeping my birthday a secret," Bianca says.

"He wouldn't do that if you're married," Hannah answers. Then she looks at Adrianne to confirm. "Would he?"

She laughs. "Doubtful."

"So does he entertain at parties often?" Ashley asks.

The rest of us glance around, unsure of how to take that. Finally, I answer. "I sure hope not."

Everyone laughs, with Ashley joining in last. I don't think she's used to my humor quite yet.

We laugh, talk, and eat a little longer. It's surreal to think that these girls are my best friends, especially Adrianne. We didn't exactly run in the same circles in high school. Knowing her like I do now, I understand that even the most put-together people don't have it all together.

That gives me a little comfort for my own life. However, it doesn't change the fact that my friends are marrying left and right, while I've never even had a real kiss.

As if right on cue, Mullet prances over and nudges my side. He really is my number-one guy.

Kyle

I lean back against the hard metal folding chair and try to get comfortable. The last thing I want to do after bending over an engine all day is sit here.

These tractor-pull meetings are a time suck for those actually working the tractor pull.

It's more of an excuse for the older men in town to air grievances and eat, my dad included. I could be at home working on some of their tractors right now, or possibly icing my shoulder, instead of listening to Wendall drone on about why we have to limit the number of hooks per tractor.

I throw my head back and spot Bradley coming my way. He's in uniform, chewing on a chicken leg. He pulls up the chair beside me and sits. A few people turn our way when the metal scrapes across the concrete floor. Bradley tips his hat, gaining approving smiles.

He's the only one I know who can equally charm children, women, and old people.

"Are you working tonight?" I ask.

"Nope."

"Then why are you in uniform?" I glance at Wendall for a moment to act interested. "And late?"

Bradley grins. "I was entertainment at a birthday party."

I twist my jaw, trying to remember if there's something going on at Double Drive since Earl Ed isn't here. "Balloon animals again, or helping with go-karts?"

He laughs and tosses his chicken leg in a nearby trash

can, making another distracting sound. I fold my arms and stare ahead as if nothing happened.

"Nope. I'm moving up in the entertainment business."

"You sang a duet with Misty at the Volunteer Fire Department?"

He laughs again. "No, I danced at a woman's birthday party."

"Oh." I perk up.

This is the most interesting news I've heard all night, including how the Tyson family is leaving the Apple Cart County Tractor Pull Association because we cut out participation trophies for pullers under age sixteen.

"Yeah, my neighbor turned twenty-eight today."

I rack my brain. Nobody has lived beside Bradley since he moved to Apple Cart. But in the country, neighbors are relative.

"Daisy, the candle-making girl, and a heck of a good masseuse, might I add."

I tighten my lips and stare at Bradley a moment. "Is that what I think it is?"

"Yep, a massage person."

I sigh. That is *not* what I thought he meant, and I'm so glad. You never know with Bradley.

"I had this whole routine made up that involved handcuffs, but I could tell she wasn't really feeling it."

"Good for her."

Bradley frowns, and I stretch my legs best I can without hitting the chair in front of me. We have quite the attendance at these meetings.

Wendall steps down—finally—and Dad steps up to read the financials of the last meeting. This is sure to open a can of worms. I bend to one side and grab my shoulder. This seat is killing me.

"We spent a hundred-fifty dollars last week on a canopy to set by the gate," Dad announces.

"More than a hundred dollars on a half tent?" an older man in the back stands up and yells.

Dad keeps his composure and nods. "It's terribly hot out there taking up money. My own mother almost had a heatstroke last year."

"Well, Maudy had no business out there," the man answers.

I scan the crowd for Gramps. He's cool as a cucumber, arms folded, and eyes drooping. But it is nearing his bedtime.

"All the able men were in here working on equipment. We had to have someone keep the gate," Dad answers.

Before anyone else can offer a rebuttal, Paul comes out of the concession stand toting several to-go boxes. He sets them down and steps beside Dad. This will be good.

Paul puts his hand on Dad's shoulder. "Donald came to me for help with a canopy, and I gave him the best deal ever." He waves his hands wide like a used-car dealer on a local commercial.

Roy, the local taxidermist, stands and stares at him. "No offense, but Paul, your store sells crap."

I wince at Bradley, who's grinning like a possum.

"Now, Roy." Dad raises a hand. Roy pouts but takes a seat. "If it makes y'all feel better, we can cement the canopy in place so we can have it ready for all events."

Mason Magill stares at Dad like he's lost his mind. "Then the rodeo and farmers' markets will use it."

"That's correct."

"So are they gonna chip in on the hundred-fifty?"

Dad runs a hand over his balding head and sighs. "That was our only expense last month aside from the chicken legs and baked beans for this meal. I will adjourn so these folks can get on with their night, and anyone with questions can ask me now."

He hits a small John Deere gavel against a folding table. People shuffle out of their chairs. Half make a beeline for the parking lot, while the other half is divided between talking in groups and rushing Dad for answers.

I sit back and squeeze my shoulder again.

"That still bothering you?" Bradley asks.

"Yeah, more so this week with all the tractors."

"Why don't you get it seen about?"

"Because I don't have time . . . or insurance."

Bradley frowns. "I get it. The benefits package is my main reason for running for sheriff."

"Yeah right," I snicker.

"What else would it be?"

"We all know you like the attention that comes with having a little power."

He kicks at my leg with his boot. "At least I use my power. You're VP of this club. Why didn't you get up there and hush them folks trash-talking your granny and aggravating your dad?"

"Donald can handle himself. So could Maudy if she were here."

"True."

I shift in the chair and groan.

Bradley narrows his eyes, then widens them. "I got it. You could get Daisy to work on you."

"The girl you danced for?"

"Yeah. She's popped a lot of people's aches and pains in place. And she'll take cash."

I rub my arm and reminisce about the days before I had ten tractors in my shop. Back when my shoulder and upper back were fully functioning and I could turn a wrench without torquing my tendons.

"I don't know."

Bradley is on his phone, ignoring me. Probably texting some girl he met. Not that it will come to anything. I know better than anyone how he's all flirt.

"Done." He clips his phone back on the holder attached to his belt.

"What?"

"I made you an appointment with Daisy for tomorrow morning."

"You did what?"

"An appointment. I told her I had a hurt friend coming tomorrow morning at nine."

"What if I'm busy?"

He stands and places his hands on his hips like a scolding mother. "Doing what? Tinkering on your Jeep or sitting in your underwear eating Fruit Loops?"

I hate that he knows me so well. "I planned on waking up early and working on some of the tractors."

"Well, your time is better spent healing so you can be more productive."

I pout.

Bradley pats me on the head like a dog. "Quit sulking. It's the house past mine. There's a chicken coop and some lawn ornaments. You can't miss it."

"I can't wait," I say sarcastically.

That is, unless she can fix me. In that case, I really can't wait.

CHAPTER TWO

Daisy

I hum to myself as I prep the massage room for my first client. Bradley texted me last night to say he has a friend with a hurt shoulder who needs a massage. Maybe he felt bad about twerking in my face and decided to send me some business ASAP.

Regardless of the reason, I have someone coming at nine. Good thing too because the sun is already blaring through my windows. If the air-conditioner guy doesn't come by soon, I'll have to offer heat-therapy massages only.

I fan my hand over the clean linens to smooth any wrinkles, then fold a thin blanket over the top. When the table is set, I stare at the variety of candles on my massage cart. I have no clue about this dude other than he's friends with Bradley.

Knowing Mr. Sheriff and his outgoing self, that could be anyone of any age and any walk of life. I opt for candles scented like vanilla with a hint of orange. That's a common favorite among most clients. And I'm almost certain vanilla allergies don't exist—at least not through inhalation.

As I'm lighting the last candle, my doorbell rings. I glance at my phone. He's ten minutes early, but I appreciate the promptness. Might as well get this show on the road before it heats up like hell's kitchen in this place.

I leave the ambiance of soft instrumental music and scented candles and cross the bright and balmy living room to the front door. A guy thinner than me stands with one arm slinked over the door frame and the other petting Mullet's head.

"Hey, I'm a little early. Hope that's okay."

"Yes, perfectly fine." I extend a hand. "I'm Daisy."

He shakes it firmly. "Slim."

I nod. I pray that's a nickname, and not an ex-convict name. You never know coming from Bradley.

"Great." I put on my fake happy-to-serve-you smile. "Come with me, and we can get started."

He steps inside. I push Mullet back on the porch and close the door. Slim lifts his sunglasses to rest on the bill of his cap and follows me to the massage room. He stops in the doorway and sniffs the air.

"Smells good to be so hot."

"Thanks." I force a smile.

Naturally, the massage client would beat the AC guy here. Why they give a four-hour repair window is beyond me.

I wave my hand toward the table. "Just undress down to whatever level you want and make yourself comfortable. Lie facedown, and I'll be back in a few minutes."

His eyebrows raise. "Undress?"

I shrug. "You don't have to take off everything. I actually prefer you don't." I laugh nervously at my own awkwardness. "But I can't massage you properly in a shirt and pants."

"Oh okay, then." He gives me a lopsided grin.

Obviously this is his first time. Of course, Bradley failed to mention that.

"I'll give you time to undress." I half smile and shut the door behind me, leaving Slim to settle in.

Mullet bleats loudly when I enter the living room. I better put him in my bedroom so he doesn't scratch the house outside the massage room. Sometimes he gets mad while I'm working and tries to get my attention. If I shut him in my room with the TV on Animal Planet, he won't sulk.

I open the door to look for Mullet. A tight gray T-shirt blocks my view. My eyes trail the shirt to a tan neck, then a handsome face outlined by dark hair that's longer in the front than back.

I swallow. "Uh, Kyle?"

Although that comes out like a question, I'm one hundred and one percent sure it's Kyle Tolbert. We went to school together from age thirteen, when I moved to Apple Cart, until he transferred to Wisteria our junior year. And Kyle has one of those faces you don't forget.

Chiseled jaw, strong cheekbones, deep-set eyes. *Why am I staring at him in silence as I write a romantic description in my head?*

Luckily, he breaks the silence. "And you're Daisy. You look familiar."

I should, you dork. Wait, no, I was the dork in high school, and probably now too.

"We were in the same grade at Apple Cart."

"Oh yeah. You changed your hair."

I gasp. He noticed. A smile, which I'm certain is goofy as all get out, blooms on my face.

"Can I come in?"

GEARED FOR LOVE

"Oh yeah." I step back and laugh.

He passes me, and I inhale a mixture of motor oil and some kind of musk. A toxic combo, really. Like I'd never dream of making it a candle, but it works for Kyle.

He rotates one shoulder, then pinches the neck of his T-shirt. He tugs at the cotton material and widens his arms. "Is this going to be like one of those heated massages?"

I stop admiring his arms long enough to string together a coherent response. "No, my AC is messed up. I've got a guy coming sometime between eight and twelve . . ."

My voice trails off and my eyes widen. Despite the rising temperature around us, shivers shoot up my spine at the realization of my mistake.

"Bradley made your appointment, right?"

Kyle nods. "Yeah, I've got this shoulder thing going on." He holds his shoulder and rotates his arm. "It's an old football injury that acts up whenever I use that muscle too much."

My eyes follow his bicep for a few seconds like a kid watching a merry-go-round. Then I shake my head and snap back to reality.

I place my hand on his stomach. It's incredibly firm, and I even pat it a time or two just to double-check I'm not dreaming.

"Feel free to have a seat." I drop my hand awkwardly. "I'll be right back."

I hurry toward the massage room and jerk open the door. Slim is lying propped on his elbows, head in hands, grinning. The first two things I notice is that he has a very prominent farmer's tan and that he chose to leave on his cap. As he starts to raise up, I notice he left on only his cap.

I slap my hand over my eyes. "What are you doing?"

"Whatever you want. The boss sent me here to service your unit."

"Yeah, my AC unit. It's not a euphemism, you moron."

"Well, if a pretty girl says undress, I'd be a fool to argue."

"You are a fool." I bend down, careful not to uncover my eyes until I'm below height of the table. I grab his pants and chuck them his way. "Put these on."

"If you insist, but I can fix your air free of charge if—"

"Get up and put on clothes!" My voice cracks as I stand and back into the hallway. I slam the door and turn to Kyle staring at me.

"Are you okay?"

I raise my hand. "I will be in a minute."

The door opens behind me, but I'm afraid to look. Slim pushes past me a second later, buttoning his shirt on the way out. Thank God, he's also wearing pants and boots. I watch him all the way to the door, then cut my eyes to Kyle.

"Give me a few minutes."

This definitely calls for a sheet change.

Kyle

I rock back and forth on my heels with my hands in my jeans pockets.

It's hot as a firecracker lit on both ends, and I'm stuck awkwardly waiting for Daisy to return from what I assume was a lover's quarrel.

Something bangs behind me. I turn to the guy who marched out a few minutes earlier lugging in a metal toolbox. It must weigh half as much as him, and I'm happy to see he finished buttoning his shirt.

"Sorry about that. I'm ready for you," Daisy calls.

I turn back to her standing in the hallway with an apologetic face.

"That's fine." I scratch my head as the guy steps beside me.

"Where's the unit?"

Daisy's cheeks flush. "Um, out back around the side of the house, to the left."

He nods, then exits again, banging the toolbox on the door frame when he leaves. I wince at the noise, then look at Daisy.

She clears her throat. "There was a bit of a misunderstanding earlier. I assumed Slim was my massage client."

I lift my chin. "Oh."

She nods and blushes more.

I smile, but clinch my jaw so I don't laugh. I'm both amused and relieved that wasn't a lover's quarrel. The only facts I know about Daisy are she makes candles, gives massages, and used to have bright pink hair, with occasional streaks of other bright colors. Still, she's way too cute and put together for someone like Slim.

Daisy pushes open the door behind her and raises her hand. I pass her and stop inside the doorway.

"Is this your first massage?"

"Yes."

"Okay, you can undress to your comfort level. I mainly need your chest, back, and lower legs bare." She swallows and fans her face. "Sorry for the heat. He's supposed to be working on it."

"That's fine. Should be relaxing," I lie as I wipe the back of my hand across my sweaty brow.

"Thanks." She glances around. A yellowish light from the candles flickers in her brown eyes. "I promise I'm usually more professional than this."

"It's fine, trust me. I have cars and tractors broken down in my living room."

She smiles widely. "Um, so I'll give you a minute to get ready. Just lie on your stomach under the sheet to start."

"Okay." I half smile as she backs out of the room and closes the door.

I suck in the fresh smell and kick off my boots. Then I take off my shirt and pants. My boxer briefs aren't in the best shape. Maybe I should've worn shorts. I was under the impression this would be a shoulder-only thing and not involve undressing. Like good old PT.

No wonder Bradley's been here before. He would sign up to have an attractive little woman rub his bare chest.

I frown and fold my clothes in the corner of a nearby futon. Then I settle on the table and pray she doesn't uncover the spot hiding my faded underwear, which may have a hole or two I can't see.

Most of my clothing splurges go to boots and church shirts, so I can't say that I've made an underwear purchase in a while.

I try and make my head comfortable, but I've never been a stomach sleeper, or rester. There's a hole in the headrest that half my face fits in. Weird, but it's either that or scoot until my head hangs off. I opt for the hole and wiggle until both my eyes are square to the floor.

A soft knock raps on the door, then a stream of light spreads across the floor.

"Kyle, are you ready?" Daisy whispers.

"Yes." My voice sounds weird with my cheeks pinched against the edge of the table hole.

The strip of light fades when she closes the door. I blink as tiny bare feet come into view beneath me.

"Can you tell me where it hurts the most?" Daisy's voice is small and soothing.

"My right shoulder blade and upper back, mainly."

"I'll concentrate there but give you a full-body massage. Let me know at any time if you feel any discomfort."

Discomfort? The idea of her seeing my decade-old drawers would qualify.

I don't dare say that. Instead, I silently pray a full-body massage doesn't involve the gluteus maximus muscle.

Daisy's hands wrap around my shoulder and melt into my skin. Her grip is both firm and relaxing, which is a combo I wouldn't think possible. I close my eyes and breathe in as she works through the kinks in my neck and shoulder blade that have tortured me the past few weeks.

Dang tractor pull.

Every year these old men decide to dig some tractor out of a back field and have me work on it right before the pull. It made matters worse when we imposed a hook limit per tractor. That only encouraged them to find more junk for me to work on with short notice.

"Relax." Daisy's breath tickles my ear.

I flinch as her hair brushes my back when she pulls away from me. Except for her hands, which dig deeper, making small circles around my upper spine.

I sigh and close my eyes.

For the first time since I remember, I clear my head. No to-do list about this job or that committee or helping my grandparents or fixing something at church. Just relaxing.

That is, until a breeze hits my bare feet and I realize Daisy is raising the sheet covering me. My heart pounds with every centimeter it raises. *Please don't uncover my butt.*

I mean, I have a nice butt. It's firm and flexible, but she may see my briefs and decide to judge a book by its cover.

The sheet stops at my upper thighs and she massages my hamstrings. I blow out a breath of relief and blink open my eyes.

Wait, is that . . . hoofs?

"Ahhh!" I raise onto my hands, cobra-stretch style.

Daisy jumps toward my face. "Did I hit a nerve?"

A loud bleat comes from underneath me. I lean over the table and come face to face with a tiny white-and-gray goat.

"Mullet, how did you get in here?" Daisy steps over and pulls the goat by its collar. "I'll be back," she calls as she marches out the door.

I reach back and straighten the sheets to ensure she doesn't get a front-row seat to my Calvin Kleins. Then I stick my head back in the hole and start plotting my revenge on Bradley.

CHAPTER THREE

Daisy

I return to Kyle shuffling the sheet behind his back.

"Whoa, what are you doing?"

He twists to look at me, loses his balance, and tumbles off the table, taking the sheet with him. I wince and inch toward him, careful not to look too close.

In all the years I've been giving massages, I haven't been flashed, until today—twice.

His arm flies above the table. "I'm okay. I just fell trying to adjust my sheet."

"Uh-huh, well, I'm gonna give you a moment to reset. Why don't you go ahead and turn on your back."

"Yeah." He pulls himself from the ground, holding the sheet tightly at his waist.

My eyes graze his chiseled chest and abs. I don't see that much as an at-home massage therapist in Apple Cart. When his eyes meet mine, my face flares and I take a step away.

"Be right back."

I rush out and shut the door, then lean against it. My heart beats faster as I imagine him climbing onto the massage table with those abs. I swallow and fan my face. This is unacceptable. I've got to go in there in a second and massage his front.

"Ready." Kyle's voice echoes from behind the door.

I take a deep breath, then go inside.

He's lying there, calm as a cucumber, eyes closed. I shut the door behind me and tiptoe in the candlelight to him.

"I'm going to massage your neck, chest, and shoulders." Despite whispering, my voice squeaks on the word "chest." I clear my throat and try again. "Let me know if there is any pain at any time."

"Okay," he whispers back.

I stand over his head and start on his shoulders. I'm short and he has a lot of knots to work out. I lean over to push into those pressure points deeper. Then his eyes pop open and meet mine.

"Sorry," he whispers, and squeezes his eyes shut.

Trying not to laugh, I reach for a warm towel.

"Here." I lay it gently across the top part of his face. "Now you can relax."

"Thanks," he mutters.

His shoulders soften when I reach for them again. I smile and continue the massage. As I work on his neck, a clinking sound bangs outside the window. I jump and Kyle's neck pulses.

My legs chill as the air kicks on. I exhale. That's one upside to Slim being here.

Kyle settles into the table and loosens his muscles. I work my way across his chest and try not to think back to high school. He was the star defensive player, and I wasn't even in the band. I was the introverted kid who didn't participate in anything aside from a few made-up clubs.

Even back then, I admired Kyle from afar. He was obviously handsome and athletic, but that wasn't why. He was also genuinely kind. Always stopping others from picking on people and refusing to participate in pranks.

We never hung out or anything, but he was a pleasant presence. So much so that it made me sad beginning of junior year when we found out he'd transferred to Wisteria High.

I rub essential oils onto his collar bone and shoulder muscles, trying every trick in the book to break apart the tension beneath his skin. Not once does he complain, so I continue kneading the heel of my hand against his muscles.

Another clank beats against the side of the house, and Kyle flinches, knocking the towel from his face.

I retrieve it from the side of the table and place it gently back on his face.

"I'm almost done with your upper body. Do you want me to finish massaging your calves and thighs?"

I stare at him for an answer as his Adam's apple bobs a time or two. "Yeah," he says quietly.

I make my way to the end of the table and start massaging his feet. He almost kicks me, so I pause and go to the other foot first. He draws in his toes and laughs.

"Are you ticklish?"

"A little bit."

I try once more and he jerks his leg. "Okay, a lot ticklish," he says.

I giggle. "I'll skip the feet."

I continue with his calves and then his thigh muscles. My fingers tingle and butterflies swarm my stomach. I'm barely above his kneecap, but my nerves are firing. I've massaged attractive men before, but for some reason, Kyle makes me self-conscious.

I move toward his calves for a moment, then turn on a small lamp in the corner of the room.

"Okay, Kyle. You're done. I apologize for the AC guy, and the goat, and the AC guy again."

He leans up on his elbows and removes the towel from his face. He smiles lazily and lifts his shoulder.

"That really helped my shoulder, so I'd say it's worth it."

My cheeks warm. "I'll let you get dressed. No rush, I don't have another appointment for a few hours."

I step into the hallway and clinch my teeth. *No rush?* Why did I say that? Will he think I'm implying I want him to stay undressed?

Why do I have to be so awkward?

Speaking of awkward, Slim bolts through the front door, carrying a clipboard.

"Miss Daisy, I got you all set."

"Thanks."

He rips off the top sheet of paper, which is my bill. I sign it. "Do you take cards or should I write a check?"

"Check is good."

"Hold on." I hurry to my bedroom for my purse.

When I return with my checkbook, Kyle is in the living room as well. Both guys stare at me.

Kyle nods at the checkbook in my hand. "Bradley said you take cash. Do I need a check?"

"No, cash is fine."

He reaches in his wallet and thumbs out the correct amount in cash while I write a check for my AC bill. Then Kyle hands me some folded bills as I hand the check to Slim.

"Looks like pretty boy here is the only one not getting paid." Slim clicks his tongue, then laughs. He clips the check to his clipboard and walks away, pausing at the door. "If you need any more units serviced, Miss Daisy, have your people call my people." He winks.

The blood drains from my face, and I try not to read too much into that statement. I play it off with a nervous laugh as he exits.

Kyle stuffs his hands in his pockets and clears his throat. "So this was great. I already feel better."

"Good. You may be sore tomorrow."

He rotates his right arm and chuckles. "I'm used to it." His eyes gravitate to my hands. "You give a mean massage for someone with such tiny hands."

"Thanks?"

He shakes his head. "Anyway, how do I get in touch with you for another massage?"

"Oh." I hold up my index finger to signal him to wait.

I go to the massage room and grab a business card from the cart. I hold up the card as I reenter the living area.

"Here."

"Thanks." He stares at it a moment, then grins at me. "I'll give you a call."

My mouth goes dry, and I can't find a response for a minute. Kyle stares at me until I manage to nod my head.

"Well, bye." He lifts his hand and walks out the door.

I stand still as a statue until his Jeep cranks. Then I lie on the floor and scold myself for acting so odd. Of course he will call me *for an appointment.*

No wonder I've never had a boyfriend. I wouldn't be able to handle the normalcy of someone like Kyle asking me out.

Kyle

A horn honks outside, which can only mean one thing. More like one person—Paul.

He loves to announce his coming and going with a honk. I stand from squatting by a tractor tire, my knees popping in the process.

Maybe I should allow Daisy to spend more time on my legs after all? Now that I know the closest she would come to seeing my boxers is me falling off the table, I should be safe.

Sure enough, Paul's junky truck is on the other side of my window. He honks again, calling me outside.

I sigh and walk to the door. He won't let up until I come out. Why he can't get out and knock like a normal person is beyond me. Then again, Paul isn't exactly a normal person.

When I exit my house/shop, he lets off the horn. I wasn't joking with Daisy when I mentioned having motors broke down behind my couch. I built a shop before a house and stayed with Dad. Then I decided to add a kitchen, bedroom, and bathroom to the shop since I'm here so much. That led to slowly buying furniture and eventually moving in full time.

But hey, barndominiums are in now, so why can't shop-dominiums be a thing too?

Paul grins at me and hangs out the open truck window. "I found this gem when I went out picking this morning."

By picking, he's referring to junk and not crops. One of the many signs pointing to Paul not needing to enter the tractor pull.

"Mind if I unload her and let you tinker around, get her ready for the pull?"

I run my hand over my jaw and sigh. "Paul, why do you want to enter the pull?"

He hops out and adjusts his massive belt buckle. "If I don't hook a tractor this year, they said they'd kick me out."

I almost bite a hole in my tongue. As club VP, I know

good and well that Paul never paid his dues. He wants to stay in the club he isn't even a part of to eat our food.

"I'm pretty backed up with everyone else's tractors." That they already owned and used before today.

Paul saunters to the tractor and pats the seat. A wad of dirt and grass falls from the back tire. He kicks it with the toe of his ostrich-skin boot and laughs.

"She ain't in too bad of shape. Sure you can't give her a look right fast?"

I cross my arms. "I'm a little busy tonight."

Paul wiggles his eyebrows. "Got a hot date?"

"Yeah, with a forty-twenty."

Paul shakes his head. "Boy, you ain't ever gonna get married working all the time."

"You're not married."

"By choice." He winks.

I shake my head. "If you can unload it, I'll fit it in this week."

Paul's face lights up as he starts tugging at the ratchet strap. I put a hand on his arm to stop him.

"On one condition."

"What's that?"

"You put a down payment on this."

"Now how am I gonna know how much my bill is before you fix her?" Paul frowns.

"That's why I'm only asking for a deposit." And to ensure that he at least pays me something.

Paul has a bad habit of paying too late and then trying to offer me something like a Trump commemorative coin instead of usable currency.

I stare at him until he breaks down and pulls a wallet from his back pocket. One by one, he unfolds wads of bills. He hands me two fifties. When I don't say anything, he throws a two-dollar bill on top.

"A little extra incentive. It's rare."

I'd argue the fifty is rarer, since plenty of older people around town shell out twos like soft peppermints, but what's the use with Paul. I fold the bills, trying to ignore that one is sticky, then slide them into my pocket.

"Thanks, Paul."

He nods. "Now help me get this beauty off the trailer."

That wasn't exactly part of the deal. I grab my shoulder, which is better thanks to Daisy's angelic touch. But I'd like to keep it that way.

"Go park on that hill with your truck facing upward." I point to the slight hill at the edge of my property.

Paul gives me an odd look, but does what I say. I assume he'd do about anything right now for my help.

I follow his truck to the hill. No sooner than he can get out, I have the trailer ramps in place and the tractor unstrapped. It rolls off into the grass, no problem.

Paul scratches his head. "Kyle, you're a genius."

I chuckle. "I wouldn't take it that far, but thanks."

"Since she's in good hands, I best be getting back to the store."

"All right. See ya, Paul."

He lifts his arm as he climbs in the truck. His taillights come on, and he starts to back up.

"Paul, the tractor!"

He stops and sticks his head out the window, laughing. "Thanks, Kyle." Then he continues up the hill, away from the tractor I'm supposed to fix.

I stare at the beast in all its glory of rusted paint and grass growing inside the tire rims. I'm mildly impressed that he got it on the trailer. Now I need to get a chain and pull it toward my shop.

There's a large chain close to the 4020 John Deere broke

apart at the edge of my shop. The one I have a date with later.

That's about the closest I've come to a date in some time. Between working all the time, my duties in the community, and church, I don't have a lot of time to seek out dates. And unlike my best friend, I don't purposely stop good-looking women to talk.

Of course, Bradley would never admit to that. He always has the excuse of thinking their tag was expired or warning them to slow down. However, some of those "warnings" pay off in him scoring a dinner date.

I've never been that forward.

Most of the local women my age are either married or someone I took on a date in high school.

Except Daisy.

She was so standoffish in school that I'm not sure I've heard her speak until my massage. I remember her moving here in middle school and having bright pink hair. She never participated in any activities. Then I transferred to Wisteria for football junior year.

That's when half of Apple Cart went to hating me, and Bradley went from hating me to being my best friend. It's safe to say that small towns take football rivalries to an unhealthy level.

I pull the chain out from around a tire and take it to Paul's tractor. My neck hitches the slightest bit, probably because of soreness from the massage.

After I move this disaster closer to the shop, I need to give Daisy a call for another appointment. Nothing else, of course. It's strictly business between us—despite me being mostly naked with her hands all over me.

CHAPTER FOUR

Daisy

"Now breathe in when you lift your back, and exhale when you lower."

"I can't breathe right with a goat on me," Samuel complains.

I pinch my lips together and ignore him.

Ashley brought him to goat yoga, claiming that they're trying to do more things as a couple. I suspect the only reason he agreed to come is because Bradley signed up to try the class. Samuel can't go two minutes without visually shooting daggers through him.

Ashley smiles tensely, as if trying to smooth over the situation. As the instructor, I move on and ignore the problem pupil.

Mullet hops off my back on the next downward dog. He trots over to Samuel and bleats loudly in his face. Samuel hops up and jumps backward about a foot.

Bradley laughs.

Samuel scowls at Bradley, then turns to Ashley. "I can't do this. You'll have to think of a better activity."

He toes his feet into his sandals and heads for the door. Ashley glances around the room, then picks up her flip-flops and hurries behind him.

I lead everyone in warrior pose as they whisper-argue at my front door.

"You can stay. Just catch a ride home with one of your friends," Samuel says loud enough for everyone to hear.

"I live too far away," Ashley answers.

He shrugs. "Well, they're supposed to be your friends."

Bradley jerks his arm up so fast that he momentarily loses his balance. "I can take her. I patrol up to the county line all the time anyway."

Samuel's nostrils flare, then he glances at Mullet. He nods at Bradley. "Thanks."

Ashley stands at the door and watches him go, then drops her flip-flops and rejoins the group.

I continue leading the class through poses as if a mini soap opera didn't just play out in my living room. After a few minutes, I give them a water break.

Ashley is almost in tears at this point, and my phone has been vibrating on the coffee table nearby.

I grab my phone while everyone drinks water and pets the goats. Two missed calls from the same number, but no voicemail. It's a local number, so I call it back.

A man's voice answers. "Hello?"

"This is Daisy Duncan. You called my number but didn't leave a message."

"Hey, it's Kyle Tolbert. I was wondering if I might could make another massage appointment."

"Oh." I didn't expect this.

"Maybe a few more until I get a hundred percent. It seems to really help."

"Uh, yeah." I glance up at my yoga class. "Hey, Kyle, can I call you back after goat yoga?"

"Goat yoga?"

"Yeah, yoga with goats, which you probably figured out." I laugh awkwardly, then clear my throat.

"Sure."

"Or I could text if that's easier."

"I can give you my cell number. This is my landline."

"Really?" I wrinkle my forehead.

"Yes. Is that okay?"

"Totally, I'm just shocked someone our age has a landline."

"Well, service isn't great where I live."

"Yeah, uh, let me call you in like half an hour to schedule something."

"That works."

"Bye, Kyle." I hang up the phone and take a sip of my own water.

Mullet prances toward me and sticks out his tongue. I waterfall a slow stream into his mouth. He swallows and marches off, satisfied.

Bradley walks to the front of the room and grabs one of the hand towels I have on the coffee table. He wipes his face, then his underarms. I snarl.

"Sorry." He looks under both of his arms and chuckles. "I didn't expect to sweat this much."

"Well, you are wearing a uniform."

"I didn't think it appropriate to take my shirt off in a room full of ladies."

I fold my arms and narrow my gaze. "But you did on my birthday."

He winces. "Sorry about that too. I thought you'd find it funny."

"Apology accepted."

"Was that Kyle on the phone?" He smirks.

"How did you know?"

"He mentioned his shoulder getting better." His lips curve into a mischievous smile. "And you said, 'Bye, Kyle.'"

I roll my eyes.

Bradley laughs. "He also mentioned Mullet scared him."

"Really? What else did he mention?" Kyle falling off the table flashes through my mind, and I bite back a smile.

"Something about an AC guy giving you an eyeful." Bradley raises one eyebrow.

I slap my forehead. "Surprisingly more awkward than your dance."

He laughs harder and wipes his face again, then pulls the towel back. I guess the pit smell got to him.

"I'll take that as a compliment." He winks, then drops the towel in a nearby basket and takes his spot on a mat.

My phone dings, and a text pops up.

This is Kyle's cell phone. If it's easier, you can text me.

I start to respond, then notice everyone staring at me. I set my phone facedown on the table and ask if everyone is ready for the last round.

Most of the women clap or cheer. There are a few exhausted nods. Bradley wavers his hand back and forth. I point to him, and he stops.

"Okay, now we're going to finish by focusing on our core."

A few groans echo in the back, including from Bradley. I laugh and lead them in a new pose. I've led yoga so many times that I can do so with my mind on autopilot. Good thing, since my thoughts keep drifting to Saturday, when I massaged Kyle.

Everything possible that could've gone wrong did. Yet he still wants another appointment. That's encouraging for my business.

But it also means I have to massage Kyle again.

It's not that I don't want to massage him. It's just that he makes me nervous. I went from thinking of him as the perfect guy in school, to seeing him occasionally around town, to having my hands all over him.

Not awkward at all.

"Let's go to the floor and stretch it out."

Sighs of relief come from my students as they break the last pose and sit on their mats. I've trained the goats to never get on my clients during cooldown. So far, they've minded.

I wish there was a market for training goats. I could make a fortune.

We stretch our arms, then legs, then I lead everyone to lie on their backs. For the last minute, I put the goats outside, then dim the lights and instruct everyone to breathe deeply.

I reach for my phone and open my appointment app. Saturday mornings really are my most free times. The timer I set dings, signaling the end of their rest. I shove my phone in my yoga pants pocket and slowly raise the light level.

Everyone chats and stretches as they gather their mats and towels. Bradley takes Ashley's mat for her.

"Thanks, everyone. Remember, you can invite a friend for free on their first visit."

"Thanks, Daisy." Carolina grins as she plunks her mat in the basket.

"Thanks," Aniston echoes, walking out.

More people pass me, dropping off towels and mats and

saying their goodbyes. Bradley and Ashley are last to leave. He tips his hat to me.

"Don't be too hard on my guy Kyle."

I nod, not sure how to respond.

Mullet squeezes back inside as Bradley closes the door. I turn off the music and blow out the few candles I lit to create a lavender scent. Then I reach for my phone.

My fingers hover over the keys as I contemplate what to text. I'll just keep it short and simple.

Would you like another Saturday morning appointment? Same time?

My stomach swirls as three little dots appear on the screen. I'm still a little scarred from all that went wrong the first time I massaged him.

Yeah, sounds good to me.

I exhale.

Good. I promise it will be cooler this time, and no Slim.

Three dots appear again, and he answers with a goat emoji and a question mark. I laugh so loud that I snort.

Can't make any promises on that one, but I'll try.

. . .

I'll try not to fall off the table, then.

He follows that text with a cringe-face smiley, which makes me grin. Kyle never seemed like the joking type to me. Then again, I've never spent any time with him before.

The first actual conversation we had was before his massage, and that was pretty much to the point.

See you Saturday.

See ya.

I set the phone down, happy to give him the last word. Whenever I keep talking too long, things get weird. I've already got to redeem my professional reputation from last time.

Kyle

Call me crazy, but after I made another massage appointment with Daisy, I immediately went to Amazon Prime and ordered new underwear.

Not that I don't trust her to keep the sheet where it

should be, but I'll rest better knowing I'm double covered. That first massage was a wake-up call that I might need to spend a little bit of this overtime money I'm making.

I'm hoping there aren't any hiccups this time around.

I turn down Daisy's driveway and blink at brightly painted metal flowers spinning in the wind. When I park and get out, a rooster crows behind me. Mullet—whose name I couldn't forget—is out front playing with a group of baby chicks.

I shut my Jeep door and walk toward the house. Daisy's head pops up behind a stack of boxes on the porch. She's wearing a bright apron, not unlike a painter or a lunchroom lady. Her hair is piled on top of her head.

"Hi, go on in." She circles the boxes and attempts to pull the top one off.

I reach and rest my hands on hers. "I've got it."

"Thanks." She smiles and slides her hands from underneath mine.

I grip the box, confused by why my hands tingled when they touched hers. The woman has given me a full-body massage and is about to again. I should be used to her touch. I guess this situation is different.

I stack another box on top of the one in my arms. "Where do these go?"

"The candle room."

I raise my eyebrows in question, as the candle room means nothing to me.

She giggles. "Oh yeah, this way."

She leads me inside to a room past the massage room. A myriad of scents hits my nostrils when she opens the door.

"It smells amazing in here."

"Thanks, it's where I make candles."

"Makes sense."

She stares at me a second and smiles. Then her eyes drift to the boxes I'm holding. "Oh, my bad. They go in here."

She opens a closet and points to a shelf. I set the boxes on the floor, then stack them on the shelf.

"Thanks."

"You're welcome. I'll get the others."

"And I'll get the door."

Daisy follows me and holds the door open. "Lift with your legs."

"What?"

She comes outside and squats low. "Use your legs to lift something low to the ground, not your back."

I start to squat and she puts her hands on my sides. "Straight back."

I move on her command like a puppet on a string, straightening like I'm about to deadlift a barbell, then lift the two boxes from the ground. Daisy steps back and nods approvingly as I walk inside. Much to my relief, she pushes Mullet back when he tries to sneak in behind me.

"I promised no goats this time."

"Actually, you said you couldn't promise that," I say, remembering our text conversation.

She laughs. "I guess I did, huh?"

I stack the last pile of boxes in the closet. "Anything else I can help with?"

She shakes her head, then glances around the room. "If you want, pick a scent for me to use during your massage."

"Hmm." I eye a nearby bookcase filled with candles and pick one up. "Duck Farts?"

She giggles. "Don't judge a candle by its label."

I shrug and unscrew the lid. "Smells good."

"Thanks."

I turn to her. "What was in there last time I came?"

"Orange You Glad It's Vanilla."

I chuckle, then pick up another candle. The label is "Woodn't It Be Lovely." It smells like pine trees with something sweet. Next, I try one called "You're Bacon Me Crazy." It smells like freshly cooked bacon with maybe some honey thrown in. I grin.

"This one."

"Ah, nice manly choice." She smiles back and her cheeks flush.

I hold the candle out, and she takes it. Our fingers brush, and we lock eyes for a split second. Then she steps back.

"You can go ahead and get ready for the massage. I'll give you enough time before going in there."

"Thanks." I pass her and enter the massage room.

It's much cooler than before. The hairs on my arms raise when I take off my clothes. I pull back the cover and snuggle underneath it on my back. I'm not smooshing my face until absolutely necessary.

A few minutes later, the door cracks.

"Ready?" Daisy whispers.

"Yes."

The door opens gently, letting in a stream of light. Daisy enters with a candle and closes the door. She lights it, and I watch her eyes glisten in the candlelight.

The scent of bacon starts to fill the room. I lie in silence, peeking at her through slanted eyes. She tugs at the back of her apron. I open one eye wider when she grunts in frustration.

"Need help?"

Her cheeks redden in the glow of the candlelight. "I don't want to lean over you with this waxy apron is all. I should've removed it already."

"Come let me help." I slide to a sitting position, careful to keep my sheet in place when it falls down my chest.

Daisy tiptoes to the table and turns her back to me. She's got the thing in such a knot that my big fingers can't undo it.

"Hold still." I lean down and undo the knot with my teeth.

My hair grazes against the small of her back as I pull away. When I raise up, her head is turned and she's staring at me. I meet her gaze and grin.

"What?" I ask as I tilt my head back and pull out the knot.

"You're gonna ruin your teeth."

"Nah." I drop the ties from her back, then reach for the neck part of her apron.

Daisy turns her head away from me. Goose bumps populate her neck as I undo the top tie with my hand. The apron falls to the floor, but she stays planted for a second before bending to pick it up.

"Thanks," she murmurs when she's at her cart.

"Welcome." I slide back down and pull the sheet up to my neck.

She comes back with a warm towel and smiles as she covers my face.

A slight breeze hits my shoulders as she exposes them. My chest and stomach are next, then it stops. Daisy begins rubbing some kind of oil or lotion on my shoulders. Whatever it is, my muscles like it.

I sink into the table and allow my muscles to melt under her gentle yet firm touch. My body is so Jell-O that I don't even flinch when she moves to my legs. Thankfully, she skips my feet this time.

I'm just getting comfortable when she covers my legs and removes the towel from my eyes. She asks me to flip on my stomach. I blink a time or two, then twist under the sheet until I'm on my stomach with my head in the hole.

Either I have an unusually large face, or whoever

designed this table has never used it. I wiggle until my eyes are in the center.

I suck in the bacon aroma and exhale as I close my eyes.

Daisy's tiny hands begin to work their magic, and I soon forget all about my face deforming in the squishy leather circle.

Whatever this woman is doing is working. My shoulders unhitch a little more every time she pushes on them. Before my brain totally turns to mush along with the rest of my body, I make a mental note to schedule more appointments.

CHAPTER FIVE

Daisy

An odd melody of clanging brass and wood circles above me when the wind blows Mom's chimes. The eave of her front porch is flanked with more than I can count quickly, of all various sizes and designs. She's collected them as long as I can remember.

The first thing she did whenever we moved someplace new was go exploring and buy a new wind chime. After Dad died and we settled here, she would buy one on a whim whenever she wanted. It's to the point where we can barely carry on a front-porch conversation on a windy day, but I don't have the heart to tell her to stop.

I may have been guilty of gifting her one or two of these as well. Something about the tradition gives me a sense of nostalgia, as I'm sure it does her.

Growing up as a military brat, I craved a sense of consistency. If that has to come in the form of Mom hoarding wind chimes, so be it.

I climb the front steps and beat on the door.

"Out here, honey," Mom calls from the side of the house.

I lean back to find her circling the porch with a bucket full of lavender in her arms. A long, lean guy around my age with scruffy facial hair follows her. He's holding a bigger bucket of mixed flowers.

Mom meets me at the porch and rests her bucket next to the porcelain gnomes anchoring the steps. She wipes her hands down her tie-dye apron and motions for the man to set his bucket down as well.

"Daisy, I don't think you've met Toby. He's my new employee."

He throws up a hand clumsily. "Hi."

"Toby, this is my daughter, Daisy."

"Nice to meet you."

He grins, then straightens his face when he turns to Mom. "Miss Tallie, what else do you need?"

Mom wipes her brow with the back of her hand and removes her reading glasses. She mouths numbers as if counting to herself, while she cleans her glasses lens on her apron.

"Bring me one more bucket this size of ginger and of mint."

He nods and walks toward the greenhouse. Maybe it's his height, but his walk is swayed. I watch him for a second, then nod at the buckets.

"How much for all this?"

Mom purses her lips. "I told you, just a hug and those candles I wanted."

"Mom." I cross my arms.

"No, ma'am." She sticks her glasses on top of her head.

Her wild curls swallow the stems and half of the frames. I

exhale, holding my stance. This lasts maybe a half minute before she engulfs me in a hug.

She's small like me, but strong and feisty. Her arms squeeze around my back as she sways me a moment before releasing me.

I arch a brow when she backs up enough for me to see her face. "Want the candles now?"

She laughs. "Sure thing. I'll have Toby load the fragrances for you."

Mom grows all kinds of organic plants, and I use many of her wildflowers and herbs in my candle mixes. A few years ago, she bought this twenty-acre property at a tax sale. It's on the way to Tuscaloosa from Apple Cart, but essentially in the middle of nowhere. The cliché location for a single, middle-aged hippie growing plants for a living.

There's no telling where she found Toby or why he'd want to work out here. Maybe he's in witness protection or something?

She offered me some land to move with her, but I was smart enough to realize my clientele wouldn't travel out here. I could've rented a place in town to do massages, but finding somewhere to give goat yoga classes might be a challenge.

Mom follows me to my car. I still drive the yellow Volkswagen Beetle she bought me in high school. The fake daisy in the flower holder by the dash is wrinkled, and worn even more than my car. Still, it doesn't have a ton of miles, and I can't seem to part with it.

I pop the trunk and retrieve the box of candles. Mom sticks her fingers in her mouth and whistles. Toby appears like Pavlov's dog.

"Toby, put those flowers and herbs back here for Daisy."

He nods and starts with the bucket he's carrying in his arms. I shift a yoga mat to the side so he has room for all the buckets. Then I follow Mom to the porch.

She stops before climbing the steps and calls out behind her, "Toby, make sure to close the trunk when you're done."

He nods. Satisfied with his acknowledgment, Mom continues into the house, and I follow. Boots rubs against my leg and meows the moment I step inside. I bend down and stroke her back and tail before she loses interest in me for a ball of yarn a few feet away.

I sit on the large beanbag in the corner. Mom doesn't have any furniture in the living room other than reclining cushions like beanbags and body-sized pillows. She said that if she doesn't have a couch or chair, she won't be tempted to sit down and waste time. I once argued that she could lie down on these. Her response was that if she were that tired, then she deserves a nap.

A native of the mountains in California, she was the exact opposite of my Southern dad. That's why it shocked me when she announced we were moving to Alabama after his death.

Aside from arts festivals and craft shows, she sticks out like a sore thumb around here. Over the years, I've taken on more of my dad's characteristics than before. Whether from living here since I was thirteen or out of subconsciousness to belong, I'm not sure.

"Want a snack? I made kale brownies this morning." Mom circles the opening from the kitchen and stares at me.

"No, thank you." I lift the corners of my mouth.

Only my mother could make brownies unbearable.

"Have you made up your mind about Trade Days?" I ask.

Mom twists her lips and considers my question. "If I can get enough harvested by then."

"Isn't that what your employee is for?" I smirk.

Mom joins me in the living room, reclining against a long pillow. Boots prances toward her and lies by her side.

"He's only a few hours a week. He's studying botany in

college and helping me out to get hands-on experience." Well, that explains a lot.

She strokes Boots before continuing. "The mayor didn't seem too receptive of my products last year."

"I told you to leave the hemp oils at home. Apple Cartians aren't ready for CBD products."

She shrugs. "You did warn me."

"I'd probably leave Toby here too."

Mom laughs. "You don't think Apple Cart is ready for him?"

"More like I don't think he's ready for Apple Cart." I snort.

"There's nothing wrong with Toby. He's a brilliant young man with a green thumb." She stops petting Boots and perks up. "Maybe you should get to know him better."

I balk. "Negative."

"And why is that? Because he's a few years younger than you?"

"No." I want to say because he's eccentric and chose to study weeds for a living. But the more I mull that over in my mind, it would be a little like the pot calling the kettle black. I'm not exactly the poster child for unearthy.

Mom grins and her eyes twinkle. "Are you seeing someone?"

"No." This comes out a little hesitant, and I'm not sure why.

I'm definitely not seeing anyone. Although my heart skipped a few beats when Kyle made standing appointments for the foreseeable Saturdays going forward.

It's strictly business—I'm a masseuse helping a man heal from an injured shoulder. The man I'm treating just happens to be handsome and kind all wrapped into one, like some blue-collar Prince Charming burrito.

"If you say so."

I flinch at Mom's words as they pop the bubble in my brain, floating around with the memory of massaging Kyle.

"I do say so," I answer firmly.

The front door opens, and we both turn to the sunlight it lets in. Toby peeks his head inside.

"Miss Tallie?"

"Yes, Toby?"

"Do you mind if I take home some of the worms I removed from your tomato plants?"

Mom clinches her jaw at the mention of worms. "Why didn't you kill them?"

Toby's pale eyes widen. "I'd never do such a thing. I want to add them to my terrarium at home."

"Sure. So you've found an apartment?"

"No, I'm still at the campgrounds right now."

"I see. Take all the worms you want." Mom's lips tighten into a thin line.

"Thanks!" Toby smiles wider than I would at a million bucks. He ducks outside and lets the door close behind him.

"Where's his camper?"

Mom arches a brow. "He's in a tent."

My jaw drops a little as I ponder his situation. "Hold up, you suggested I consider a guy who lives in a tent and collects worms?"

She shrugs.

I snort. I may be weird, but my pot's never been that black.

Kyle

With every tractor I've fixed, I've counted the days until my next massage. Not that I'd admit that out loud and run the risk of sounding soft.

I've been called nice, and even compassionate, but soft would go against my upbringing. When you're raised by a single dad who rebuilds engines for a living and go to college on a football scholarship, you can't stoop to soft.

It was only junior college, but still took a lot of hard work and competition to earn that.

I drop the wrench in my hand and slide out from under the International hunk of junk I'm working on. The red paint flecked with rust blurs my vision as I sit up quickly and arch my back.

My stomach growls. I stand and walk toward the kitchen for a snack. The sound of the front door opening catches my attention.

No knock, which could mean it's either Dad, Bradley, or someone here to rob me.

Dad's tall, balding head bobs through the opening, followed by the rest of his large frame slinking inside. He shuts the door and makes it to my side in time to stop my hand hovering a cereal box over a bowl.

"You need more than that to eat if you're gonna mess with all these engines."

I set the box of Frosted Flakes on the counter. "I wouldn't even be taking the time to eat this if my belly button weren't scratching my back."

He chuckles. "Let's go to town and eat."

I slant my eyes to him. "I plan on staying here and starting on that next John Deere so I can relax some tomorrow."

"I'll help you tomorrow. You need a break."

I press my hands on the counter and sigh. My bad shoulder twitches under my shifting weight.

"All right." I close the box of cereal and return the bowl to the cabinet.

"Good. I'll clean up some while you shower and change."

I glance down at my grease-stained hands and sigh. "Give me ten."

He nods. I walk to the bathroom as he heads toward the mess of tools I have strewn around the tractor.

Even though we will go back to the same tractor tomorrow and use the same tools, Dad instilled the importance of neatness in me. I thought it a waste of time when I was younger, but now I appreciate that teaching. It especially comes in handy since when I took Tolbert Auto to the next level, I decided to live in my shop.

It made more sense than to waste money on an additional building for my home while I was single. One day, if I ever marry, I can build a house on the property.

I shed my jumpsuit and underwear, then step into the shower. The idea of marrying someone hits me almost as abruptly as the cold water when I turn on the showerhead.

I step back while the hot water kicks in and assess my situation. I'd always assumed I'd get married and have a kid or two, but I never wanted to leave Apple Cart County.

Throughout high school and college, I dated a lot of girls. Pretty, popular, and smart girls, but none of them really stuck. The last few years, I've been stuck in a routine of working, community clubs, and hanging out with my guy friends. It's not like I don't want a woman, it's just that time passes on while I'm busy.

Not to mention that a lot of the good-looking girls I've known are already settled down or moved away chasing better things.

I step into the warm water and shower quickly, making sure I soap my hands enough to get rid of most of the grease.

My nails are another story. Maybe since I'm now a believer in massages, I can try a manicure.

Nah, that would get me called softy for sure.

I turn off the water and shake the excess drips from my hair. Then I dry off and cinch the towel around my waist.

The best idea I had when building this place was adding an extra door to the bathroom that goes to my bedroom. I retreat that way for clean clothes.

In my top dresser drawer is the new boxer briefs I ordered from Amazon last week. Since I hadn't bought new underwear in . . . well, maybe never. I think Dad bought my last pack, which is sad. I ordered a large assortment.

If I don't gain too much weight, this should last me another decade.

I snatch one of the clear packs and pull until it breaks open. Underwear fans up and onto the floor like I've popped a party favor. There are several solid colors, but also a few wild designs. I assume the bulk packaging is Amazon's way of getting guys like me to buy the crazy pairs.

I bend down and examine a pair with hot chili peppers, another with rubber duckies, and a third with daisies.

Daisies.

My throat catches when I pick up that pair. What are the odds of this? I frown at them and start to stuff them back in the drawer, then stop.

The hope is that Daisy will never see my underwear and keep the sheet where she's obligated to as a professional massager. But on the off chance that she might accidentally get a peek, I can't resist a good laugh.

I step into the boxer briefs covered in daisies and admire my rear from my dresser mirror. Not half bad.

Jeans, boots, and a button-down later, I'm back in the main area staring at Dad. He's cleared my mess and is fooling with the TV remote. He lifts his head at the sound of my boots on the concrete floor.

"Let's go." He tosses the remote on the couch, having not yet managed to turn on the TV.

For all his mechanic skills, he sucks at everyday technology. It took me years to convert him to a smartphone.

I grab my keys and wallet from the kitchen counter where I put them every time I come in. Then I follow him outside and climb in his old pickup.

We ride into town in mostly silence, as I lean my head against the seat. It's nice to sit back and soak in the air-conditioning. My stomach flips, and I close my eyes. Mental images of food from Mary's and Big Butts BBQ circle my mind. Whichever Dad picks is fine by me.

The truck stops, and I blink awake from my momentary food coma. We're in the middle of town, sideways against the ditch circling the town square. Vehicles surround us, and tents cover the center of town.

"Trade Days."

"Yeah, Mary's and Big Butts are set up like always. So is the cookie lady and some of those trailers that make the roasted corn and funnel cakes. Figured we could have our pick of food tonight."

My jaw hitches. I despise Trade Days. For the town, they're great. Vendors coming in, renting booths, and bringing revenue to local shops and such. But it's the one thing I refuse to help with in town. I don't like the random crowdedness and the carnival people complaining when I try and check the stability of their rides. One year helping, and I was done.

Dad's eyes twinkle when he spots the roasted-corn stand, so I can't deny him. I open my squeaky truck door and climb out.

He adjusts his belt, which keeps his pants snug under his

growing belly. For a man in his fifties, he's still in good shape, but the middle-age pudge is starting to show a bit. I never poke fun, as I'm well aware I'm built just like him. Tall and broad, but not immune to spreading around the middle.

Good thing, or my massages might not be so pleasant for Daisy. Wait . . . why should I care what she thinks? It's her job to massage me, and I'm paying her for it.

Daisy.

While I'm standing in line for hot buttered corn, her cinnamon hair flashes against a white tent and green grass, giving it a holiday effect. I watch as she stacks candles on the table in front of her and chats with an older couple browsing her booth.

"And for you, sir?" The man peddling corn catches my attention.

Instead of answering him, I turn to Dad. "I'll catch up with you later. I need to check on something."

He nods, quickly abandoning his mission to make me eat and relax in favor of his own hunk of corn. I step out of line and trail toward the Country Candle Company sign that is decorated with daisies, not unlike those covering my backside.

I'm not sure why, but I suddenly got the urge to see her and ask if she'd like to get something to eat with me.

CHAPTER SIX

Daisy

"This one is a little fruitier if that's what you're looking for."

I unscrew the lid on a jar of "Isn't That Just Peachy" and hold it for the older lady to sniff.

She puts a feeble hand on the mason jar and lowers her head. "Oh my, that's lovely." She smiles and lifts her eyes to mine. "A good choice for a kitchen candle."

"Exactly my intentions," I say, returning her smile.

"I'll take four of these."

"Yes, ma'am. Let me get those."

I turn and rummage through the boxes of candles I stuffed at the back of our tent. When I return to the woman with a hefty paper bag and four candles, I notice Kyle standing at our other table. And he's talking to my mother.

My pulse picks up as I silently pray she doesn't say or do something to embarrass me too much. Of course, the fact that she's out here barefoot isn't helping with that.

I pull my money bag from my camping chair and hand change to the lady before rolling her individual candles in heavy paper. The last candle almost rolls off the table as I sneak a peek at Mom with Kyle. I catch it with my thighs and finish packing the merchandise.

"Thank you, dear."

"You're welcome. Enjoy your night." I smile as the woman shuffles off carrying my paper bag on one arm and her small purse on the other.

I fumble with the zipper on my money bag, not unaware of Kyle watching me. It's perfectly normal for him to be here, in the middle of town, like everyone else. Yet it makes me nervous, since I can now picture him with his shirt off—lying on my massage table.

"Thanks," I hear him mutter to Mom. Then he steps toward me. "Hey."

I drop the money bag in the chair behind me after fooling with the zipper far too long. My eyes trail up Kyle's chest to his face, framed by slightly wet dark hair. He has a clean, masculine scent that complements my candles marvelously.

Hmmm . . . maybe I should bottle his scent—literally. But what would I call it?

"Kyle in a Can." No, "Mr. Clean." Dorky. How about "Heaven Scent"? Okay, I'm officially a weirdo.

"You okay?"

I blink, realizing I've been staring awkwardly at him while analyzing his scent like a drug dog. "Fine," I squeak out.

"Fine." That would work too.

I wince at my cheesy thoughts. "I'm good. I guess the heat is getting to me."

"It has been a hot one." He gives me a lopsided grin that melts my insides more than my perspiring face.

I manage to smile and lean slightly into the table as my knees buckle. I've never been great at talking to attractive guys. Huge understatement. More like I've never been anywhere near normal talking to them.

Massaging Kyle is bad enough, but we're quiet then, and he's my client. I'm doing my job, and he's on my turf. Trade Days is a fair playing field, and I hold no upper hand.

"If you're not too busy, I thought maybe you'd like to grab a bite to eat." He runs a hand over his hair.

I focus on the veins and muscles flexing on his arm when he does. My mouth goes dry, so I reach for my water bottle.

"With you?" I somehow choke out after a quick sip.

He lifts then lowers a shoulder. "Yeah."

"Uh, yeah, that sounds great." The last word is a little clipped as I bite down on my tongue.

My tone sounded more eager coming out than I'd meant for it to. I glance at Mom, who's replenishing some of her essential oils for display.

"Let me ask my mom."

"That's your mom?"

Despite the heat, my body chills. "Yes," I say slowly.

"Huh. Her hair's much lighter."

Relief runs through my veins, warming me slightly. I expected a comment about her eccentric look or something similar. Most women her age don't wear multicolored fringed vests with cut-off shorts and no shoes. At least not in this decade.

"My dad had dark hair." I tug at the fishtail braid hanging over my shoulder. "And to be honest, I'm not sure what color my hair is supposed to be anymore."

He laughs, and I find myself smiling. I let go of my braid and hold up a finger before stepping toward Mom.

"Mom, do you mind if I go ahead and grab some food before it gets busy? I'll come right back."

"Sure, honey." She pats my arm, and her multiple metal rings heat up my skin.

"Thanks, we'll only be a few minutes."

"We?" She raises a thin brow toward Kyle and nods.

"Yes, that's Kyle. A client, and kind of a friend."

A mischievous smirk crosses her face. She pats my arm again. "Take all the time you need."

I tilt my head.

She nods. "Seriously, if you don't enjoy the night with him, I will."

I roll my eyes.

"Don't try me, Daisy Mae."

"Yes, ma'am." I twist my mouth as she laughs. "My money bag is in my chair," I call as I turn toward Kyle.

I circle the table and step out of the shade from my tent. Several food trucks and carts line the perimeter of the trade grounds.

"What would you like to eat?" Kyle asks.

"Doesn't matter, but I'm partial to Mary's food."

Kyle nods. "Mary's it is, then."

We walk side by side toward her food truck. I scan the area, checking out vendors who arrived since we set up shop, making mental notes on what tables I want to visit later. A few local people whisper when they see us.

My skin itches as the shock registers on their faces. Kyle and I have never done anything together, like ever. Well, there's the massages, but not anything in public. He's always with Bradley or neck-deep in some town event. I'm usually with Adrianne or doing something with goats and chickens and candles.

Wow, that last thought makes me sound like a modern-day fairy-tale witch.

We reach Mary's truck before I get too much in my head. I scan her limited menu on the side of her window. Her idea of limited still offers plenty of variety, just less than inside her actual restaurant.

Two people are ahead of us in line. I stand close to Kyle, his arm brushing my shoulder. Fresh man scents waft my way, and I inhale. I much prefer his scent to fair food and Mom's essential oils.

The hairs on my arms prickle as he moves his arm, causing it to brush against mine again. I try and act casual, as if hot guys brush against me all the time. No big deal. I've had my hands all over his upper body—shirtless.

Wrong thought.

My throat closes up as Kyle on my massage table flashes through my mind once more. To kill the shirtless Kyle mirage, I look at fully clothed Kyle. He smiles down at me, which has the opposite effect of calming me.

"What you want, sugar?" Mary's smooth voice calls from the other side of the window.

Kyle faces the menu and starts ordering. His voice is muffled as my pulse beats in my ears. I run my eyes over the menu once more and clear my throat before it's my turn to order.

I manage to say, "Chicken finger basket and water," in a normal voice. Then I reach for my back pocket, where I stuffed a twenty in my shorts earlier. I pull out the bill, and Kyle's large hand lands on mine.

I stare at it like a foreign object has landed on Earth rather than another human hand landing on mine. His fingers are long and strong, with neatly cut nails lightly outlined by oil or grease stains.

"I've got it. My treat," he says.

I'm still staring at our hands when he pulls his back. I tuck the twenty back in my pocket and force my gaze to the window. Freezing in front of all Apple Cart isn't going to help my reputation for weirdness.

Mary flashes her white teeth with a noticeable gap in the front. There's a mischievous twinkle in her eye I know all too well.

She gives many young people this same look . . . right before they get together.

Kyle

Daisy and I stand to the side and wait on our order from Mary's. I fumble with the paper number in my hand as people pass us on the concrete walking trail that serves as an unofficial border to separate the food from the other vendors.

A woman pushes a large stroller with a tiny dog inside. The dog is wearing a dress, and the woman is wearing pants that are not near thick enough. Not caring to count her rolls, I turn to Daisy.

Her reddish-brown hair is twisted in some kind of intricate braid that I couldn't do if an Eagle Scout medal depended on it. She's wearing a light-pink shirt that makes her skin look extra smooth. Her legs are tiny like the rest of her, but toned thighs peek out from her khaki shorts. Her toenails are painted bright green. Like glow-in-the-dark green.

I take my time scanning her from the feet up, as if really looking at her for the first time. In high school, she had hair colors as crazy as her toenails and wore a lot of black and white. I like her better with pink on her clothes rather than in her hair.

When my eyes reach her head, she turns and meets my

gaze. Her eyes are like almonds in shape and color. She isn't smiling, so I turn back to the crowd.

For all I know, she watched me checking her out just now and decided I'm a pervert. I suck in a breath and hope she's not just sticking around for free food.

She has her own money. She can leave at any time.

Reminding myself of this gives a little reassurance. But of all the girls I've hung out with, Daisy is different.

In a good way.

She doesn't seem to care what people think, and she's content in her world. She's also pretty in an unconventional way. I'm used to majorettes and cheerleaders who all dress alike and wear a lot of makeup. They're usually tall and travel in packs like zoo animals.

Daisy is small but still feminine, and I kind of find that cool next to my large frame. She has pretty hair and eyes that aren't like everyone else's, and she has the softest skin I've ever touched.

Okay, more like she's touched my skin. But hands are usually the roughest part of someone's body, so if her hands are that soft, I can only imagine how the rest of her feels.

"Order number thirty-seven."

Mary's booming yet soothing drawl brings my mind back to the present. I take a few steps to the window and retrieve our food.

I rejoin Daisy, and we head toward the gazebo and picnic tables.

"Let me help you." She reaches out and I hand her the drinks.

Our hands brush lightly, reminding me of her smooth touch once again. The same tingle that hit my hand when I stilled hers before she paid rushes up my arm again. I recognize this sensation all too well, even though it's been a while since I've felt it.

I like Daisy.

"Where do you want to sit?" Her voice travels up to me through the background of kids playing and someone singing in the distance.

The picnic tables are filling up fast, and the gazebo is overtaken with little kids climbing on the rails. I raise a brow and scan the area. "I know a place if you want somewhere quiet."

"Okay." She follows me.

We go behind the flatbed trailer set up as a stage in the bank parking lot. The woman front and center sings a Faith Hill song as a bluegrass band tunes fiddles down below. I suppose they're up next.

I lead her to the small neighborhood on the other side of the bank. Before the houses begin, there's a narrow creek with a few benches.

Daisy stares at the creek and smiles. "This is so peaceful."

"Yeah, it's kind of a hidden gem people don't know about unless they live in this area."

She nods.

I've never lived in town myself, but I dated a few girls who did. I leave that detail out in case she already thinks I'm a little slimy for staring at her.

We sit and eat in silence for a few minutes. Not awkward silence, though. More like we're mutually enjoying the sound of the creek and being out of the crowd.

"How did you get into massaging?" I ask, wanting to know her better.

She takes a drink of water before answering. "My mom is pretty eccentric and always swore by holistic medicine. I'm not quite as extreme as her, but I do think massages and stretching can do a lot for your overall health. Plus, I like the calmness of it all."

I smile. "Goes well with candles, huh?"

She laughs a little. "I guess it does." She eats a few fries, then turns to me. "What about you? Did you always want to be a mechanic?"

I shrug. "I guess I was destined to. I started college but never went as far as I intended, and moved back here."

She nods. "And your dad's a mechanic, right?"

"Yep. I helped him my whole life, so it came easy, and I enjoy knowing I can fix something other people can't."

She grins. "I get that. What about your mom?"

My jaw tightens as I regret opening the door to this get-to-know-you conversation. I often forget it's a two-way street. The worst part is that this question still bothers me after two decades.

"I don't know. She hasn't been around since I was six."

Daisy sets down her water and puts a hand on my knee. "I'm so sorry. I had no idea."

"It's fine. My dad raised me, along with the help of his parents. I just hate I don't know much about her."

Daisy slides her hand off my knee, and a small piece of me breaks off with it. I start to reach for her hand, but hold back.

"My dad died when I was thirteen. That's when we moved to Alabama."

"Sorry to hear that."

She lifts one side of her lips. "Thanks. He was a great man. Military, very matter of fact and to the point on things. Opposite of my flighty mom." She lets out a laugh laced with sadness.

"I guess we have something in common, then, both being raised by single parents."

She lifts her head and smiles. I smile back, happy to have alleviated some of her sadness. Then I pop the last bite of my steak melt into my mouth and wad up the wrapper.

She closes her food box and tucks it neatly beside her. I

want to stay out here and get to know her better, but I also don't want to scare her off or make her sad. We got deep—fast. In all honestly, I'm not sure I can handle much more diving into my own past right now.

"Is there anything you want to do before I have to return you to your post?"

She taps her lip with her finger. "Hmm, maybe ride the Ferris wheel."

Crap. Why did I ask?

I'm certain the tan has left my face as I feel blood drain from my head. She could've said take a bullet for her and it wouldn't bother me as bad as this. Despite clocking in at six-foot-four, I have a fear of heights.

"Okay," I mutter.

I stand and gather our trash, willing myself to put on a brave face. Not quite as brave as when I lined up against someone on the football field. I don't want to scare her away. More like the face I wear for the older men at the tractor-pull meetings when I really want to roll my eyes and tell them all the reasons their ideas are garbage.

We stroll back toward the town square, my feet heavy like I'm walking the green mile rather than green grass to a festival. I stop at the first trash can and get rid of our boxes.

Then the large wheel of terror comes into view. *Why do those seats have to swing? And why do they stop people at the very top?*

A buzzer rings behind us, jolting me to attention. I turn to a row of fair games in the center of the square. Shooting targets with water guns, throwing rings at bottles, and my favorite—tossing footballs through toilet lids.

Part of me is excited about throwing a football, and the other part wants to delay an untimely death suspended on carny cables.

"Ooh, let me win you something."

I grab Daisy's hand and lead her to the football booth. My body instantly relaxes, though I'm not certain whether it's from tossing a football instead of being suspended in the air or holding her hand.

The woman behind the booth grabs the five I slap on the counter and replaces it with three footballs. She explains how the game works, while meticulously balancing a cigarette between her teeth. Throw three balls at a toilet seat. The more you ring the hole, the better prize you get. Good thing it's simple, since my focus is on the dangling cigarette with about an inch of ashes on the end.

"Got it?"

"Yes, ma'am."

"Okay." She moves out from in front of my targets.

I drop Daisy's hand and grab a football, then turn it in my hands as the carnival worker finally taps the end of her cigarette. A small pile of ashes hit the edge of the counter like someone used a pepper shaker with a loose lid. She swipes them away with a weathered hand.

I grip the laces of the football, oddly energized from holding it. Even though I played defense in college, I played both ways for Apple Cart and Wisteria. I rear back and hit the hardest target on the board.

Daisy cheers behind me, bringing a smile to my face. I throw the next ball through the same hole. Then the last one.

When I turn to the carnival gal for my reward, her mouth is open, and the cigarette falls to the ground.

"What in tarnation? Nobody's done that good yet. We even rigged that top toilet seat to fall if a ball hits the edge."

I raise a brow. I'd always heard they rigged these games, but never expected someone to admit it. I smile over my shoulder at Daisy. Her cheeks are rosy, and her eyes glisten in the lowering sun. I give her a quick wink, then turn to the woman.

"So I'd say we get a big prize, then, huh?"

She laughs, which quickly turns into a smoker's cough. "Get whatever you want, hon."

"What do you want?" I ask Daisy, motioning toward the prizes.

She takes a step forward and bounces on her toes, which I find adorable. I watch her eyes move from side to side across the row of prizes hanging from hooks on the back of the booth.

"That." She points enthusiastically at a huge pink chicken on top.

The woman snorts. "Finally. We got that in with our Easter inventory. A pink chicken don't make much sense to me. I've been hanging it every weekend hoping someone will win the dang thing."

Daisy hooks her arm through mine and stares up at me. "Well, we're happy to take it off your hands."

She uses a mop handle to unhook the chicken. Daisy beams as it falls toward us and the woman catches it effortlessly, as I'm sure she's done a million times.

"Here, hon." She hands Daisy the chicken before lighting a new cigarette.

The only downside to Daisy's excitement about the stuffed animal is that she lets go of my arm to grab it. She hugs the chicken, which isn't much shorter than her and way bigger around.

This time Daisy grabs my hand and shuffles the chicken to one side like it's the size of a real chicken rather than her.

"My turn to pick."

She pulls me toward the Ferris wheel. I dig my heels in the dirt for a second before giving in.

We join a dozen or so other people in line. Some I know, and some I don't. But they're all staring at Daisy and me together. Maybe she notices their stares too, because she drops my hand and uses it to better hold the chicken.

I try and convince myself it's because of the chicken, not me. My insecurities about Daisy soon take a backseat to panic as the wheel stops and people exit beside us. A couple with a child at the front of the line gets in the cart.

The kid can't be more than five. If he can do it, so can I. *Right?*

One by one, the people in front of us load into seats and move up the wheel. I shove my sweaty palms in my pockets, wishing Daisy were holding them instead.

My stomach bottoms out when we step on the platform in front of an empty swinging seat. Daisy sits down first and adjusts the chicken beside her. I sit on the other side of the chicken and suck in a breath as the guy running this thing lowers the bar.

Normally I wouldn't trust someone with a tattoo around their entire neck, but what choice do I have?

We're in here now, buckled and moving upward. I close my eyes and breathe in the scent of barbecue and sugar. I haven't heard of anyone dying on this . . . yet. But that also doesn't seem like something people would advertise.

"Are you okay?"

Daisy's sweet voice echoes in my right ear. I peek one eye open and find that we're stopped almost at the top. My feet are now higher than the bank roof. This is not cool.

"Uh . . ." My voice is breathy and panicked.

Daisy's hand finds mine and grips it. "Are you afraid of heights?"

I shake my head quickly, then regret doing so as it rocks our cart.

She gives my hand a gentle squeeze. "It's okay. Just focus on one thing."

Daisy.

I turn to her, but see the stupid chicken between us. Luckily, she leans forward and smiles. We stare in silence, and I take in her unique beauty. The way the sun glistens behind the treetops, highlighting the red tones in her hair. A light breeze catches it, sending a few waves across her cheek. I want to brush them away so I can see her full face, but one hand is holding hers, and the other has a death grip on the bar beside me.

When I can no longer resist, I move my hand from the bar and use it to brush the hair from her cheek. I tuck the strand behind her ear and linger my fingers on her cheek. It's even smoother than I expected.

She swallows and closes her eyes. I'm not certain if she wants me to kiss her, so I inch closer. Maybe that will encourage her to make a move.

I close my own eyes and decide to give her a few seconds. If she doesn't make a move, I will. The worst that can happen is her not wanting a kiss, in which case I'll simply stop.

But that's not the worst that could happen . . .

After counting to five in my head—Mississippis included—I lean in, close enough to feel her breath on my face. Then a loud clank comes from below and we speed down toward the ground.

I jerk my head back and clinch my jaw, then squeeze Daisy's hand.

"It's okay," she whispers beside me.

I turn my head, hoping to calm my nerves with her sweet face. Instead, I'm eyeball to eyeball with the giant chicken. I shriek. Daisy's hand reaches across the chicken and lands on top of our locked hands. I realize I'm probably cutting off circulation on her other hand and lighten my grip.

"Look at me."

"I tried, but there's a giant chicken in the way."

She giggles and leans forward. "Just breathe."

I suck deep breaths in and out until my heart rate returns to a semi-normal speed.

"I'm sorry I suggested we go on this."

I shake my head. "I thought I could handle it. I've never told anyone I'm scared of these things." I swallow. "Until now."

She smiles. "It's okay to be scared sometimes."

"It helps having you here with me."

"It does?" Her smile widens.

"Yeah." I stare into her eyes, contemplating if I should try and kiss her once we're back on solid footing.

The classic rock song "She Drives Me Crazy" starts playing out of nowhere.

Daisy rolls her eyes. "That's Mom's ringtone. I better get it."

She pulls a purple phone from her back pocket and answers it. I close my eyes and try to imagine we're anywhere but here. Then I realize I'd rather be here with her than anywhere else with someone else.

"I'm selling out of candles. She asked if I could come back and take orders. People are asking questions she can't answer."

"Oh, well that's a good thing, I guess."

"Yeah." She smirks. "I'll head over there once we land."

I nod, trying to put on a happy face. I'm glad her business is doing well, but not so glad for this night to end.

And to think that I wanted to stay home and eat cereal.

CHAPTER SEVEN

Daisy

Last night was one of the best, yet most confusing, nights of my life. I sold out of every candle scent I brought except for "You Butter Believe It." And rightfully so since I still haven't mastered the scent of real butter.

Even better and more surprising, Kyle and I connected somehow.

He had this sultry look on his face at the top of the Ferris wheel. Either he wanted to kiss me, or he had to puke. My limited experience with guys wouldn't allow me to make that judgement call, or allow me to kiss him.

Adrianne would've kissed the guy in my situation.

But I'm not Adrianne. Or Hannah, Ashley, or Bianca. I'm not even Carolina, with a sweet guy best friend to fall for me. I'm just Daisy.

From football captain to heading up clubs all over town,

Kyle has always been a leader. Tall, handsome, and sure of himself. Why would he want to kiss me?

Yeah, he totally had to barf.

Still, that doesn't mean all the hand holding and smiles my way didn't stir something inside me. I've never had a close guy friend before, so maybe that's how they act? Other friends have grabbed my hand to pull me someplace, so why should Kyle be any different?

Friends. That's what we are.

I stare down at my chunky sandals and grunt. If it's only friendship, why did I take extra long on my hair and makeup this morning, put on my cutest sundress and sandals, and light bacon candles all over the house?

I stare at the giant pink chicken in the corner of my bedroom. The one Mullet has grown to love in less than a day's time.

I know why, and it's killing me. I have a crush on Kyle Tolbert.

Bad, Daisy. So bad!

He is super off-limits. Not only is he forever out of my league, but he's also a client!

I'd be breaking all kinds of masseuse/client codes. My hands grow clammy as I reach for my phone. He will be here any minute for his weekly massage. Time to lock Mullet in the room and report to duty.

I laugh at myself. Some duty. Talk about mixing business with pleasure. I'd massage Kyle for free.

But he can't know that.

The living room is lit up like a seance. I move from table to table blowing out bacon candles so Kyle doesn't think I'm attempting to seduce him.

There's a knock on the door, but I hurry and blow out the candles on the mantel. As I lean over to blow out the last one, a fringe on the collar of my sundress catches the flame.

It flickers as I beat out the small fire. Now I'm left with a singed dress that smells like a campfire. There's another knock, leaving me no time to change.

Shoot. I jerk my hair down from the updo that took me half an hour to create and fan it over the shoulder of the singed collar. Then I rush to the door and put on a smile like nothing weird just happened.

"Oh, it's you." My face falls.

Toby frowns. "Sorry. I guess you were expecting your mother."

No, not really.

"I have some cinnamon and sage for you in my trunk."

"How much? I can help you get it on the porch."

"I'll help him." Kyle's voice booms from somewhere beyond the porch.

I peek around Toby, trying not to look too giddy about seeing him. Toby follows my eyes and turns to Kyle.

"Thanks, man." He turns back to me. "Where you want it?"

Kyle steps on the porch. "I can take it inside if you want. Same place as last time?"

"Yeah, great. Y'all go ahead. I need to check on something before your massage anyway."

"No problem. I'm a few minutes early." Kyle grins at me, and my stomach dances like I've eaten at Enchilada.

I hurry to my bedroom and lock the door behind me before stripping off the singed dress. I toss it on the stuffed chicken I still haven't named and rummage for a cute top and shorts—my usual attire.

How silly of me to try and fix up anyway. This is my home/office/studio. I reach for a ponytail holder to pull back my hair, then stop. It's in soft waves around my shoulders, and I kind of like it. Besides, there's nothing wrong with having good hair today.

Mullet nudges my dress until it falls from the chicken, then curls up beside it. I really should name that thing, but what's a proper name for a hot-pink stuffed chicken that's bigger than me? Nothing comes to mind.

Big Bird. Wait . . . is a chicken a real bird? I should know this.

Maybe Big Chicken. Big Chick! That's it.

Content with naming my new roommate, I stroke Mullet's little mullet and shut him in the room with Big Chick. I follow voices to the candle room.

"And that's how you can use medicinal plants to heal hemorrhoids," Toby says from his spot propped against the door frame.

"You don't say," Kyle answers as he fits the last of the boxes into my closet.

He turns around and spots me. We make eye contact and I mouth "sorry." He winks, causing my heart to thump.

"That's all of them, Daisy," Kyle says after closing the closet and walking toward us.

He extends a hand to Toby. "Thanks for the help, man."

Toby shakes his hand weakly. "Thank you. It was my job and you did all the heavy lifting."

Kyle waves a hand dismissively. I bite back a laugh, knowing full well that a box of dried herbs and flowers weighs about as much as an armful of baby chicks.

Toby wipes a hand across his buzzcut and sighs. "I best get back to your mother."

"Thanks, Toby. Tell her to text me what candles she wants. I plan on making more this afternoon." He nods and sways out of the room.

That leaves me alone with Kyle.

Not unusual, except for last night. Somehow holding his hand was even more intimate than massaging his entire body.

Okay, not his *entire* body. I wince. NOT what I should be thinking about.

"You ready for me now?"

"No!"

Kyle jerks his head back.

"I mean, yes." *To the massage only.* "Go ahead and make yourself comfortable."

Kyle half grins, then brushes past me. He sniffs the air as he leaves the candle room. I step out as well and try not to sniff him.

"It smells great in here, by the way. You been cooking bacon or something?"

I giggle nervously. "No, the bacon candles are pretty potent." *When you light like twenty all over the house.*

"I like it." He smiles, then turns and disappears into the massage room, where the only lit candles remain.

I suck in a breath and relax my shoulders. In a few minutes, I'll walk in the next room and put my hands all over a shirtless Kyle. It was nerve-wracking before, given my teenage admiration for him.

I can't really call it a crush, per se, since I admired him from afar and never really talked to him. More of a celebrity crush. The way some girls pasted posters of Justin Bieber on their walls in high school, I looked at Kyle IRL.

My stomach flips like there's a tiny gymnast bouncing around my gut. I recall last night and try to overanalyze all the hand touching and what each instance meant. I'm deep in my thoughts when I realize Kyle has been in there a while now.

I push myself off the wall and knock on the massage room door. "You ready?" I call as I crack open the door.

"Yes," his muffled voice says from inside.

Now aware of my bare feet, I tiptoe in, close the door, and dim the lighting. I'd kicked off my sandals to step in my shorts and never slid them back on. Oh well, at least my toenails are painted. And as far as feet go, mine are attractive. They're tiny and all my toes line up nicely.

A rerun of the show *Friends* introduced me to "foot flirting." I've never considered trying it, since it didn't fare well for Phoebe.

After rubbing some oil on my hands, I press them into Kyle's shoulders. I close my eyes and will myself not to overthink last night. This is a new day, and Kyle is my client. He has a huge knot in the center right of his back, which concerns me. But it helps me keep things professional too.

I make a mental note to address that after everything else. Then I continue with our routine massage. The knot somehow takes center focus in my mind, helping me keep things normal. After I massage his front, I peel back the cloth from his eyes.

"Kyle, you have a huge knot on your back."

He reaches under the sheet and rubs his side. "Yeah, I know."

"I can apply more pressure if you're good with that. It may hurt a little, though."

He nods. "Anything to help."

The sides of my mouth uptick. I don't use this move unless I'm certain someone can take it. Something tells me Kyle will have no trouble holding my small stature.

"Flip over."

I wait for him to turn beneath the sheet and settle his head in the hole. Then I pull a small stool out from under the nearby table and use it to climb on top of Kyle.

My feet balance on his back as I hold to a small band suspended high above the table. I use it for my own yoga practice sometimes, but keep it here for this very reason.

The ashiatsu massage.

Holding to the band for balance, I walk across his back

with both feet. I apply more weight when I reach the pained spot. I rock back and forth until I feel the knot break apart under his skin.

I curve the front of my foot around his sides and work my way up and down his back. I'm nearing his rib cage when Kyle jerks and lifts off the table.

Instead of grabbing the band with both hands like I intend to, the hand actually on it releases. I fall toward Kyle.

Closing my eyes, I pray for a soft landing. At least one that involves the table rather than the floor. I have no idea if Kyle is still under me until two strong arms cradle me, breaking my fall.

My breath hangs in my throat as I blink my eyes open to Kyle's bare chest. He is kneeling on the table, holding me.

"Are you okay?" he asks.

I stare at his chest, afraid to lift my head that close to his. "Yeah. Are you?" I clear my throat to regain more of a voice. "I literally walked all over you."

He laughs a little, and his chest vibrates against me. I swallow.

"It felt really good. I'm just ticklish some near my rib cage."

"Duly noted." That's the first time I've grazed across his actual side, as I always massage his back, then front.

Pressing against his warm, bare chest is too much for me, so I wiggle my way to standing and hop off the table. Kyle starts to shuffle back to sitting, holding the sheet to slide under.

But not before I catch a glimpse of his boxer briefs that are covered in . . . daisies!

The flowers. Not photos of me. Thank God! But still, a little ironic, and strange yet flattering.

"Um, I'll let you get dressed." I drop my eyes and march

toward the door, thankful I'm in a room I know like the back of my hand.

Once I'm in the properly lit hallway, I close the door and make a beeline for the kitchen. The living room smells too much like bacon—a scent I now associate with a shirtless Kyle.

I grab a glass and fill it with cold water, then down it like a drunk needing alcohol. I'm returning to the sink for a refill when I hear boots clicking across the tile floor.

"There you are. I need to pay you."

I turn around, forcing my eyes to Kyle's face this time. He's smiling and holding out some folded cash. Why do I suddenly feel like a prostitute?

"I added some extra for getting out that knot in my back."

"That's not necessary."

"Sure, it was worth it. Take it." He pushes the money toward me.

I shake my palm at it. "No need to tip, you did buy me dinner last night."

Wow, could this be any more like Pretty Woman *right now?*

Kyle grabs my hand and lays the money in it.

I stand corrected, it could be more like *Pretty Woman*. I clutch the cash and withdraw my hand from his, as if letting it linger might put me in danger of driving a sports car in a blond wig.

"Hey, are you going to that?"

I lift my eyes from the wad of cash in my hand to Kyle. He's staring at my refrigerator. I turn to the invitation for Carolina and Tanner's couples shower. I'm not technically a couple, but somehow made the guest list.

"I was invited, but I think I'm supposed to bring someone with me, by the wording."

"Same. I don't mind going solo, but I don't know how to buy a gift for stuff like that."

I walk over and take the invitation off the fridge. "Says they registered at Buc-ee's. The problem is you can't buy it online."

Kyle scratches his head and sighs. "I could just give them money, but that seems a little impersonal."

Tell me about it. I stuff the cash he just gave me in my back shorts pocket, as it's started feeling slimier by the minute in my hand. If only I hadn't seen him in those daisy drawers.

"Would you want to ride to Buc-ee's with me and help me pick out a gift?"

My ears ring. Did he just ask me to ride over an hour with him and shop for Carolina's shower? Kyle lifts his eyebrows as if waiting on my response. I guess he did just ask that.

"Sure." What other choice do I have?

Better than the alternative response: "Thanks, but it would be too awkward since I break out in hives when we're close and overanalyze whether you were making a kissing face or barfing face at the fair."

"Great, I can pick you up tomorrow after church if that's good with you."

I nod. "Works for me."

"Be ready by twelve and we can grab lunch there if you don't mind waiting. They have great brisket."

"They do," I choke out through a nervous smile.

"See you tomorrow." He turns and walks out of my kitchen, then my front door.

I'm plastered to my kitchen floor, trying to make heads and tails of what just happened. I glance down at the invitation in my hand. This little slip of paper is to thank for me spending an afternoon alone with Kyle. Or it's to blame.

Only tomorrow will tell which one.

Kyle

I just committed an unpardonable sin in the Baptist Church. At least, according to my grandma. I walked out during invitation to beat the crowd.

But I had a good reason. I wanted to get out of dodge before everyone started talking, holding me up, and before Granny cornered me to invite me to lunch. Not that she would have to invite me. It's always a standing invitation for Dad and me to eat there after church, or anytime really.

However, I have other plans this afternoon. Plans that involve an afternoon with Daisy, who I hope is wearing that dress I spotted her in yesterday for a split second.

I turn down her driveway and drum my thumbs on the steering wheel. I've never been one to get nervous around women. For the most part, they would come to me. If not, I assumed they didn't like me and let it be.

I've never really had to work to find out if a girl likes me. Until now.

Daisy gives me a lot of mixed signals. The fact that she massages me every week muddies the waters between us even more. I think I scared her by catching her yesterday, but I wasn't going to lie there while she fell.

Besides, her falling on top of me would make things even more awkward. Mostly because I wouldn't mind it at all, but I somehow think she would.

I pull up to her house and park. A few chickens peck

around the porch as I climb the front steps. The top step shakes a little under my boot. I knock on the door, and she answers almost immediately.

She isn't wearing the dress from yesterday, but she is wearing a flowered shirt and a jean skirt. Very cute. Her hair is braided.

"Hey, you ready?"

"Yeah, let me grab my purse." She smiles and disappears behind the door.

I watch the chickens until she returns with a brightly colored bag and locks the door behind her. On impulse, I take her arm and tug her toward the other side of the porch.

"That top step is wobbly on that end. I don't want you to fall."

She turns to me with rosy cheeks. "Thanks."

We walk down, and I let go of her arm once we're in the yard. I walk to the back of my Jeep and grab a small toolbox I keep on hand.

"Go ahead and have a seat. I'm going to secure that step before we go."

She scrunches her brow in confusion, but gets in the Jeep. I jog back to the porch and put a new nail in the loose wooden board, then step on it to test it out. There, fixed.

When I get in the Jeep beside her, she's smiling.

"That was nice of you to fix the step. I've been meaning to get someone out here to do that."

"No problem." I smile back and turn my Jeep toward the main road.

While traveling out of town and down the interstate, I allow her to lead the conversation. If she asks about my mom, I'll answer her. Thankfully, she doesn't. She doesn't ask about my past at all.

Daisy talks about my business and all the things around town I'm involved in now. It's refreshing to have someone show interest in the current Kyle without digging up the past.

My mom left when I was in kindergarten. Then I changed schools my junior year for football, causing half the county to love me and half the county to hate me. It depended on whether they rooted for the Apple Cart Armadillos, who I supposedly abandoned, or the Wisteria Mudcats, who I helped win back-to-back championships.

Then there was my quick stint at that junior college in Mississippi. I lived it up as a college football player for a little more than a year before my social life got the best of me. One DWI and I was off the team for good. Back to Apple Cart County without a college education. Nothing like the school of hard knocks to grow me up and make my hard drink of choice sweet tea.

Daisy perks up when we turn off the interstate toward Buc-ee's. "They have the best candles, especially the ones made of goat's milk. I get a lot of ideas here."

"Huh. That's cool. I get brisket." I smirk at her.

She smiles back, then stares at the truck-stop sign.

I pull my Jeep into a parking space and we climb out. Daisy walks beside me until we come close to the entrance. Then she abandons me for the beaver statue. Daisy pets the thing like it's a real animal rather than a plastered mascot dressed like Alvin from the Chipmunks. I laugh and pull out my phone, snapping her photo.

She smiles for the photo, then lets go of the statue. I catch up to her, and we walk past rows of lawn chairs and grills, and then through the sliding doors.

The scent of brisket and candied nuts hits my nostrils when we go inside. I turn to Daisy. "Lunch first?"

"Sure."

Thanks to the long drive, the usual buzz around the center area with all the sandwiches has died down some. We walk right up and make our selections. My stomach growls, so I grab a bag of homemade chips too.

As we're fixing our fountain drinks, I glance around. "I forgot they don't have tables. I guess we'll have to eat in the Jeep, then come back in to shop."

"Unless . . ." Daisy stabs a straw in her cup and nods toward a pile of women's stuff.

Among a hodgepodge of towels and signs are two chairs. They're that weird style that people do nowadays, painted then chipped off in places.

I grin at Daisy, both surprised and impressed that she would suggest we eat on merchandise. "Think that thing would hold me up?"

She laughs. "Of course, it's a full-size wooden chair."

I follow her to the register, where we pay for our food. I'm not quick enough to pay for hers this time since she jumped in front of me with her purse open.

As soon as we're both paid up, we take our bags to the chairs near the food. Daisy moves a few towels and pillows off the seats, arranging them neatly on the nearby table. It's not that hard to enjoy my brisket until a woman leans around me to check the price of my chair.

Daisy's cheeks wiggle, and she laughs loudly after the woman walks away. I laugh with her, and we catch the attention of an employee. Khaki pants step in front of me. I trail my eyes to a red collared shirt with a Buc-ee's lanyard at the waist. It reads "Danielle."

I swallow my bite of brisket and wipe my mouth with the back of my hand. Danielle stares at us like we're on exhibit. In a way, we are.

"Sir, ma'am. Is there something I can help you with?"

Daisy is taking a bite of her club sandwich. Her face goes pale, and she blinks up at Danielle.

I open my mouth to say there's no seating, but something entirely different comes out.

"Yes, we need to find a wedding registry."

"Oh, of course." Danielle beams. "Right this way."

I pop the last bite of my sandwich in my mouth and ball up the wrapper. Daisy folds her leftovers in her paper and stuffs it in the bag with my chips.

We stand and Danielle leads us to a kiosk near the back of the section we're in. She taps the screen and types a few things.

"Input all your information, and then I'll get you a scanner to start your selections."

Daisy laughs. "I'm sorry, we should've clarified. We are looking for our friends' registry, not wanting to open a registry."

"Oh." Danielle's face drops. "Then you put in their names, do a quick search, and hit 'print' on the registry."

"Thanks." The color returns to Daisy's cheeks.

I try and ignore the shock in her tone when she corrected Danielle's mistake. Is it really that funny of a notion for Daisy and me to be together?

She steps forward and types in Carolina's info. Danielle stands awkwardly beside us as we wait for multiple pages to fall from the printer below. She doesn't speak until the printer stops.

"If you guys need anything else, please let me know."

"Thanks," Daisy answers. I nod, happy to see Danielle walk off.

Daisy shuffles through the papers. "Looks like some of these items are already fulfilled. We can decide what we want to spend and then find something in that price range not already bought."

"Sounds like a plan." I smile, relieved I brought her.

I would pick up something I thought they might like and

call it a day. Probably from Walmart too.

We discuss a few items, and Daisy flips through some sheets.

"How about this for Tanner?" She points to a few items.

I lean down to get a better look. Her soft hair tickles my cheek, and I suck in its flowery scent. She tilts her head toward me, putting her lips dangerously close to mine. We both move back an inch on impulse, even though I'd prefer to move an inch closer.

She clears her throat. "Grill accessories?"

"Yep," I say, straightening to my full height.

Daisy leads us toward the area indicated on the sheet. There is quite a variety of items along the way. She stops at every candle display to test out the scents and read their ingredients. For some reason, I find that endearing.

"Try this one." She sticks a candle toward my nose.

I bend down and take a sniff. It has a masculine scent.

"Like it?"

"Yeah." I do, but I'm more aggravated that it's blocking the scent of her hair in front of me.

After selecting some items for Tanner, Daisy concentrates on finding something for Carolina to use in the kitchen.

My eyes widen when I spot an entire display of goat stuff. "Look, Daisy."

I hold up a pillow that reads, "Crazy Goat Lady."

She giggles. "I had a shirt like that once."

I set it down where I found it and make a mental note that Daisy might like that.

She leads us to another table with trays and bowls like women use to put out a lot of food. Daisy picks up some kind of ceramic bowl/tray shaped like the state of Alabama and says it's on the list. Then she gets a towel to go with it, also from the list.

"I think that will do it," she says.

I hold up my spatula and brush combo. "Hope they can cook."

"If not, they can learn." She smirks. "They did pick this stuff out anyway."

"True." I glance around the displays behind us. "You need anything else?"

"No, I'm good." She twists her lips. "Maybe a quick trip to the restroom."

"Okay, want me to hold that?"

"Sure." She hands me her items, and I make sure to touch her hand.

It's only for a second or two, but enough to satisfy my craving of her soft touch. For now, at least.

She heads toward the bathroom, and I jog toward the goat display. If she's anything like the other girls I've dated, she'll take a few minutes.

Wait . . . is this a date? We never really defined that.

Not having time to let that thought percolate, I grab the pillow and rush toward a register.

"You're fast." Daisy's voice calls from behind me as I'm paying. I grab the bag and hope she doesn't notice how it's mighty bulky for some slim grilling supplies.

I step aside as she pays for her items.

The pillow burns through the bag under my arm. I'm not used to hiding things, especially a surprise.

Daisy stuffs her card in her wallet and grabs her bag, then turns to me. We exit the way we came in, through all the summer sale items out front.

The sun blinds me as we make our way to the Jeep. Daisy waves goodbye to the beaver statue when we pass. I slow down and admire her cheerful stride toward the parking lot.

If she gives me even the slightest clue that she wants to be kissed . . . let's just say I hope she doesn't mind brisket breath.

CHAPTER EIGHT

Daisy

"Hey, Daisy, let me take your gift." Hannah greets me at the door of the lodge and takes the gift bag from my hand.

I continue inside and follow the voices coming from the kitchen. A group of all women stands around the countertops talking. Jack is behind them pulling a pan from the oven.

"Appetizers are out," he announces as he sets the pan on a rack.

"Let me get a tray." Bianca circles him and opens a cabinet.

I smirk at the fish oven mitts on Jack's hands. Looks like something I might wear if they were goats or chickens instead.

"Hey, girl." Adrianne comes over and drapes a long arm around me.

She's wearing heels, so I almost fit under her shoulder. I smile at her.

"Where's JoJo?" Unless it's goat yoga or a dedicated girls' night, it's rare I see her without her new husband.

"Outside. The guys have congregated around a firepit even though it's more than seventy degrees outside." Adrianne rolls her eyes.

I laugh. Alabamians have a weird habit of building bonfires outside all times of year. I found that strange when we first moved here, then quickly accepted the ritual of making s'mores year-round.

"Excuse me, ladies." Bianca slides in front of us with a wooden tray.

She meticulously places deer poppers in a row using a pair of tongs. Jack pops one in his mouth, disrupting her array of rolls. She slaps at his hand playfully, then he kisses her cheek with a full mouth.

"Go join the guys. Your work here is done."

He grabs one more, this time from the pan instead of the tray. That earns him a smile from his wife. Then he disappears out the kitchen door.

I stare toward the back patio as the door opens and closes just enough for Jack to exit. I didn't see Kyle's Jeep when I parked, but that doesn't mean he isn't here. The lodge has plenty of places to park in the back, and he may have just gotten here or rode with Bradley.

"I'm taking these to the dining room. There are more appetizers in there, so help yourselves. I'll alert the boys." Bianca sways out of the kitchen, balancing the large tray in her hands.

I will myself to stop wondering if "the boys" includes Kyle, but I can't. He's supposed to be here. He said he would, and he bought a gift. It shouldn't matter, and I shouldn't care.

But I do. A little too much.

We had such a fun trip yesterday, talking and browsing around Buc-ee's. I usually go by myself to check out candles and bath products for ideas. Or with Adrianne, who stocks up on earrings and maybe some novelty things like a swimsuit with the Buc-ee's mascot across the rear.

My friends continue to chatter around me, and I comment now and again to act interested. They're busy discussing the house Carolina is flipping with Jonah.

Bianca blows back through and out the back door about the time Ashley walks in with Samuel.

"Sorry we're late," she announces.

"Just in time," Hannah says. "We finished setting out refreshments." She takes their gifts and waves toward the dining room.

"You don't have to tell me twice," Kendra comments.

She was Carolina's college roommate. I've only met her twice, but I like her. Mainly because she makes me feel more normal. Of course, she has dreadlocks and talks about juice cleanses all the time. But hey, I'm not the oddball when she's in town.

We head toward the dining room, with Kendra leading the way. She piles a plate full of raw veggies and takes a seat in the corner of the room. The fact that she's happily married gives me hope.

Deep voices call my attention toward the opening between the dining room and kitchen. I crane my head to see around my taller friends. Jack, Jonah, Bradley, JoJo. No Kyle.

I finish fixing my plate, then step aside.

Adrianne elbows me. "Where are you sitting?"

I shrug. "Doesn't matter."

She nods, holding her plate. JoJo walks up to her and asks what she wants to drink. She agrees to fix him a plate while he gets their drinks.

An odd sensation curls through me. One I haven't felt in a long time. So long that it takes me a minute to identify it as jealousy.

My best friend is beautiful—and tall—but that's not the reason for my envy. She has someone who loves her, as do all the other women in this room. I never minded much before, until I started hanging out with Kyle.

He may not even think the same about me, but at least he would keep me company if he were here.

"Come on," Adrianne says, bursting my Kyle thought bubble. Probably for the best.

I follow her to the dining room exit that leads to the living area, where JoJo is walking toward the couch. He sets their drinks down on the coffee table, and I realize I still need a drink.

"I'll be right back." I set my plate by theirs and head for the kitchen.

Hannah is at the counter beside the refrigerator, pouring drinks. "What you want, Daisy Mae?"

"Water is fine."

She fills my cup and hands it to me with a smile. I start toward the living room, then bump into Bradley on the way. My water sloshes, but doesn't spill on either of us, just the floor.

"Sorry," he mutters.

I stand back, holding out the cup. "I'll get us a towel."

He stays plastered where I bumped into him, and I notice he's staring at Ashley and Samuel, who are seated alone at the kitchen table.

"Allow me." He takes the towel from me when I return and mops up the water.

"Thanks, do you know where the laundry is?"

"I'll take it." Hannah comes by and holds out a hand.

She smiles as if I'm handing her a hundred dollars rather than a soaked dish rag.

"You okay?" I ask Bradley.

"Yeah." He cocks his head at me. "Kyle couldn't make it tonight. I brought his gift."

"Okay." I force a smile and head to the living room.

I don't want to question why Bradley brought up Kyle or why he thought I'd care that he couldn't make it.

Even worse is the fact that I *do* care.

I table that thought as we eat our snacks and make small talk about our weeks. Adrianne has a funny story about Misty as always, and JoJo talks about his new lumber mill. Carolina chimes in that she and Jonah need wood flooring soon for their reno.

"Steaks and potatoes are ready," Jack announces. He's in the foyer with those fish mitts on his hands again.

One by one, people stand to fix their meal plates. I hang back and stare at the deer heads on the wall.

"Word of advice?"

My shoulders jerk as Bradley's voice startles me. "What?"

"You like Kyle, don't you?" He sits in the recliner opposite me.

My face heats up like the bonfire out back, and I quickly scan the room to see if anyone overheard him. I'm so guilty.

"I could say the same about you and Ashley." I take the less mature road and deflect it back on him.

"She's with the banker. I just like talking to her is all."

I raise an eyebrow. "And Kyle's just my massage client who I like talking to."

"Who you also have been spending time with outside of massages."

I narrow my eyes. "He told you that?"

Bradley laughs. "No, darlin', guys don't gossip, but

everyone else in these parts does. You're forgetting I'm like the king of Apple Cart County."

"Oh." I laugh so hard I snort. "The king, huh?"

He shrugs, some of his cockiness diminishing. "Well, I'm sheriff of the whole county, which kind of trumps both mayors."

I nod and smile.

"Anyway, we're not talking about me, but Kyle. I usually mind my own business, but he's my best bud, and I can tell he likes you too."

"You can?" I perk up, then relax on the couch to try and hide my interest.

"Yeah. Know him like a brother, and he doesn't go around offering girls rides or walking with them around the fairgrounds."

I stare at my almost-empty plate and sigh.

"I don't know you that well, and we didn't go to the same school, but you seem like a great little lady. Anyone who can manage goats like you do and make a candle that can fumigate the jail cells is a winner in my book."

I grin. "Thanks?"

Bradley tips his hat. "I mean it, Daisy. I think you'd be good for Kyle, that's all I'm saying. He needs a good woman in his life."

"But you just said he doesn't go around doing things with women. What makes you think he wants one?"

Bradley shrugs, then folds his arms behind his head. "Not sure that he does. But what a person wants and what a person needs are two different things. Kyle works all the time. He's at home now tinkering with some new crap Wendall brought in."

"I'd think he could take a break to come here."

Bradley grits his teeth. "Not Kyle. Not when he's

promised people to get stuff done. Dude's such a Boy Scout. I just didn't want you thinking he was dodging you."

"Why would—"

"Skootch." Adrianne returns with a real plate of steak and baked potato. JoJo is beside her with a plate holding at least double her food.

I slide to the other end of the couch and make eye contact with Bradley. He winks at me, and I'm not sure what that means. Is he trying to assure me Kyle wasn't dodging me or trying to let me know Kyle likes me too?

Whatever the case, I take the opportunity to leave Bradley's awkwardness. I shuffle between the couch and the coffee table and head for the kitchen. The only people there are Jack, Bianca, and Hannah, who are all hosting. Well, and Kendra, who questions Jack for details on how the potatoes were prepared.

I'd forgotten she was vegan. Her husband comes in and puts an arm around her waist. He mentions something about the vegetables they had out for appetizers.

"Oh yeah." Jack snaps his fingers. "We have more in here. I didn't get them all out." He slides past me as I put a well-done steak on my plate.

I eat meat, but I draw the line at pink and bloody. I move to dress my potato with bacon bits and butter and cheese, all of which Kendra protested.

Jack pulls a Tupperware of vegetables from the refrigerator. "Take all you want."

Kendra beams and takes the bowl. "Thanks."

They walk out while I'm salting my potato. Jack chuckles. "There goes my baby deer's midnight snack."

Bianca rolls her eyes. "Don't act like you weren't going to smother the brussels sprouts in oil and bacon later for me to roast."

"Us Southerners know how to make vegetables taste good." He nods at my potato. "Like Daisy's doing now."

Bianca shakes her head. She lived in Atlanta until marrying Jack. He often teases her about not really being from the South.

I grab a fork from a ceramic caddy nearby and start toward the living room. Bianca and Jack banter behind me, and that little green monster makes its way back to my mind.

I've never had a boyfriend or even a real kiss in my life. Now I'm twenty-eight, and suddenly jealous of every real relationship around me. What's my problem?

Kyle

What a week it's been.

I last saw Daisy Sunday afternoon. Hanging out with her was so enjoyable that I didn't even mind wasting an entire afternoon driving to and from Buc-ee's. We had a fun time together with no crazy mishaps.

Unless you count me almost running off the road to keep her from reaching in the back for her leftover sandwich. I managed to grab it before she could find the pillow I bought her, and we didn't wreck.

I woke up easily this morning, in anticipation of seeing her again. My stride lengthens as I walk to her front porch. I climb the steps two at a time, almost knocking over a chicken on my way to the door.

I knock and wait a minute or two, then I knock again. The door swings open and Mullet stares up at me.

"Mullet?"

He bleats loudly.

I wince. "Where's Daisy?"

"Come on in," I hear her call from somewhere inside.

I step around Mullet and shut the door. Daisy walks past me carrying a load of laundry in her arms.

"Go ahead and get ready. I'll be there in a minute."

I head for the massage room, my ego slowly deflating like a tire with a pinhole. Not the warm greeting I expected.

When I dropped her off Sunday, we sat in the driveway for a good fifteen minutes talking before she got out. I debated kissing her at least twenty times that day and wanted to especially then. However, I couldn't read her well enough to make myself make a move. Most girls are so obvious when they want to be kissed. Not Daisy.

I go through the routine of undressing and climbing onto the massage table. There's a candle lit, but it isn't bacon. A woodsy scent mixed with something sweet. Even though I prefer bacon, this is nice too.

Today I chose plain black boxers in case we have another mishap. I hope she didn't see my daisy drawers last week. If she did, would she have mentioned it Sunday?

The door cracks, and I center my head in the hole on the table.

"Ready for me?"

"Yes," I mumble, trying not to take that question the wrong way.

Daisy eases the door closed behind her and dims the lights. She doesn't ask where I'm hurting or say anything in greeting as she normally would. Instead, she drops something hot on my back.

I jerk, lifting onto my hands. Something hits the ground with a loud thud.

Daisy reaches down and picks up a large black rock with a towel. She sets it on her tray and meets my gaze.

"I'm sorry, did that hurt?"

I stare at the stone. "It's a little hot, but mainly unexpected."

She sighs. "I thought you might want to try something different. Maybe you were tired of me rubbing all over you."

A goofy laugh escapes my mouth. That is the exact opposite of what I want.

"No, it's fine. I like your massages."

"Thanks." Her lips curve upward.

"Are you okay?" I fold my arms and rest my head on them.

"Of course."

"Good, you seem a little mad or something."

She narrows her eyes. "I'm not mad. I just don't want to do anything that makes you uncomfortable. Last week got a little crazy, then when you didn't go to Carolina's party . . ." She sighs and shrugs. "I don't want to bother you."

"Bother me?"

"Yeah."

"Daisy, you're not bothering me. You've never bothered me. You help me. More than you realize. I couldn't do the work I do without your massages, and you helped me find them a gift. The only reason I didn't go to that party was because I stayed up until two a.m. working on something for Paul."

"Really?"

"Yeah. I would've loved to have been there with you and all our other friends, but I had to work. I already skipped the tractor-pull meeting and knew if I showed up someplace else, the farmers in town would have my hide. I took that as the perfect opportunity to work. I would've slept in today, but I didn't want to miss this."

She smiles, and although the room is very dimly lit, I detect a slight blush in her cheeks.

"So I don't get on your nerves?"

I laugh. "Quite the opposite. I'm so sleepy right now, but I set two alarms to make sure I made this appointment. You help my back and shoulders, sure, but you also brighten my day."

Her smile widens, and I return it. A small part of me aches in realizing she really thought herself a bother rather than a help.

"What do you want? Help me help you."

My smile widens. "Your soft but firm touch. No rocks, just you."

A lump slides down her slim throat as she tiptoes toward me. I begrudgingly stick my head back in the hole, then relax my shoulders as her tiny hands knead my muscles. Her palm skids across my shoulder blades like warm butter on a roll. My skin melts at her touch.

I close my eyes, take a deep breath. The scent of the candle starts to fade as my eyes grow heavy.

The next thing I know, I'm blinking my eyes open in a dark, cold room. My face feels like someone stuck a plunger to it. How long did I lie with my head in that hole?

I twist to see if Daisy's in the room. It's just me and the door is shut. I raise up and notice a note on top of my clothes folded on the futon. Not taking any chances, I lock the door before going for it.

Just because I'm wearing nice-looking underwear today doesn't mean I want anyone to see them. I pick up the note.

I let you sleep. Take as long as you need. When you wake up, I can fix you lunch.

• • •

Daisy

I don't know what I find most endearing about the note. That she let me sleep and offered to make me lunch, or that she dotted her "i" with a flower.

I run my thumb across her signature like a love-struck teenager. Except I'm close to thirty and I'm not sure how she feels about me. That's all it takes for me to drop the note and get dressed.

After I slip on my boots, I yawn and fold the note in my back pocket. I stretch, then leave the massage room.

Mullet greets me in the hallway, making his signature sound. I pet his head and keep an eye out for Daisy when I walk through the living room.

No sign of her.

I continue outside, hoping the sunshine will wake me up more.

"Sleeping beauty has awakened," Daisy calls from somewhere in the yard.

I crane my neck to get a better view from the porch. Reddish hair sticks up beside the chicken coop. I step off the porch and head that way.

"Hey." Daisy greets me when I get within a few feet of her.

She's dumping some kind of grain in a small trough for chickens. I shove my hands in my jeans pockets and watch the chickens scatter from their perches. Some come and eat, while others peck along the ground.

Daisy spreads the grain evenly among the two small troughs, then exits the fence surrounding the coop.

I nod toward it. "Why do they need a fence if they're normally outside?

"The fence is more to keep bigger animals out than to

keep them in. That feed could poison my goats."

I widen my eyes. "Really?"

She nods. "That's why they have a door."

I follow her gaze to a small door on the other side of the fence. It's just large enough for a chicken or other small animals like cats and puppies to go through.

"Thanks for letting me sleep."

She smiles. "You're welcome. I didn't have the heart to wake you up. I tried to flip you and get your front, but you were too heavy."

"*You* tried to flip *me*?" I laugh.

"I'm stronger than I look."

"You could've woken me up."

She shakes her head. "Anyone snoring that loud needs to rest."

I grit my teeth. "Sorry about that."

I've heard from others that I snore, but I never believed them. When it comes from someone like Bradley or Dad or my old college roommate, it's easy to think they're joking. I've never heard myself snore, so I have no solid proof.

But I believe Daisy.

"It's okay. Are you hungry?" She holds up the feed bucket.

I make a strained face, and she laughs.

"For real food in the house?"

"Oh, yeah. Not necessary, though. You've done enough."

Daisy reaches over the short fence and hangs the feed bucket on a hook on the chicken coop. The coop and small fence look cute next to her, like they are Daisy-sized as well as chicken-sized.

She wipes her hands down her shorts and starts walking toward the house. I fall in line with her steps.

"It's no problem. I threw something in the oven before I came out here."

We climb the porch steps together, but I reach out and open the front door. It isn't hard to beat her to it since my arm is about as long as her whole body.

"Thanks." Daisy passes me and hurries toward the kitchen.

I stroll inside and take a seat at the small table across from her kitchen counter. Her phone rings and she rushes to the counter to answer it.

"Hello?" She cradles the phone with her shoulder when the oven beeps next.

I stand and circle the counter. We make it to the oven at the same time. I motion for her to take the call and open the oven door. It's a pizza, and it appears to be done.

I shove my hand in a nearby oven mitt and pull out the pan. My hand stings as I drop the pan on the stove.

"I'll talk to you tomorrow, thanks." Daisy slams the phone on the counter and rushes to me.

She cradles my hand in hers. "Are you okay?"

"Yeah, I had a mitt on." I make a fist, then stretch my fingers out.

She eyes the oven mitt and pouts. "That one is no good. It's old and thin and you have to wear it backward to protect your hand."

"Wear it backward?"

She wavers her head. "Not to me. I'm left handed, but to most people."

"Huh."

I never noticed she's left handed. Massages are all hands on deck, so it's hard to determine a dominant hand.

"Sit down while I get something for that." Daisy slides her hands out from around mine.

I sit and rest my hand palm up on the kitchen table while she disappears down the hall. A minute later, she's at my side, rubbing some kind of cream on my hand.

The burn cools, then numbs. I slump down in my chair and relax.

"Better?"

I lower my head to Daisy staring at me. I swallow hard and try to focus on her question, rather than her kneading some sort of miracle cream into my hand.

"Yes."

She releases my hand again, letting it rest gently on the table. "Good. You feel like eating?"

"Yeah."

It pains me to say that, even though I'm hungry. Part of me knows I could milk this slight wound and have her rubbing my hand half the day, but that wouldn't be right.

She goes into the kitchen and rummages around in the cabinets. I stare out the window at goats and random yard ornaments until she returns with two plates of pizza and some drinks.

"This okay? I remember you drinking Mountain Dew."

I smirk, flattered that she remembered me getting that at Buc-ee's.

"Perfect."

Our eyes meet for a split second, and I force myself to refrain from kissing her. If this were a movie, I'd slide the pizza and drinks off the table with one swipe, then lay her across the table and kiss her senseless.

But it's not a movie, and I have no clue what she really thinks of me. Is she attracted to me the way I am her? Does she think of me as a new friend? Or am I just some local guy who keeps needing her to nurse him back to good health?

I glance at my numb hand before picking up a slice of pepperoni with my non-dominant one. Whatever Daisy thinks of me, I'll take it.

As long as it keeps me near her.

CHAPTER NINE

Daisy

I tend to make any and all excuses not to show up at Apple Cart County High School. My time there as an odd little wallflower weren't exactly the best years of my life.

While everyone else was busy making memories, I was busy trying not to be remembered.

My evil plan obviously worked since Kyle didn't remember going to school with me, and some of my now-friends barely did as well. That's saying a lot for a school in a town this small.

Most people go back for reunions, games, and other events. I go back for one thing—money.

This is my second candle-and-soap fundraiser for the school, and it's been quite profitable. The principal happened to call and check on the order on Saturday when Kyle was still at my house.

He overheard our conversation and offered to help me

transport the candles today. After we fixed his hand, of course. That must be why he offered. It can't be my frozen-pizza chef skills.

Kyle's Jeep pulls up beside my Beetle, and my stomach churns. Ten years ago, I recall popular, pretty girls waiting on their boyfriends to meet them in the parking lot.

I'm still not popular, and he's not my boyfriend.

However, it's a little satisfying for Kyle Tolbert to meet me in the parking lot. Even if his only intentions are to haul a few big boxes of candles.

I open my door and hop out. "The janitor said he would leave a rolling cart out by the old gym."

As opposed to our "new gym," which is older than Kyle and me. I never saw the irony in that until I gave someone directions to the new gym and they got lost looking for a new building. That didn't exist!

"Cool, I'll get it."

Kyle jogs across the parking lot and goes inside the gym. He comes out pushing a large cart that makes me glad he offered to help. Last year, I made three or four trips myself.

I reach for a box when he rolls my way.

"Stop, I'll get it." Kyle snatches the box before I can pick it up.

He continues lifting boxes and placing them on the cart. When he fills the top of it, he bends to put a box on the bottom.

"Bend with your legs," I remind him.

"Yes, madame masseuse." He smirks at me and squats.

I enjoy his jeans pulling across his butt a little too much, and my face heats up. I stare at the trunk of my car rather than his trunk and hope he continues to bend properly. It's for the best.

"All loaded up."

I turn my gaze cautiously, thankful he's now standing.

Not that he looks any less attractive not squatting, but it doesn't put certain "assets" on display.

We walk the cart toward the office. And by we, I mean Kyle does all the pushing, and I hold on to the side like a toddler tagging along.

The first person I see is Mrs. York, the school counselor. Her mouth curls into a wide smile when she spots me.

"Always good to see you, Daisy." She hurries toward me and wraps me in a huge hug.

We're close to the same height, but she's probably double my weight. I suck in a breath and attempt to hug her back, but she has a kung-fu grip on me. At last she lets loose. I exhale and smile back.

"Good to see you as well."

"You were always so smart." She pats my cheek, which does nothing to debunk my feeling like a toddler.

She looks up at Kyle. "Daisy was my star student in Battle of the Books."

I bite my bottom lip and scan the hallway for an exit strategy. My eyes land on the trophy case, where a football photo of Kyle sits front and center. So much for hiding.

Mrs. York narrows her gaze at him and straightens her glasses.

"We haven't seen you here in a while, Kyle."

He clears his throat. "I transferred junior year."

She nods, then widens her eyes, as if remembering why he transferred. I was even further removed from sports than Mrs. York, if that's possible, and I remember what happened.

Wisteria wanted him for their football team. Kyle lived on the city-limit line between the two towns. They used his dad's shop address rather than his house address so he could move to Wisteria and play ball without a wait.

Small-town sports politics at its finest.

"But I'm here today to help Daisy transport candles."

Mrs. York blushes. "Always such a strong man."

She pats Kyle on the arm, then continues walking past us. We stand there a beat before she turns and motions for us to follow.

"We're going to organize everything in the media room." She smiles back at me. "We had some good times discussing books in there, didn't we?"

"Yes, ma'am," I whisper.

I did have a good time discussing books, but I don't want to come off as the biggest dork ever in front of Kyle.

We follow her into the library. I don't even pretend to help Kyle push the cart this time. Mrs. York opens a door against the wall for us to enter the media room. It's like stepping back in time, but with more technology. This must be how Marty McFly felt.

One guy is on the corner computer. Mrs. York greets him before turning to us.

"That's Augustus. He's working on the yearbook. There shouldn't be anyone else here to bother y'all. The cheerleaders aren't due to pick up their orders until this afternoon."

"Cheerleaders?"

"Yeah, they're the group who sold the candles."

I had no idea who was running the fundraiser since they started it end of the school year and said it would end in the summer. My only obligation was to fulfill the orders on time.

For some reason, the mention of cheerleaders selling my candles while standing in the media room is all too much. I pull out a chair and sit.

"Are you okay?" Kyle asks.

I nod. My face must be pale, because I feel faint. Not from sickness, though. I just need a minute to shake off the bad memories of high school.

I'm just regaining my strength to stand when a bell rings.

Chill bumps travel down my spine. I flinch and almost fall out of my chair.

Mrs. York laughs. "I don't know why they don't turn those things off in the summer. Gets me every time, too, dear."

I stand slowly and walk to the cart. Before I can reach for the first box of candles to start organizing, Mrs. York rushes over to me with a large scrapbook.

"I knew it was in here somewhere." She blows dust from the top, and we both cough. "Sorry, dear."

She opens the cover, and seventeen-year-old Daisy with pink-and-purple hair, dressed as a medieval princess, stares back at me. Could she embarrass me any more in front of Kyle?

"This is memories from the Shakespeare club Daisy started in high school." She turns the book toward Kyle. "Unfortunately, the group fizzled out once she graduated."

Yep, she can embarrass me more. Now I'm just waiting for her to pull out that Juliet costume and ask me to try it on for an encore.

Kyle tilts his head and studies the photo, while I die of mortification. My limbs numb as he turns the page and looks at more photos.

God, please make it stop!

My prayer halfway works. Kyle doesn't stop looking at the book, but I do gain the strength to move a box of candles. A moment later, he follows suit and starts unloading as well.

Mrs. York gets the idea that we're here to work and not remind me of how different I am from Kyle. Maybe not the latter, but she understands the first.

"I'll let you two get to work. The room is yours long as you need it." She tilts her head to the boy at the computer. "Augustus won't be a bother."

He continues typing on the computer, not even acknowledging us, proving her point. Mrs. York closes the scrapbook, sending more dust my way.

I hold back a cough as she stands on her toes to return it to a shelf. Part of me wants to chunk it in the trash when she leaves, but I don't.

Instead, I busy myself unloading candles. One box has a master sheet of orders and bags to put them in. I learned before that it's best to bag on site. Otherwise, I end up with clanking candles that are harder to transport and still want to check everything when I'm there.

"Here's the list. If you want, I can organize the orders, then you can bag them. I have labels we can stick on the bags as well."

I hand the back few sheets of paper, which are filled with name labels, to Kyle.

"We can use the boxes to group the orders by person who sold them once they're empty."

He smiles at me. "You're good at this."

I shrug sheepishly. "It's just organizing stuff."

"No really. You made all this too. That's cool. You should be proud."

"Thanks."

My cheeks heat, and I'm certain they're blushed. I lower my head and continue working, hoping Kyle won't notice.

We work together in silence, except for the few times we call out a name for an order. A good half hour passes, and I forget Augustus is in the room until he clears his throat at one point.

When everything is organized and the labels are added, I stand back and survey our work. I slide one box with the toe of my shoe to straighten it.

"Now we're done."

Kyle laughs. "What about these empty boxes?"

"I'll grab them if you can take back the cart."

"Good deal."

He pulls the cart through the door, while I gather the two leftover boxes. It's a little odd exiting the media room with a guy. Like a real guy, not a Shakespeare buff.

Most guys like Kyle only graced the media room when they wanted to sneak and make out with a girl, or if Coach had them come borrow the large-screen TV for game-film viewing.

I wave to the principal as we exit into the hot summer sun. Kyle veers off toward the old gym to return the cart. Do I wait on him, or go to my car?

It's these awkward details I never learned as a teen. And it doesn't help much that I have no idea what Kyle and I are.

Assuming we're just friends helping one another out, I walk slowly toward my car. As suspected, he catches up to me before I can open my trunk.

"Here." He opens it for me.

"Thanks." I toss the boxes in the back and shut it.

Nerves bounce inside me like Mexican jumping beans. I have to address what happened in there or it will bother me every time I see him.

"Kyle, about the book battles and the Shakespeare reenactments . . ."

"What about them?"

I shrug. "I was a total dork in high school."

He kicks some loose gravel in the parking lot and studies my face. Assuming he's waiting on me to finish, I continue.

"I saw your photo in the trophy case, so you must think my high school days were pretty lame."

I wince. The way I drug out the words "pretty lame" solidifies my lameness.

His face falls. "Daisy, no. I would never think that, and I didn't think that then either."

My eyes widen. "You didn't?" Surely he's just being nice.

"No." He tilts his head at me, obviously reading my doubt. "Honestly, I didn't. Everyone has their own interests. Mine just happen to be football and working on things. I thought your dress in that photo looked pretty neat."

"You did?" I blink. He's beyond being nice now, and either flat out lying or delusional.

"Yeah. I've never seen anything like that. Closest thing would be when they do the Civil War reenactments in Moonshine County and some of those women dress up like from then."

I laugh. "Civil War reenactments?"

"Yeah. My grandpa used to be in them. Back before his hip got too bad to lie on the ground and play dead."

I laugh so hard I snort, and Kyle laughs with me.

"They still do them. I need to take you sometime. Good Southern entertainment."

I smile. That sounds like the lamest thing in the world, but if Kyle is there, I want to go.

He stares at his feet and kicks gravel again. I clear my throat from laughing.

"Kyle?"

He raises his eyes. "Yeah?"

"Thanks for today."

"No problem. My shoulder can handle lifting a few candles now, thanks to you."

He rotates his trouble shoulder.

"I don't just mean for the candles."

He nods. "You're welcome. Thank you too."

I smile and hurry inside my car before I say something stupid. It's been a great morning, and Kyle isn't totally turned off by a younger me wearing a homemade Juliet costume with rainbow hair.

Best leave before I ruin it.

Kyle

"Hey, big dog?"

I turn, a little startled by Bradley's voice. It's the middle of the day, and I'm in the zone with this tractor.

I slide my rolling chair away from the metal beast and turn around. Bradley leans against the back of my couch, facing me.

"What brings you by this time of day?"

He shrugs. "Patrolling nearby. Thought I'd check on you, seeing how I didn't hear from you all weekend."

"You knew I was working. That's why I missed the party."

Bradley adjusts his cowboy hat and smirks. "What about yesterday?"

"What about it?"

I stand and wipe the new grease from my hand with a rag before it dries on the old grease that will take more than a rag to wash off.

"You weren't up at the school with Daisy?"

I face him and toss the rag near the tractor. "Are you patrolling me now?"

Bradley chuckles. "Nah. Just saw your vehicles parked together and heard you helped her transport some candles."

"Which would qualify as working and helping a friend."

Bradley laughs louder. "If you say so, big dog."

"What's that supposed to mean?" I cross my arms to prove I'm not kidding.

"Nothing, but I don't see you helping any ugly girls move candles on a Monday morning."

"No ugly girls have needed my help moving candles on a Monday morning." My tone is dripping with sarcasm.

"Ah-ha." Bradley points to me. "So you admit she's good looking."

I snort. "Well yeah. Don't you think Daisy's pretty?"

"Yeah, she's pretty. I prefer long legs, but she's downright hot for a pint-sized person."

I laugh. Bradley has an odd way with words. I used to think he's still single because the one woman he loved moved to Atlanta and married a doctor. Now I think it's just him.

"You know she likes you."

I make a straight face. "Well, yeah. We've become friends and I'm a likable guy." I grin, hoping to change the subject.

Of course, Bradley picks up on that and takes it even further.

"What's wrong with dating Daisy?"

"Nothing's wrong with Daisy." Honestly, I can't think of one thing wrong with her.

"I didn't ask what's wrong with her, I asked what's wrong with dating her?"

"Nothing, I suppose." I run my hand through my hair, then regret doing so given my grease. "Unless you're her massage client and you live in a garage where your work never ends."

"You don't have to work this much, you know."

I glance at the tractor parts spread across the floor and the other tractor waiting in the wings behind it.

"What do you want me to do, be a cop so I can ride around and bother my friends at random hours?"

"That hurts." Bradley holds his hat to his heart and throws back his head.

I roll my eyes. "Daisy and I are friends, and I felt like I owed her one after feeding me lunch."

He returns his hat to his head. "Do tell more."

I shake my head, regretting saying so. Bradley spends way too much time questioning all the town gossips—my grandma included.

"My massages are Saturdays."

"Yeah."

"I fell asleep from being so tired after working all night Friday. Daisy let me sleep, then fed me lunch before I went home."

The corners of Bradley's mouth uptick. "You fell asleep at her house?"

"At like ten in the morning, while she was giving me a massage. It's totally normal, I paid her."

Bradley bursts out laughing, obviously taking the payment part the wrong way. As he does everything.

I reach out and punch his arm. Not hard, but hard enough for him to stop laughing and rub his arm.

Bradley opens his mouth to say something else, then pauses when his radio beeps. He picks it up and answers the call. A dispatcher on the other line says he is needed at the Apple Cart Piggly Wiggly ASAP.

"Ten-four. I'll be there in ten."

He clips the radio on his side and backs toward my front door. "We'll continue this talk later, big dog."

I twist my mouth and watch him hurry out the door. Last time he got called to Piggly Wiggly was during the monthly meat sale.

They marked down all bacon to a dollar a pack. People went nuts and started fighting over it. Two women picked up the last pack of Oscar Mayer brand at the same time.

I wasn't there, but word on the street is they pulled so hard that one hit the concrete floor and the other fell back into the sausage links. One had a concussion and the other a broken wrist.

And yet, Bradley wonders why I prefer to sit at home and work on engines.

I grab a bottle of water from the refrigerator and down half of it. Then I find my chair and roll back to the tractor. This one is almost ready. A few more adjustments, then I can put it back together.

Turning a wrench is a lot easier than it was Friday night, all thanks to Daisy and her magic touch.

Her smile flickers in the back of my mind like a low-burning candle. It's always there, lighting up the room when I least expect it.

I do like her, and I have for weeks now. The fair did it for me.

Ever since that night, I've wanted to get to know her better. That's why I took such interest in that photo album at the high school. It had enough dust to kill a house cat, and the photo was faded. But Daisy was in it.

Daisy in high school, the Daisy I don't remember. I was either moved to Wisteria by then or too busy living my own teenage life to notice.

Not that it would've mattered at the time. I doubt she would've wanted to date an athlete back then, and I wouldn't have been into a girl with pink-and-purple hair. But now . . .

I'm clearly past my glory days, and her hair is the color of red dirt. I mean that in a good way. It's shiny and smooth and has tints of brown mixed in.

I turn the wrench another time before dropping it and leaning back against my chair. Since when do I analyze people's hair color so closely?

Since never. Same as every other detail I analyze about Daisy. I can't quite decide the color of her eyes. They're brownish gold with hints of yellow when it's bright outside.

I've seen and dated a lot of pretty girls, but none as uniquely beautiful as her—or as unique in general.

That's the problem. I can't get a good read on how she feels about me. I've never had to ask a girl if she likes me. If I didn't have to in junior high, I'm not about to start in my late twenties.

My phone buzzes, kicking Daisy to the back burner. At least for now. Her flame will keep flickering in the back of my mind like one of those trick candles. The kind you blow out like five times before it ends.

I pick up my phone and frown at the message. It's Bradley.

Can you come to the Pig and pick up a lawn mower?

I shake my head and call him. Some things are easier understood over the phone.

He picks up on the third ring. "Hey, Rufus wrecked his lawn mower."

"And you need a wrecker for that?"

"It's stuck in the side of the Pig."

"What? How?"

"That call I got was about him driving his lawn mower downtown."

"He does that a lot."

"Yeah, well, today he was extra drunk and got in the middle of the road. An out-of-towner came up the hill and laid on the horn. He swerved and made it off the road, but ran right into the side of the Pig."

I sigh. "Okay. I'm coming."

Rufus has had so many DWIs over the years that he's permanently lost his license. As a one-time offender, I can partially sympathize. However, instead of giving up the bottle like I did, Rufus decided to drive his lawn mower everywhere.

He's on it so much that he even started a lawn-care business. He drives to people's houses, then puts the blades down and starts mowing. Only downside is he can't be trusted with a weed eater.

I guess fast living has finally caught up to him, as he managed to total the slowest vehicle known to man.

I best go get the wrecker, since I'm sure everyone who wasn't already at the Pig has made their way over to see the wreck.

CHAPTER TEN

Daisy

People who think small towns are boring have never shopped at Piggly Wiggly on a Tuesday.

One minute I'm picking out bananas, and the next I'm dodging a rogue buggy shoved by a panicked woman.

When the shock simmers down enough for me to focus, I follow the crowd like a mindless zombie toward the front of the store. The nose and two front wheels of a smoking lawn mower stick out through a huge hole in the metal wall.

Half the town stares at the tractor, while the other half rushes outside. I didn't hear the crash, but I was in deep concentration in the produce aisle. Not to mention that the store manager cranks up nineties' country pretty loudly over the speakers. No cliché grocery store music in Apple Cart.

Reba belts out the last verse of "Fancy," and I glance around for someone with half enough sense to tell me what just happened. I come up with nobody, so Morgan will have to do.

She's still at her register, filing her nails. I push past the crowd gathering near the lawn mower to reach her.

"What happened?"

Morgan nods at the tractor and smacks her gum. "Lawn mower came through the building."

I want to say I can see that much, but refrain from sounding snarky.

"Someone said the dude was drunk. Looks like Rufus's lawn mower, so I wouldn't be surprised."

I turn to the wreck, then back to Morgan. "I'm more shocked that a lawn mower can do this to a building."

She shrugs and tosses her nail file in a drawer near the register.

"I've worked at this circus almost a year now and have four kids. Nothing surprises me."

I nod. "I'm sure."

I smile at Morgan, then remember my purse is still in my buggy. I jog toward the bananas and find it as I left it. There aren't a lot of common crimes in our small town, but we do have some outliers who aren't above picking off someone's cash to drive across the state line and buy lottery tickets.

It's happened to me before.

Luckily, fruit was the last thing on my list. I pick out some strawberries and head for Morgan. She's watching something on her phone. She laughs crazily, then takes a swig of her gas station Icee. I have every item smooshed on the belt by the time she notices me.

"Oh, sorry." She pockets her phone and scans my first item.

I fold my arms and stare past Morgan toward the tractor. The smoking has ceased, but it's still in the wall. A police siren echoes from outside. Maybe nobody is hurt.

"Eighty-two fifty-four."

I turn my attention to Morgan, who's already pulling out her phone to watch more videos. I swipe my card and wait for her to hand over my receipt. She circles something at the bottom before doing so.

"I'm obligated to tell you that you can fill out this survey for a chance to win fifty dollars free groceries."

"Thanks." I grin and take the paper.

Heat rises from the lawn mower as I pass the crime scene. The closer I get to the sliding doors, the more voices and commotion I hear outside.

Bradley's cop lights glisten in the sunshine as he talks to a tall bald guy I've never seen before. Rufus is in the back of the cop car with the window down. Typical, since he did cause all this damage, but he's not dangerous.

At least not to others. Just to himself, and apparently the Pig.

"Hey, girl."

I glance over to Ashley. "Did you see it happen?"

"No, I was processing a loan. People in the teller line rubbernecked and the drive-through stalled, so I knew something was up. I told Samuel I'd see what happened."

I sigh. "Apparently Rufus wrecked his lawn mower . . ."

My voice trails off as Kyle drives up with his wrecker. I almost drop the sack of groceries in my arms when he parks near the lawn mower and hops out of the cab like a hero. In some ways, he is.

Bradley, always wanting a piece of the limelight, gets out of his patrol car and lifts a hand.

"Stand back, folks. He needs room to work."

I resist the urge to roll my eyes at our county sheriff. Kyle uses some tool to grip the lawn mower and pull it from the building. The side of the Pig now has a hole large enough to see inside.

I step forward to see around some of the taller people. Morgan waves at us from inside, where she's leaned against the grocery belt, snacking on something.

Once the lawn mower is completely moved, the store manager steps toward the building and examines the curled metal outlining the sides. He puts his hands on his hips and shakes his head.

People start to scatter now that the lawn mower is loaded. Ashley tells me bye and crosses the street to the bank. I watch Bradley talk with the manager while Kyle climbs back in the wrecker.

My heart beats faster as he drives away. I feel like the biggest dork admiring him right now. It's not like he saved a kid from a burning building. He pulled a lawn mower out of the Pig.

The remaining crowd shuffles around me to their cars, and I squeeze to the side to let a larger man by. Moisture glazes my arm from the grocery bag.

Shoot. It's probably my ice cream melting.

I hurry to my own car and put the groceries in the back. Then I jog back inside the store for new ice cream. Adrianne will whine if I don't have some for our next girls' night.

Morgan is standing by the hole, taking selfies. The manager sticks his head in and reprimands her. She drops her shoulders and returns to her register.

In her defense, there wasn't anyone waiting in line. Besides, it's not like someone runs into the side of the Pig every day—thankfully.

I hurry for the ice cream aisle before my milk has a chance to ruin as well. A large sign in the refrigerated section announces a sale on steaks.

Hmm . . . what if? I dismiss the crazy idea and continue toward the Blue Bell.

Something compels me to circle back to the steaks and

pick up a few. Not because I really like steak, but because I have a friend who says he does.

Kyle

I finish the tractor that's consumed half of my day, then turn to the lawn mower that's consumed the other half.

Normally, I work on things in the order they come into my shop. However, this lawn mower is Rufus's only means of transportation, and he already put a down payment on the damage.

Well, for me to haul and fix the lawn mower. I get the sense he will have to cut a lot of grass to pay for the damage to the Pig. Maybe the store's insurance will cover it, as Rufus didn't have lawn-mower insurance. Though he should consider getting it the way he drives that thing downtown.

I stare at the bent front and realize I can only do so much before getting new parts. That's a good enough excuse for me to take a break and shower. I'll get online and order some parts after that, then maybe tinker with my next tractor.

I turn on the shower and unzip my grease-stained jumpsuit. It's been a weird week so far, and it's only Tuesday.

Steam rises from the shower, and I step inside. The hot water beats on my back and shoulders, soothing them. If Daisy could massage them right now, I'd be in heaven.

I grit my teeth, ashamed of thinking that. I'm in the shower, buck naked. Not the time or place to want a massage.

After washing my hair and using my "normal" soap, I

reach for the bottle containing my grease-fighting mixture—Dawn dish soap and sugar. This one home remedy is almost worth all the castor oil and apple cider vinegar Granny forced on me as a kid.

As I lather my hands to remove as much grease from under my fingernails as possible, Daisy's soft, tiny hands come to mind. What does she think of my hands? Does she think they're dirty from all the stains around my nails? Are they so calloused that she doesn't want to hold them?

I've never given it much thought until now.

My entire life has consisted of football, fishing, and working on engines. I can't remember a time my hands didn't have calluses or a little grease around my nail beds. It never bothered me until I started admiring the softest, cutest hands in the world. The hands I want to hold. The hands I hope want me to hold them.

I watch the sugary suds fall from my fingers, content with the amount of grease that disappeared. If I stay in here and scrub any longer, I'll be out of hot water.

My dad's dog howls in the distance when I cut the water. I wouldn't think much of it except that it's followed by a knocking sound. Raccoons have been getting in our trash recently, and this may be Girl's way of telling us they're back.

Yep, Dad named his dog Girl. It started as laziness on his part because she's a girl. She was a stray that kept coming around until he gave in and let her stay. Now he likes to refer to her as "his girl" to throw people off. I don't find the humor in it, but he's always been corny.

Another knock sounds louder. I secure a towel around my waist and grab the nearest shotgun. The one I keep right inside my bedroom door for weird situations like this.

I slip on my boots because it's not safe to walk barefoot through my house when tractor parts are strewn across the floor.

Cocking the gun, I march toward the door, ready to end the drama with these trash pandas. I open the door to Daisy, wide-eyed, holding a picnic basket.

"Daisy?" I lower my gun and click the safety.

Her chest rises and falls as she inhales and exhales deeply. "You pointed a gun at me."

I sigh and swipe the hand not holding the gun down my face. "I didn't mean to. I heard knocking sounds and assumed it was raccoons."

"Like this?" Daisy knocks on the open door.

"Yeah."

She blushes. "The doorbell was a little high for me to reach with my hands full, so I knocked."

"I'm so sorry. I didn't mean to scare you."

"It's perfectly fine." Her voice lowers on the word "fine" as her eyes stare at my bare chest.

Crap. I realize I'm in nothing but a towel and a pair of work boots. And here I was worried she'd be turned off by grease stains around my fingernails.

"Uh, come on in. I'll just go and change real fast."

She grins through flushed cheeks and steps past me. I catch a whiff of her flower-scented hair when it fans under my nose.

With one hand on the gun and the other securing my towel, I hurry to the bathroom. Not so fast that the towel might fall, but fast enough to end the embarrassment.

Once the door is closed and my gun is secure, I swipe on deodorant, then stare in the mirror. Normally I would shave after a shower, as I had planned to before hearing the supposed coon outside. But I can't shave now or Daisy will think I shaved for her. Even though I do want to shave for her, I can't let her know that. I run my hand across my jaw. That doesn't mean I can't wear a little aftershave.

I splash some on, then open the door on the opposite

end of the bathroom that's connected to my bedroom. Out of habit, I almost put on new work clothes. Instead, I reach for my best pair of jeans and a nicer T-shirt. Not that T-shirts are nice, but I can't wear a church shirt. Then she would know I mean to impress her. But I do wear my church boots.

Daisy is in the kitchen when I return, unpacking the picnic basket. She's so cute behind my tall counter with the basket. Kind of like Little Red Riding Hood with that red hair.

"Oh, I brought you dinner. I didn't know if you had eaten." She pauses pulling things out of the basket and looks up at me. "I should've texted first."

"No, I haven't eaten yet, and it smells great."

She smiles. "Thanks. I know you mentioned liking steak, so I grilled some and made some sides."

My stomach growls audibly at the mention of steak. Daisy giggles, and I'm embarrassed again. At least I'm properly dressed this time. I swear, every time I do something stupid in front of this woman, I'm shirtless.

"That's so nice of you to cook for me." And to make my house smell like steak rather than motor oil for once.

She shrugs. "I was actually at Piggly Wiggly today and saw you moving the lawn mower. I figured you'd work late tonight to catch up, so I wanted to make sure you ate."

"Thanks, Daisy. You're so sweet to always take care of me."

She blushes and bites her bottom lip.

"I mean it. I really appreciate you."

She rubs her lips together, and my insides twitch. I want to thank her with a kiss, but I can't risk running her off.

"Anyway, I have some steaks and potatoes and green beans." She touches each container as she lists its contents. "I would've made bread, but I didn't have time."

I cross the room and take her arms in my hands. "It's fine. You didn't have to do anything, but you did."

"You're welcome," she whispers.

I can't stand it any longer. Her almond eyes twinkle up at me. This is it. I need to kiss her. I have to kiss her.

I start to lower my head, but she dips hers before I can and digs in the basket one more time.

"I almost forgot, here's some more cream for your oven burn in case you need it."

"Thanks," I say, taking a bottle of lotion.

Did she totally miss my signal or is she not interested in *that*—or in me? Maybe she does just care about my well-being as a client?

We stand for a beat of silence, then Daisy grabs her basket from the counter. She takes a step back from me.

"I'll let you eat and relax some. I know you have work to do."

My face falls at the announcement that she's actually leaving and not just cleaning the counter so that *we* can eat.

"You don't want to stay and eat?"

She shakes her head. "I ate earlier, and I promised my mom I'd help her press some oils."

I have no idea what that entails, but it obviously takes enough time and attention to not stay with me a while.

"Well, thanks for this. I'll treat you to dinner sometime."

"Sounds great." She smiles, then bounces toward the door and shuts it behind her.

I stare at the closed door for a minute before going to my room and changing into gym shorts. If I have to eat alone, the least I can do is make myself comfortable. I don't bother putting on another shirt, which is fitting for the occasion.

I'm now the stupid guy who tried to kiss the same girl twice in one month and failed both times.

CHAPTER ELEVEN

Kyle

I've had Daisy on my mind all week. That's kind of common lately, but my thoughts of her have intensified since Tuesday. Not only is she sweet, quirky, and uniquely gorgeous, but she can cook too.

Usually tiny people and good cooking don't go together, especially in our generation.

My heart skips a beat when I turn into her driveway. I try and talk it down since I've had two failed kiss attempts and still don't know for sure how Daisy feels about me.

When I get out of the Jeep, Mullet bleats from his position in front of the porch. We've become cordial, but I get the sense he's guarding the place. Luckily, I've come prepared.

I open a box of graham crackers I bought at the DG on my way. He gets excited when Daisy hands him these, so I figured it might help me win him over. And maybe if the goat likes me, his mom will as well.

I pull a brick of crackers from the pack, then close the box. Mullet notices them in my hand the moment I start toward him. He sniffs the air and prances my way.

Holding the crackers high enough where he can't reach them, I pet him with my free hand.

"Good boy."

I lower the block of crackers when he quits butting his head and allows me to pet him. When they're within reach, he bites the end and wags his tail.

The nub is still wagging when I climb the porch steps and knock on the door. I'm a few minutes early. Partly because I couldn't wait to see Daisy, and partly because I wanted to talk about the last time I saw her.

On the ride here, I mulled over whether I should bring up the fact that I intended on kissing her or simply mention that night and see what she says. Either way, I'd like to bring it up to try and read her feelings about it.

While I'm waiting on Daisy to answer, I put pressure on the top porch step to make sure it's still intact. Yep, that nail fixed it. I walk over all the porch steps from side to side again to test them as well.

I'm on the last step when the door creeps open. I lift my face to a muscled-up guy wearing a flannel shirt with the sleeves cut out, a leather vest, and a leather skullcap. Weird, since I didn't see another vehicle here.

He stares at me, squaring me up, then shuts the front door. I freeze on the bottom step as he passes me and disappears around the side of the house. A motorcycle cranks in the distance while I'm walking up the steps.

I turn and watch him drive off, Mullet following until he can no longer keep the pace. I reach my hand to knock again, but Daisy opens the door.

She's wearing a yellow sundress with her hair pulled back.

123

The yellow makes her eyes extra golden, and I'm immediately jealous that the biker dude saw her like this.

"Morning."

"Good morning." I clear my throat and step inside.

Mullet follows me in and runs toward the pink chicken I won her at the fair. I smile at the memory of that night, then frown when I see what Mullet does to it.

"Mullet, take Big Chick to the other room." Daisy snaps her fingers and points toward her room.

Mullet grabs what's left of the chicken by the neck and drags it with him, spilling stuffing on the floor.

Daisy sighs. "I swear, he's so messy with his toys."

She bends to pick up some of the stuffing, and I stare at her slim shoulders and upper back exposed by the dress and her hair. They're graceful like a ballerina. When she straightens, I raise my eyes to meet hers.

"I'll throw this away while you get ready." She holds up the wads of cotton and hurries toward the kitchen.

I go in the opposite direction and open the massage room door. My limbs relax when I smell bacon. I go through the routine of undressing to my underwear and positioning my head in that little hole, with the cover securing my rear.

The door cracks, sending the line of light in my view. Daisy enters and shuffles around at the table. I've heard these same sounds so much that I can calculate how long before her hands land on my shoulders.

I anticipate her touch, then a mental image of the biker guy flashes in my mind. His biceps were twice the size mine ever were. In my prime when playing college ball, I was pretty stacked, but never to the point of veins popping like that dude. His arms were so ripped, it made his tattoos look lumpy.

"You're tense. Try and relax," Daisy whispers.

Normally that smooth voice would lull me into submission and have my bones sinking into the table. Not today. One muscled-up man has me contemplating all the guys Daisy massages. Are there more like him? Maybe some just as muscular but not as burly? Some that look similar to me but who have actually read—and liked—Shakespeare?

I might could compete with an older biker dude for her affection, but not someone of similar age and stature who also knows medieval literature.

Daisy applies more pressure to my shoulder blade area. I try and enjoy it without the lingering thought of other men enjoying the same touches. Men who I may or may not can measure up to in her opinion.

What does Daisy want in a man, anyway?

I've had little trouble attracting girls my entire life. So much that I've never really tried. When you're a six-foot-four lineman with dark hair and manners and ambitions, it's not that hard.

Until Daisy.

I still haven't figured out what makes her tick. But I want her to tick for me more than I've wanted any other girl.

I'm still a ball of nerves when she asks me to flip over. I clumsily do so and close my eyes. The warm towel drops on my face. I spend this part of the massage mustering up the courage to point blank ask Daisy out.

She hasn't read any of my signals. Granted, they've been a little grainy, as I'm out of practice and I can't really read her. Regardless, it's time to man up and ask her to dinner.

By the time she finishes massaging my legs and steps away from me, I have a plan.

Daisy removes the towel from my face. I pop open my eyes while she's still standing there. She half smiles, then quickly turns to her table and shuffles things like always.

If I don't say something, she'll leave again for me to get dressed. Given our track record, I have a better chance of embarrassing myself shirtless. But I don't want to wait any longer. I sit up, securing the sheet around my waist.

"Daisy?"

"Yeah?" She turns at the door.

"I owe you a dinner."

She bats a hand and giggles. "No, I told you it's fine. I wanted to help. No need to repay me."

Seriously? Am I going to have to kidnap this woman for a date?

I cinch the sheet behind me and hop off the table like I'm in a sack race on elementary field day. I shuffle over to Daisy, who's wide-eyed at my odd behavior. When I'm within a few inches of her, I resist the urge to kiss her and talk.

"Daisy, I'm trying to ask you out."

Her eyes widen even more—if that's possible.

"On a date," I continue.

She points to herself, then me. "Me, and you, on a date?"

I shake my head. "Unless you don't see me that way. I understand that I'm your client, and you may have a boyfriend for all I know. We haven't really talked about that—"

"Yes."

Now my eyes widen. "Okay, then. This weekend?"

Her cheeks redden and she smiles. "Friday would be good."

I clinch my jaw. "I have the tractor-pull barbecue. I can't miss it."

"Do they feed you there?"

"It's a barbecue."

"Right . . ." She blushes more.

"I'd love for you to come with me, if you don't mind a lot of boring tractor talk with old men."

She giggles. "If I minded that, I wouldn't be living in Apple Cart."

"Good point." I chuckle.

She nods at my waist. "I'll let you get on some clothes."

I stand still while she backs out of the room, closing the door behind her. We didn't get to have the conversation about any of my kiss attempts, but I did get the point across that I want to date her.

Maybe that's good enough to earn me another shot at kissing her. I pray the third time's the charm.

Daisy

My hand shakes as I put on my mascara. I steady it with my opposite hand to make sure I don't look like Kiss for my date with Kyle.

Date with Kyle.

That one sentence makes me want to vomit. But in a good way.

Never in my lifetime did I think I'd have a shot with someone like Kyle. Maybe the fact that he never finished college and my hair is now a God-given hair color puts us on a more even playing field.

Still, that doesn't counteract the fact that I'm . . . me.

I love myself, I really do—and so do my mom and friends. But that doesn't make me lovable in a romantic sense.

As my friends have made it clear, it will take one weird and brave dude to live with a bunch of goats. Though I have transitioned to having Mullet only in the house since their little "fake" intervention.

It took twice as long as usual to apply my minimal makeup, but it's done. The anticipation of going on an actual date and not wanting to mess it up led to me getting ready super early. As in I picked out my clothes last night, then changed my mind about them every time I walked past what I'd laid out.

I'm now in a jean skirt and my one pair of cowgirl boots. The pair Adrianne insisted I had to buy from Paul before we went to a Luke Combs concert. I did, and haven't worn them since. Sure, they're cute, but when you're barely five feet tall, boots go over your knees.

These hit just below my kneecaps, so they aren't quite as bad. They also have some shiny accents that pair nicely with my gold earrings.

A little much for a tractor-pull barbecue? Maybe. It's not like I frequent those.

I'm debating between two tops when I hear a knock at the door. I drop the shirts on my bed and hurry toward the door.

Halfway there, I realize I'm in my bra!

I hurry back to my room and rip the one I like best from the hanger. When I make it to the door, I'm still shoving the hanger loop inside the shoulder. I straighten the bottom, pull my hair over the shirt, and open the door.

Kyle is smiling. He has on a button-down shirt with nice jeans and boots. His hair is combed neatly, and he's holding a bouquet of daisies. My stomach swirls. The only guy who's ever given me flowers was my dad.

Well, unless you count the corsage from my oddball prom date. I don't, since most of that night is blocked from my brain.

As the two shortest people from Battle of the Books, we decided to go together. He drove his grandpa's vintage car and had to sit on a textbook to see over the steering wheel.

We paid for our own meals, and a week later, he sent me a bill for the seven-dollar corsage.

So technically, *I* bought that flower.

"Do you like daisies? I just assumed."

I smile at Kyle, a little embarrassed for staring so long at the bouquet. I can't possibly explain that it's not his flowers, but rather my lack of getting flowers that caused me to stare. He may decide this date is a bad idea and run for the hills.

"Yes, I love them." I take the flowers.

He smiles wider. "Good."

I sniff them. "Can I put them in a vase where Mullet can't reach them?"

"Of course." He follows me inside and closes the door.

Kyle has been in my home every weekend for the past month, but today is different. He isn't here for a massage or a trip to Buc-ee's. He's here for me.

I hurry to the kitchen and find a vase on top of the refrigerator. That will require my stool.

I have a wooden stool my dad made me as a little girl. I keep it in my closet, but carry it around the house when I need a few inches. I'm certain he didn't think I'd still need it as an adult, or maybe he did. Neither of my parents were big people. I'm more disappointed that he didn't live to see me as an adult.

It's a hassle to get it out sometimes, but a nice reminder of Dad. It's like he's still here to help me in some ways. I like that.

When I get back to the kitchen with my stool, Kyle is filling the vase with water. I didn't even realize he had followed me into the kitchen.

I smile when he plucks the flowers in the vase. He holds it out for me.

"Thanks." Our fingers brush, and my body heats up to match my face.

"You can arrange them however to make it pretty."

"They look great." I laugh a little and set down the stool in my other hand.

Kyle follows me to the mantel, where I center the vase.

"Perfect," he says.

"It is." My voice is raspy and a little embarrassing. Probably because the "perfect" I'm referring to is him.

"Ready?"

"Yeah," I answer in a clearer voice.

He opens the house door and his Jeep door for me. Living in the South, I'm used to guys opening building doors for me, but the car door thing is new.

I cut my eyes toward Kyle when I buckle my seat belt. He's far from needing a textbook to see over the wheel. He's closer to giant sized compared to me, but I prefer that. I feel safe with him, like he can take down anything that comes against us.

We ride toward the multipurpose building where all of Apple Cart County hosts events like rodeos, tractor pulls, and livestock shows. It's essentially a metal building closed on three sides, with a big dirt center. There's a large concrete end with tables and a kitchen area for concessions.

Like I expected, the barbecue dinner is set up on the concrete. I've only been here a handful of times, when it rained so badly that we needed to move Trade Days inside.

Tools, gift cards, caps, local honey, and other items line a long table near the entrance. I browse it and turn to Kyle.

"What's all this?"

"We do an auction as a fundraiser."

"You should've told me. I could've made a gift basket."

He chuckles. "That would be helpful. Half the guys here have never smelt near as good as your stuff."

I smile. "I'll take that as a compliment."

"What's this?" I point to a metal bucket filled with everything from a fly flat and gardening gloves to a bottle of Tylenol.

Kyle rolls his eyes. "Gotta be from Paul."

I nod. "Makes sense."

An older version of Kyle strolls up to us. He scans me head to toe, then turns to Kyle. "Aren't you gonna introduce me?"

"Dad, this is Daisy."

"Pleased to meet you, I'm Donald Tolbert." He holds out a hand.

"You too, sir." I shake his hand.

"Daisy?" He lets go and wags a finger at me. "You're the one who's been massaging Kyle."

"Yes, that's me." My face heats up at the thought of Kyle mentioning me to his dad. Even if it is in the context of getting a massage.

"Thank you. He's had a time with that shoulder. I've helped him work some too, but I'm no spring chicken myself."

"Yes, sir." I grin at Donald rotating his arm the same way Kyle does at times.

"You two better grab a plate and get settled. You don't want to be left standing when the auction starts. They'll assume you're standing for a bid."

"Good point. Let's go." Kyle takes my arm and leads me to the long tables of food.

Brooke hands us plates and smiles. She was a little younger than me in school, but very popular. It makes sense for her to be here since her family runs an apple orchard. I imagine that would require tractors.

We move down the line as various ladies ask if we want whatever dish they're standing behind with a spoon. It's pork and chicken legs, with all the usual fixings of a barbecue.

Kyle piles his plate high, making me happy I sent him all

the steaks. I did eat before bringing him food, but not a steak. I got the feeling he could eat three if given the chance, and I still order off kids' menus.

A lot of the seats are taken once we get drinks. Kyle scans the room with his super-human ability to see over people's heads. Not really a superpower, but for someone my size, it is.

"Let's go back here." He motions toward the tables in the back.

I like the idea of sitting away from the crowd. Old people in Apple Cart start planning your wedding when they see you together for the first time. The fact that we've been seen before now at the fair will only make it that much worse.

"Sounds good."

I follow him to a back table with only two chairs. Good choice. Now if they want to gossip, they will have to seek us out.

An older man in overalls whistles to get the crowd's attention. He thanks everyone for coming and prays over the food. I peek at several older men in the crowd who already have a mouthful of food. All of them cease chewing except for Paul. He never checks up and continues chowing down.

How he spoons baked beans into his mouth with his head bowed is beyond me. I'm certain he's had practice.

The man in overalls tells everyone to enjoy their meals while he calls out auction items. He starts with individual bottles of honey. The first few all go for ten dollars. The last bottle goes for a little more. Must be the scarcity tactic.

Paul's bucket of crap surprisingly goes for twenty bucks. Whoever strategically placed the Tylenol on top knew how to market.

Two men move what resembles a large scale to the front of the table. It's painted green and yellow, with "John Deere" on the side.

"We saved this beauty for last," the announcer calls out. "A handmade, one-of-a-kind John Deere seesaw."

Several kids gasp and point. Their parents perk up as the bidding opens at fifty dollars. We eat and listen as the bidding increases, ten to twenty dollars at a time.

It gets to two hundred and people quiet down. The man with the highest bid sits down with a satisfied grin. Kyle wipes his mouth and stands. I expect him to go to the bathroom or back to the buffet.

Instead, he lifts a finger and yells, "Two-fifty."

My jaw drops, but not as far as the guy who bid two hundred.

The announcer scans the crowd before saying, "Going once, going twice, going three times—sold!"

Kyle smiles at me, then marches up front and collects his winnings. He easily lifts the long wooden contraption that took two men to move.

My heart contracts when I watch his arm muscles flex against the weight of the seesaw. He walks it back to our table like it weighs the same as a baby goat. The top board sways slightly when he rests the base on the ground.

"Do you have a child I need to know about?"

He smirks. "That's for Mullet."

My eyes widen, and my heart beats faster. "My Mullet?"

He laughs. "I don't know another Mullet."

I smile, then wrinkle my forehead as I study the seesaw.

"I noticed him balancing on things around your house, like the loose board I fixed on the porch. Maybe if he has a toy, he won't go toying with things that he shouldn't."

A tiny part of me is a bit offended that he dissed my baby. But the other ninety-eight-ish percent is melting over such a kind gesture—one that proves he pays attention to my number-one animal.

Kyle just might be the GOAT.

CHAPTER TWELVE

Kyle

It's evident I didn't plan on purchasing a seesaw by the long wood plank sticking out the back of my Jeep.

I drive slower than usual to make sure it doesn't bounce around and get scuffed up. Not that it should matter since it's going to a goat, but someone spent a lot of time on that thing.

The guy with two kids stared daggers at me when I upped his already huge bid. If he knew what kind of kid this toy was for, he would really be mad.

I glance at Daisy, whose profile is highlighted by the full moon. Her milky skin almost glows. We hit a bump in the road, and I face forward, remembering my back cargo.

I want to reach out and hold her hand, but it's too dark to tell where it is. It's not smart to feel around in the dark while driving. I might get slapped, then wreck.

My mind jumps ahead ten or so scenes all the time. It's both a blessing and a curse, as it's kept me out of trouble. The one time I lived for the moment was my drunken arrest and the end of my college athletic career. Best to play it safe with Daisy, no matter how badly I'd prefer to pull over and kiss her.

Instead, I settle for small talk and hope she realizes it's not common for me to buy a woman an expensive gift. Especially when that gift is intended for her goat.

When we reach her driveway, my stomach sinks. I don't want to leave her yet. But it's not worth pushing my luck. My goal tonight is a simple kiss. Maybe that will earn me points to hang out more and do more kissing next time.

I pull up to her house, careful not to hit any chickens running loose. Neon green swirls in front of my headlights, followed by a goat's eyes glowing when it raises its head.

"Uh, Daisy, what's that goat got on its horns?"

"Pool noodles."

"Why?"

"Hoss likes to butt all the other goats during mating season, so I have to secure his horns."

I chuckle as several jokes come to mind—though none appropriate to share with Daisy. Then I cut the engine, and Hoss loses interest once the headlights dim. He runs in the opposite direction of the house as we get out.

"I'll go turn the porch light on so you can see how to get the seesaw out."

"Thanks." I'd almost forgotten about it thanks to the pool noodles distraction.

Daisy hurries to her house, effortlessly dodging animals and lawn ornaments. I'm afraid to move that quickly around her place in broad daylight. It's like a minefield of moving targets between here and the porch.

The yard lights up once she opens her front door. I hop

out and open the back of the Jeep. Hoss lifts his pool-noodle horns and bleats at me when I lift the seesaw.

"This is for Mullet. You'll have to ask him to share."

I carry the contraption and set it in front of the porch. Daisy bounces down the steps with Mullet.

He immediately steps on the downward slope. He crosses the plank and rides it down, then does the same in the opposite direction. Daisy giggles and claps.

The way she smiles at me is worth it all.

"Do you want me to move it someplace else?"

"Actually, do you mind moving it on the porch? I've trained the other goats not to come on it. That way Mullet can have it to himself."

"Sure." She does nothing to hide her favoritism with animals. I wonder if it would be the same with real kids?

Stop thinking about having kids with Daisy. You haven't even kissed the girl.

I lift the seesaw again, careful to bend with my knees instead of my back. Partly because Daisy is watching and partly because it has helped my aches and pains.

She shuffles Mullet out of the way so I can climb the porch. I set the seesaw down and push it to the place she points. The porch is rather large, and her flower bushes hide it from view off the porch. Mullet seems to approve as well, since he prances over and climbs on the board.

Daisy walks up to me, grinning widely. "He loves it. Thank you so much."

I intend on saying, "You're welcome." Instead, I lean down to kiss her. I've waited long enough.

Third time has to be the charm. Or is it?

I'm hovered over the seesaw to try and bend down enough to reach her lips. Mullet walks under us right before our faces meet, and I end up kissing her nose instead of her lips. Then Mullet walks into my chest, pushing me back.

My backside hits the porch, and I grunt. Daisy offers a hand to help me up, but Mullet beats her to me. He swipes his tongue from my chin to my hair in one big lick.

I cough as I bite back vomit. His breath did not smell good. Daisy laughs, and I blink. Refocusing on her hand, I take it and allow her to help me up. More like I allow her to think she's helping me up, as there's no way someone that tiny could lift me.

She smiles up at me, still holding my hand. "I'm sorry. I think that was Mullet's way of thanking you for the gift."

"That's not how I planned on the night ending." I untuck my shirt and wipe my face with the end of it.

She laughs again, and we lock eyes for a few seconds. Bad as I want to, I can't bring myself to kiss her with goat breath, even if it is her goat.

Like an awkward teenager at a middle school dance, I take my free hand and pull her in for a side hug. Her head nuzzles under my arm, magnifying our height difference. I should've started bending down sooner to beat Mullet out of the way.

I could stand here all night with her cuddled under my arm. But that would be a little awkward since the moment for a kiss has passed yet again.

I slide my arm out from around her and drop her hand. A chill runs through my body like I've lost a part of myself when I'm no longer touching her.

"See you in the morning?" she asks.

"In the morning," I confirm before begrudgingly heading for my Jeep.

Lucky for me, her hands will be all over me in the morning.

Daisy

I just thought I was nervous about massaging Kyle last week. I'm even more nervous now that he's kissed me.

On the nose.

Not as romantic as I'd fantasized, but Mullet can be to blame for that. Maybe it's for the best, as I now have time to muster up the courage to kiss him back when he kisses my lips.

If he still wants to.

I shake my head and try not to think too much about it. My weird prom date tried to kiss me, but I closed my mom's front door before he got the chance. Before that, I had a brief encounter with another nerdy guy during a night of gaming that gave way to a game of Spin the Bottle. I blame it on the goth girl from another school someone invited. That kiss lasted maybe a second, and he had an allergic reaction to my Bath & Body Works spray.

And that is how I've made it to my late twenties without a real kiss.

Regardless of my nerves, I swipe on some lip gloss in case Kyle tries anything. The kind of lip gloss that's barely noticeable but tastes like watermelon if you lick your lips. The strawberry flavor is even better, but I've never known of anyone with a watermelon allergy. Best to play it safe given my limited experience.

There's a knock at my door, and I drop the lip gloss while trying to screw on the lid. I frantically close it and set it on the bathroom counter before hurrying to the door.

I take a deep breath and open it to . . .

"Toby."

My face falls flat with my voice.

"Heya, your mom sent over more stuff she said you needed."

"Eucalyptus and lavender?"

"Yeah. That's it."

I nod. I agreed to lead some homeschoolers in making soap one day next week and needed more scents to mix in.

"I'll help you get the boxes."

He tilts his head and sniffs. "You smell nice."

"Thanks." I half smile.

It's nice that he noticed, but I actually don't care what he thinks. The guy I care about is pulling into the driveway now.

I swallow and look around Toby's slim frame as Kyle steps out of his Jeep. Mullet prances toward him. They've become closer recently, and reached a whole new level last night when Mullet licked his face.

Kyle pets him, then walks toward the porch. Toby turns his head and follows my gaze, which is fixed on Kyle like superglue on, well, anything.

"Hey." Kyle greets him and holds out a hand.

"Hi," Toby answers without shaking his hand. He glances back at me. "I'll start unloading."

"Thanks." I return my gaze to Kyle as soon as Toby steps off the porch.

"Need me to help him?" Kyle hooks a thumb behind us.

"Nah, it's just dried herbs. Not heavy at all, and I wasn't expecting him either. I don't want to keep you waiting."

Kyle smiles. "Thanks, although I wouldn't mind."

My cheeks heat up as he passes me through the open door. I follow him inside and close it. Kyle continues to the massage room, and I allow my eyes to trail him.

A muffled sound comes from outside. I open the door to Toby fumbling with the knob. He balances a box on his knee and almost falls on his face as the door swings back.

"Sorry, Toby."

He sighs and lets go of the doorknob. "No worries. Could you leave this thing cracked for me?"

"Yeah." I step back for him to enter.

He moves the box from his knee to his arm and steadies it beside another box in his opposite arm. Although the contents are light, the boxes are big.

I leave the door cracked and head for the massage room. Kyle should've had time to change by now, but I knock to make sure.

After hearing a muffled "ready" from the other side of the door, I fluff my hair and enter the room. My limbs tingle at how silly I'm acting. Putting on lip gloss and fluffing my hair. Wearing a new top and nice sandals.

Even if Kyle does want to kiss me, he's here today on business. A situation that will require me to rub oils and lotions all over his naked back and torso, but he's paying me money, which makes it a business transaction.

Wow, that did *not* make me feel better.

I move from my table to Kyle, who's facedown with his bronzed, muscular back staring at me. Now that I'm certain he wants to kiss me, I shouldn't be so nervous. Yet for some reason, that makes me even more nervous.

I suck in the scent of warm bacon and rub my hands together once more before placing them on his shoulders. My fingers melt into his skin, and I instantly relax. Strange, since he's supposed to be the one relaxing from this.

For the first time, there are less knots in his shoulders than usual. Maybe he's relaxing too.

I move down his back and apply pressure. A loud clank down the hall causes me to pause. I continue the massage until the door opens, and Toby stares at me.

"Woah, my bad."

I sigh and walk to the door, pushing Toby into the hall. I close the massage room and clinch my teeth.

"I'm in the middle of a massage."

"Yeah, well, the goats got into some of the eucalyptus leaves."

"It will be fine. Please clean up what you can, and I'll take care of the rest after my client leaves."

"Client? I thought you two were . . ."

I cross my arms. "Yes, he's my massage client. I am a massage therapist."

"I thought you made soap and stuff."

"I do that too, just like you go to school and do whatever my mom has you do."

I open the door and back inside, locking it behind me. I'm now acutely aware of every sound Toby makes behind the wall. When it's time for Kyle to flip over, I give him a sympathetic smile. "Sorry about all the noise today."

"It's okay." He smiles back, then closes his eyes.

I drape the warm towel over his face and massage his collarbone area. It's probably for the best that Toby is a few feet away, making all sorts of distracting noises. Otherwise, I'd be tempted to kiss Kyle.

Not that I'd know what to do.

The sounds die down as I finish his massage. I step back and remove the towel from his face.

"I'll let you get dressed." I turn toward the door as he starts to sit up.

A goat bleats loudly down the hall, and I pick up my pace. I rush out the door, closing it behind me, then stop in front of the candle room.

"What is going on?"

Boxes lie strewn across the room, while Mullet and Hoss chew on crushed leaves mashed into the carpet.

"Hoss, you're not supposed to be in here."

He snorts and prances out of the room, knowing he's in big trouble.

"Mullet followed me, and I didn't see the one with the green horns until he started head-butting boxes."

I look at Toby standing in the room and pinch the bridge of my nose. "I thought you'd cleaned it all up."

"I did, but he knocked them over again. I didn't know what to do. I've never seen a goat with green horns."

I shake my head. "Thanks, Toby. I'll take it from here."

I pull his sleeve to politely shove him out of the room. Then I point to Mullet. "Go outside. You're grounded."

He hangs his head and walks away like a shamed child. Good. That was the response I wanted.

I puff up my cheeks and go for the vacuum in the hall closet. Kyle steps out when I'm in the hall.

"Hey, I've got your money."

I'd forgotten all about that. "It's fine. I doubt you were able to relax during any of this. Just keep it."

"No, you gave me a service, and I'm going to pay you."

I shake my hand at the cash he's holding. "Seriously, keep it. I wouldn't feel right charging you for that."

Kyle frowns. "On one condition."

"What?"

"I will put this toward taking you out on a date."

He waves the cash, then steadies it in front of my eyes. "No tractor-pull barbecues. A real nice dinner without all of Apple Cart around."

The corners of my mouth curve. "Deal." I hold out my hand for him to shake on it.

He takes my hand and kisses my knuckles. Goose bumps drift up my arm as his lips linger on my hand.

"Daisy Mae, you ready for me?"

I jump back and pull my hand from Kyle's. He lifts his head and clears his throat. Paul struts in from the living room in a bathrobe and boots. Except where most people would secure the robe with a tie, he's wearing his signature belt and belt buckle.

I glance at Kyle, then back at Paul. I'd totally forgotten about his appointment.

"Give me a few minutes to change the table. We had a little goat-tastrophe in the next room."

"All right."

As he adjusts his belt, I look away. The last thing I need today is for a skinny old man to have a wardrobe malfunction.

I head back to the massage room to change the sheets, while Paul talks to Kyle about the tractor pull.

When the table is ready, I step out and let Paul know. He holds his belt buckle and marches in the massage room. I step toward Kyle and smile. He reaches out and cups my face in his hand. My stomach swirls like tennis shoes in a dryer.

This is it. He's gonna kiss me. Not on the hand or the nose. On the lips!

I moisten my lips in anticipation, happy to taste a little watermelon still left on them.

"Daisy."

I jump, causing Kyle's hand to flinch. Paul is shirtless with his head out the half-open door.

"Yes?" I ask in a breathy tone. Partly from the shock and partly from the effect Kyle is having on me.

"Mind if I keep on my boots? I've got these bunions on my feet nobody needs to see."

"Uh, sure."

He nods, ducks behind the door, and slams it. I blink at the noise and clinch my teeth.

"See you Friday night," Kyle whispers close to my ear.

"Friday night," I repeat.

He steps away and waves bye. I lift my hand and watch

him exit the front door. I have almost a week to muster up the courage to let this man kiss me. Unless we have even more interruptions.

I inhale and blow out a long breath. Speaking of interruptions, I have the perfect antidote to get my mind off kissing Kyle.

I've got to massage Paul Bunion.

CHAPTER THIRTEEN

Kyle

I walk slowly to Daisy's front door in an effort to avoid all animals. I'm wearing khaki pants and don't want hoof marks or tongue prints on them before we go to dinner.

The chickens don't care about me, but I spot Hoss across the yard. He might be a problem. I make it to the front door and stand where he can't see me on the porch. Then I knock.

The door nudges open about an inch. I pull it open more to Mullet standing in front of me. He bleats.

I wince, and crane my neck to make sure he didn't call Hoss toward us. Luckily, Hoss is busy scratching his horns on a tree and tearing a hole in the pool noodle.

Daisy appears when I turn toward the door.

"Hey, you look beautiful." She's wearing a flower-print dress with her hair pulled over one shoulder.

She steps past Mullet and smiles. "Did he open the door?"

"I guess so." I frown at the little goat, who tilts his head as if that shouldn't surprise me.

"If it's not completely shut, he'll do that." She steps onto the porch and closes Mullet inside.

The top of her head comes to my shoulder rather than my armpit. "Did you grow since Saturday?"

She holds up a slim leg and wiggles her foot to show off bright pink high heels.

I admire the way the sun shines on her smooth legs and smile.

She returns my smile as I offer her my arm. We descend the steps together and start toward my Jeep. I'm opening her door when something butts at my butt. I turn around and meet Hoss's stare. He snorts.

"Shoo." I shake my hands toward him, and he backs up a step.

Daisy laughs. "He's being protective, I think. He can tell this is a real date."

I start to say that the tractor-pull dinner was a real date too, but then decide it probably wasn't. Tonight I hope to make up for that, along with all the other times I've tried to kiss her and failed miserably.

I hurry to my side of the Jeep and hop in. After closing the door, I sigh.

"Uh, Daisy, I hate to ask you this, but can you check if he did any damage to my pants?"

"Are you asking me to check out your butt?"

I laugh nervously. "Well, it sounds bad when you say it like that."

She smirks. "Turn around."

I lift off the seat and twist so she can see my backside. A few seconds tick by, and I'm more interested in if she likes what she sees rather than if there's a hole in my pants.

She laughs. "You're good. Saved by the pool noodles."

"Good." I sit down and wiggle to get comfortable. I may have a bruise tomorrow thanks to Hoss.

"Where are we going?" Daisy asks.

I start down the driveway, glaring at Hoss in my rearview mirror. "Lakeside Landing, ever heard of it?"

"Yeah, they're known for having really good shrimp, right?"

"I think so. It's supposed to be really nice, and just far enough away that there's a slim chance Apple Cartians will be there." I smile at her.

"Even better." She smiles back.

Once we're on the main highway, I glance over and notice her hand on the console. I reach for it and curl my fingers around her tiny palm. She closes her fingers on my hand, and my chest swells at the softness of her skin melding with mine.

We make small talk like always, but it somehow seems deeper with her holding my hand. I almost regret making a reservation, as I'm enjoying our ride so much. But Daisy looks too good not to take someplace, and it's time I take her on a nice date like I've wanted to for so long.

I'm relieved when the restaurant gives us a quiet window seat so we can continue talking. Dinner is somewhat of a blur. I hang on Daisy's every word as I stare into her honey-colored eyes. They change colors slightly as the sun sets over the lake beside us.

Even though we've shared some serious details about our parents and growing up, there's still a lot I don't know about her.

"What made you want goats?" I ask in between bites of my seafood platter.

"I have to say that goats wanted me first."

"What?" I laugh. That's not the answer I expected.

"I already had chickens for eggs, and I was feeding them

one day. I heard something and saw a tiny goat with a mullet nearby. He had his horn tangled in a blackberry bush at the edge of my yard. I untangled him and fed him, then I tried calling around to find his owner. To this day, I don't know where Mullet came from."

"Interesting. And the goat yoga?"

She giggles. "Also Mullet's idea. I've always been into yoga, and he decided to do it with me—or on me. I'd heard of goat yoga before, so researched the proper ways to do it. Then I got certified to offer classes."

"Cool."

Her face beams.

We continue talking about all her other ventures, from making candles and soaps to how she got into massage therapy. The candles and soaps were also a by-product of having goats, since she uses their milk in the mixtures.

We're deep in conversation when the waiter returns. "Would you care for any dessert?"

I look to Daisy for an answer. She smiles, then glances at her plate.

"I'm good, but thanks."

"I'm good too. Just the check."

"Yes, sir." He nods and walks away.

Daisy gazes out the window at the lake below. I study her profile and focus on the curve of her lips. No matter what stands in my way tonight—it could be goats, gangsters, or even gorillas—I intend on kissing her.

The waiter brings our check, and I pay with cash. I leave enough for a good tip and push back my chair. Daisy follows my lead, and we take the staircases to the exit.

"Enjoy the night," the hostess calls when we open the front door.

"You too," we say in semi-unison.

I take Daisy's hand, happy that it's easier to reach with

her in heels. The sun lowers behind the trees, shining just enough to brighten her hair.

I release her hand to open the Jeep door for her before circling to the driver's side. When I turn my head to back out of the parking lot, Daisy smiles.

"I feel bad. We've talked so much about me. You mentioned leaving college to become a mechanic when we talked before. Was that to help you dad?"

"Partly." I face forward and head for the road.

"You just didn't like college?"

I run a finger under the collar of my shirt. The truth about my mistake was bound to come out sooner or later. Might as well be sooner than later. That way if she has an issue with my past, I'll know before my feelings get too deep.

"I was studying business, and I did like college. I actually liked it a little too much." I grip the steering wheel tighter and take a deep breath before continuing. "I went on a junior-college football scholarship. Everything was going great. I was starting defense, my grades were good, and I had a lot of friends. Just not the right friends."

I glance at Daisy. She's looking straight ahead, so I can't gauge her reaction. Regardless, I need to keep talking and get it all out.

"We partied. A lot. I had drank maybe one or two beers in my life before then and never cared for the stuff. But all the other guys drank, so I did too. One night, I thought I could drive and got behind the wheel."

I swallow. The memory of what happened still haunts me, but the thought of what could've happened is even worse.

"Thankfully, a cop pulled me over before I had a wreck or anything. I got a DWI and spent one night in jail. Because I was only nineteen at the time, I was kicked off the team indefinitely. That meant no more scholarship. Everything that was once free—room and board, food and tuition—would now cost full price."

Daisy continues to stare ahead in silence. I loosen my grip on the wheel as I flip on my blinker to exit toward Apple Cart.

"I didn't want to stay there anyway, since I let down all my coaches and teammates. I could've enrolled at Apple Cart when I came home, but decided I wanted to lie low a while. I started working with Dad, since he had a full-time job elsewhere. Turns out I was good at it and enjoyed it. The rest is history."

We drive in silence for a full minute, which feels more like a full hour. My stomach churns as I analyze what might be going through her mind. Will she think I'm an awful, irresponsible person? Will she worry that I still have a drinking problem?

"Kyle, I'm so sorry. That must have been really tough." Daisy reaches over and squeezes my hand.

All my nervous energy loosens at her touch. I can't begin to explain to her how much her comfort means to me. So I continue opening up to her.

"The worst part of all was having to call my dad from jail. Then admitting to him and my grandparents what I'd done, and what I'd been doing for months."

Daisy squeezes my hand again. "We all have things in our past we're not proud of. For some of us it's partying, for others it's Shakespeare reenactments."

I laugh, then catch myself. "Sorry."

"No apologies needed. I was a total dork. I still like Shakespeare today, but I know better than to go out in public dressed like Juliet."

Daisy dressed like medieval royalty flashes through my mind. Part of me hopes she still has that Juliet dress stashed away somewhere. Good thing she says something else to derail that train of thought.

"You were always a good guy in high school. Even though I didn't know you well, I could tell. Don't beat yourself up over a stupid mistake when you were nineteen. You're still a good person, and you've more than made up for it in the way you are now."

"It means a lot to hear you say that." I rub the back of her hand with my thumb.

I turn into her driveway, both sad that this night is coming to an end and excited because I know a kiss is on the horizon. If anything good came from that hard conversation, it was getting Daisy's support and assuring myself she would want me to kiss her.

I park the Jeep and cut the engine. "Can I walk you to the door?"

Daisy smiles shyly.

We open our doors at the same time and meet in front of the Jeep. She rubs her arms, so I pull her close. It's not cold outside, but a good bit cooler since the sun went down.

Her slim, bare arm is covered in goose bumps, but is still silky smooth. I cup my hand around her elbow and pull her under my arm to keep her warm.

We climb the porch steps together as I glance around for any rogue goats wanting to boot me away. No animals are in sight, and all I hear are crickets among the trees.

This is it. No animals, weird townspeople, or loud noises to distract our kiss.

We stop in front of the door, and I turn her toward me. A few seconds tick by as I focus on her face. My eyes adjust to the dark shadows and I move my hand from her arm to cup her face.

"I want to kiss you."

Her jaw moves under my hand, then she takes a slow

breath. She steps toward me the slightest bit and lifts her head. I take that as a yes and dip my head.

My heart beats a million miles a minute when our lips meet. Her lips are even smoother than her skin, and they taste like fruit. I linger for several beats, then pull back to judge her reaction.

Her cheeks blush against the moonlight, and her eyes sparkle. Then she curves her lips and steps closer so our bodies are touching.

That's the only hint I need to kiss her again.

I tilt her chin upward and kiss her in a way I've imagined since the fair. The way I've attempted to kiss her several times now. She kisses me back, making it all the sweeter. I move my hand from her face to the back of her head and finger her soft curls.

She leans up slightly to kiss me deeper. I'm lost in all the loveliness that's Daisy until something knocks into my knees, pushing my chin into her head.

"Ouch." She moves back and holds her head.

I turn around to Hoss snorting at me. "What did I do?"

He bleats in response. I shake my head and turn back to Daisy. "Are you okay?"

She pats the side of her forehead. "Yep, just a little sore."

"I'm so sorry." She took the brunt of it, as my chin came down on her head.

"It's fine, really." She sighs. "Everything before that was perfect."

Perfect. I bask in the idea that for a few minutes, we did have it perfect. Before a stupid goat pool-noodled the back of my knees.

I nod toward Hoss. "I guess that's my cue to leave."

She giggles. "They're not used to sharing me yet."

"Yet." I grin.

Her cheeks blush, and she smiles slowly.

"I had a perfect time all night. Except for the accident." I chuckle. "Thank you for going to dinner with me."

"Thank you for asking."

Hoss bleats louder, causing me to flinch. I turn around and groan. "Okay, I'm leaving."

I shake my head at Daisy as she laughs. "See you tomorrow."

"Tomorrow," she whispers.

I take one last look at her in the moonlight, then I jog down the steps to my Jeep. Maybe it's for the best that crazy goat cut our kiss short. A few more minutes, and Daisy Duncan would own me.

Daisy

I yawn and lean against the back pew in the Baptist church. I hardly slept a wink all night. Partly because I kept replaying the perfect kiss with Kyle in my head, and partly because the outside of my head was throbbing.

When Kyle drove away, I closed Hoss in the time-out pen I reserve for misbehaving animals. It's small, away from everything else, and has no toys.

Serves him right.

Although, I'm not sure how much more kissing I could've taken before my knees gave out and I tumbled to the floor. I now get why people describe a good kiss as making them weak in the knees. It's not a metaphor.

That kiss was perfect.

Not that I have anything to compare it to, but wow. So worth waiting twenty-eight years.

"Daisy, hello?"

I blink and whip my head around to Adrianne snapping her fingers at me.

"Huh?"

"I thought we lost you there. I need your help with floral arrangements up front."

"Oh, sorry." I laugh and follow her to the front of the church.

"We've got to be on our A-game. I told Carolina we'd handle it all, and I want it to be as beautiful as she would do it."

"Geez, no pressure, huh?"

Adrianne narrows her eyes. "Seriously, it must be perfect."

Perfect. Last night was perfect. I want to go back.

"More purple on this side, don't you think?"

"Yeah," I agree to whatever Adrianne just said.

I've got to get my head in the game and quit thinking about Kyle. Maybe it's because he was at the tractor pull this morning instead of getting a massage. I missed my weekly Kyle fix.

I sigh.

"What?" Adrianne's face is full of concern.

Come on, Daisy. Make something up. "I think more pink would help too."

"Great idea. Grab those roses when you get the hydrangeas."

"Okay." I twist my mouth, a little proud of pulling that one out of nowhere.

Once I secure the extra flowers in place, Adrianne and I agree that adding more pink and purple was perfect.

Ah, perfect.

Adrianne's phone twinkles, buzzing me back to reality. She grabs it from the first pew.

"Shoot, that means it's time for hair and makeup." She points dramatically down the aisle. "To the basement. Carolina is meeting us there."

I fight the urge to roll my eyes and follow her downstairs. I'm beginning to regret volunteering my help today. Even though she's my best friend, I mainly did it to save her from Misty. She would be more of a hindrance than a help, and I couldn't do that to Adrianne—or Carolina.

We take the stairs, and I rush to keep pace with Adrianne's long legs. By the time we reach the landing, Carolina is coming in from the back with a rolling suitcase.

"Perfect timing." Adrianne beams.

Please quit using the word "perfect." That is reserved for kissing Kyle, as nothing else compares.

"Are you okay, Daisy?" Carolina asks.

"Yes."

Adrianne shakes her head. "She's acted loopy all morning. I blame it on that new candle scent she came up with."

"There's nothing wrong with goat breath."

Carolina frowns.

"That's the candle scent, not the real thing."

"No." Carolina steps closer and pushes my hair behind my ear. "I mean this bruise on your head. Did one of those goats butt you?"

I touch my head lightly. "No, just a little clumsy accident I had last night." I giggle nervously.

Adrianne narrows her eyes, as if not convinced by my story. It's a true story—just not the whole truth.

"We're burning daylight, let's get you wedding ready." Adrianne pats Carolina on the shoulder, then turns her in the opposite direction.

I fall in line, and we head for the bridal suite, which doubles as a prayer room and occasionally an extra nursery.

Adrianne immediately unpacks a bag of makeup we brought in earlier and checks the curling wands we plugged in an hour ago.

"Have a seat, Carolina." Adrianne pulls a chair in front of a desk where we set up a lighted mirror.

Carolina does as she's told, while Adrianne instructs me on gathering certain hair products from yet another huge bag.

My arm is enveloped by the deep bag as I dig for a certain brand of hair spray. I never understood why she's so picky about every product, but she does always look flawless. I don't complain since she's fixing me up next for my payment.

An hour passes as we chat about everything from Carolina and Jonah's honeymoon plans to their newest renovation project. She smiles wider than ever whenever his name leaves her lips. I hope I'm lucky enough to feel that about someone one day, and even luckier that he will feel the same for me.

Luckiest would be if the he were Kyle.

I shake that thought from my head and finish the task at hand, which is steaming Carolina's gown while Adrianne finishes her lipstick.

When her lips are set and the dress is smooth, I hold it out for her to step in it. Carolina laughs after I zip the back of her gown.

"What's funny?" Adrianne has a worried look on her face.

"Nothing, just that it fits me much better than Bianca's dress did."

Adrianne arches a brow. "As it should, and why would you try on Bianca's dress?"

"Never mind, a story for another day."

Adrianne shrugs and checks her phone. "Ah, not a minute to spare. Let me add a little more holding spray."

Carolina closes her eyes and I stand back as Adrianne dusts the place with hair spray. I cough when a cloud of fumes fills the room like someone tossed a hand grenade.

"There, flawless."

Thank you for not stealing perfect again.

Carolina turns in front of the mirror and smiles. She reaches out to hug us, but we do so from arm's length to not mess up our work.

"Thank you both so much."

"You're welcome," we say in unison.

"Knock, knock," someone calls from outside. "It's your mama."

Carolina tiptoes to the door and opens it slightly. Her mom grins widely through the crack. Carolina opens the door all the way.

"The photographer is here for family photos."

"Okay." Carolina slides out the door and waves to us. "Thanks again."

We wave and mutter our welcomes as the door closes. I plop down on the couch in the corner and raise my eyes to Adrianne staring at me, arms crossed.

"What?"

"You've been acting odder than usual, and you have a knot on your head. Spill."

I lean back and sigh. She grabs my hand and pulls me from the couch. "And do it here. We're getting the remaining bridesmaids in a minute, and I want to give that Kendra hippie a proper makeover."

I sit on the chair in the front of the mirror and tilt my head to get a better look at the battle scar. It does look pretty bad when my hair is pushed aside.

"Kyle hit me."

Adrianne chucks the brush in her hand and balls up her fists. "He what?"

I laugh. "Not like you're thinking. You know how we went on a date last night?"

"Yeah?" She perks up, but keeps a skeptical face.

"We kissed."

Adrianne's eyes widen. "For real? Or on the nose again?"

I sigh, wishing I'd never told her about that. "It was a real kiss. Like a really real kiss."

Adrianne claps, then hugs me. When she pulls back, a smile stretches across her entire face. "And you didn't tell me until now?"

"To be fair, it happened last night, and we've been busy today."

"True." She fumbles in her makeup bag, then stops and wrinkles her brow. "If y'all kissed, then why are you acting all moody today? Shouldn't you be happy? And how did you get the bruise?"

"I am happy, but kind of nervous too. He didn't come for a massage today, but he'll be at the wedding. I don't want to be weird and mess this up. Oh, and the bruise was goat interference."

She nods, then puts a hand on my shoulder. "You won't mess it up."

"Easy for you to say. You're happily married and never had guy trouble."

"Hey, that's not true." She grabs a comb with her free hand and levels the pointy end at my face.

I stare at it cross-eyed. That thing could do a lot of damage, especially in Adrianne's hands.

"Sorry, you're right. We've had different guy troubles, but troubles all the same."

She flips the comb around and starts parting my hair. I swallow, regretting what I'd said. Adrianne is traditionally beautiful and has a magnetic personality. She also doesn't foster goats and attempt to sleep-train roosters.

So I'm a little more eccentric with my hobbies. That doesn't mean she's had it easy. Her boyfriend before JoJo was a lying, cheating jerk. A handsome jerk, but a jerk all the same.

"Adrianne, I'm really happy for you and JoJo. Y'all give people like me hope."

She stops combing my hair and smiles at me in the mirror. "Oh, honey, you're too sweet. Your Prince Charming is out there, whether he's Kyle or someone even cooler we haven't met yet."

I half smile back. I appreciate her perky encouragement, but I'm not quite ready to accept that the love of my life may be someone besides Kyle.

CHAPTER FOURTEEN

Kyle

I grit my teeth as Bradley and I pull yet another wrecked tractor off the track. Another tractor with just enough damage that it's fixable for a later event, but it needs fixed by me.

This is the part I hate about the tractor pull. Aside from recent shoulder pain, I enjoy working on tractors and truck engines. It's my job, and I get paid well to do it. But when a tractor breaks down at the pull, the owner somehow expects me to fix it on the spot.

I will be sending out invoices this year.

That's the least I can do to justify staying here all day. Not to mention getting here super early and missing my weekly massage. And, man, did I want to make that appointment more than ever after last night.

I sigh when Bradley brings over the parts that shot off when the driver wouldn't let up and accept defeat. He had to keep bouncing and twisting, raising his front wheel to try and gain those last few inches. He didn't. Instead, he ended up with a few loose screws.

Half of the drivers here have a few loose screws, or I'd be having a relaxing day. Oh, to be one of the older guys who waves a flag or flips burgers at the concession stand.

Bradley slaps a hand on my shoulder and gives it a shake. "Gotta run, big dog. I'll see you tonight."

I nod. "See ya."

He's playing the guitar at Jonah and Carolina's wedding. I hope to make the wedding, but the odds are stacked against me today.

Speaking of odds, Paul and Wendall walk up, both eating snow cones. Wendall has a napkin tucked into his front overalls pocket, and Paul is wearing a green and yellow striped shirt to match his John Deere trucker hat.

"Kyle, I sure am glad you got some sense, son." Wendall's high-pitched voice cracks around a mouthful of shaved ice.

I blink at him, not sure how to respond. Do I say "thanks" or question what brought him to this unusual conclusion? Luckily, I don't have to say anything, as he follows with his reasoning.

"All these young'uns are running off to that wedding like their life depends on it." Wendall shoves another spoonful of colored ice in his mouth, then chews loudly. "And that Jonah should know better. You don't plan a wedding on tractor pull Saturday. It's like the Iron Bowl of our county."

I bite back a laugh. These old dudes take tractor pulling way too seriously, as does the rest of our state with the Iron Bowl.

He shakes his head, then leans toward me. "At least we got you. You're a trooper, and we can count on you to stay with us 'til the end."

I wince when an ice chip flies from his mouth to my

cheek. Wendall slaps me on the back and continues walking with Paul. My stomach pits as they hobble over the dirt mound bordering the edge of the track.

Like it or not, I'm stuck here.

I wipe the melting ice from my face with the end of my T-shirt. My shirt soaks through, which I attribute to lots of sweat mixed with the one drop of ice. I assess the damage on the tractor in front of me before turning to my toolbox.

An easy enough fix, but it might take me a bit. The rush is always guys entering multiple pulls. They change out weights to pull the same tractor in several classes. If something breaks before they're done with that tractor for the day, they look to me for rescue.

A few years back, I gladly accepted all engines—big and small, work and leisure. I'd like to move away from that, but I'm stuck now, especially since several Apple Cart residents drive tractors more than vehicles. Which reminds me of Rufus's lawn mower in my living room. It's still waiting on a part. Probably for the best since Bradley pulled his "license" for a while.

The owner of the tractor stomps over and watches me work. If there's one thing I despise more than a time crunch, it's having someone watch me work when I'm in a time crunch.

I try my best to ignore him.

After a few minutes, the announcer warns everyone to stay away from the track since a truck class is starting. That sends the guy running behind the tractor trailer set up as a stage for the announcer and scoreboard operator. I'm plenty enough away from the main action, but most people get farther than that.

At least I won't be bothered while I work.

With one part left to go, a loud engine roars behind me.

I scrunch my face, wishing I'd put in earplugs. Smoke bellows above, and the crowd screams.

A huge chrome bumper lands within inches of my feet. I crane my neck to see the teenager hanging out the window of a jacked-up pickup. Ervin waves a red flag toward him, yelling for him to cut his engine.

He finally does, and the truck bounces, then pops. Gasps come from around the arena. The kid hops out and rushes off the track.

I blow out a breath, then drop my wrench. Time to get the wrecker.

Why, again, did I allow them to nominate me as an officer for this association? Everyone else my age is eating cake by now. Except for maybe Earl Ed, who's waiting in the wings to pull his new truck.

I pull the wrecker toward the smokestack clouding the wrecked truck and prepare to load it. I'll stick to my word and fix what I can—for a while. However, I'm not staying all night if things keep messing up.

For the first time in my life, I actually want to attend a wedding. Simply so I can ask Daisy to dance.

Daisy

I down another cup of punch and lean back in the folding chair. The music blurs in the background as older women chat at a table beside me. One laughs about her husband choosing the tractor pull over the wedding.

It's not so funny to me since I know that's where Kyle is now.

He *needs* to be there. Still, there's a little part of me that whispers he wants to be there instead of here . . . instead of with me.

For all the time I stayed up last night replaying our kiss in my mind, I've stewed over it today. The high of that perfect kiss slowly gave way to worry. I've analyzed everything about it and debated what all could've gone wrong.

Not with the goat interruption and head butting, but with my execution.

Kyle has had way more practice than me. He once kissed Adrianne at the movies when we were teenagers. That alone is enough to make me self-conscious about my own lack of experience. Then when I think of all the other pretty, popular girls he's kissed over the years, my insides burn.

What could I possibly have to offer him? Other than a good deep-tissue massage. But he's paying me for that, so it doesn't count.

I stare at the half-eaten cake in front of me until a hand hovers over it. I flinch and turn to Bradley standing beside me.

I push my plate toward him. "You can have the rest."

He laughs. "No, I was offering my hand, hoping you would dance."

I frown. "Did you mistake me for Ashley?"

"Why does everyone think I have a thing for Ashley? Can't two attractive adults of the opposite sex just be friends?"

"No."

He grins. "Touché."

I drop my head to the table, barely missing my plate. After a moment of realizing Bradley isn't going away, I lift my head.

"Uh, you got a little something." He licks his thumb and reaches toward my face.

I swat at his hand like it's a rogue fly. "Stop!"

He drops his hand and pouts.

"Tell me where it is instead of wiping grandma spit at me like I'm a toddler."

One of the older ladies from the table beside us huffs when I say "grandma spit." I ignore that and widen my eyes at Bradley.

"Right above your eyebrow."

I wipe my fingertips across my forehead, then stare at him. He grits his teeth and hands me a napkin. He tilts his hat up and swipes at his own forehead.

I run the napkin harshly across my forehead. He gives me a thumbs-up after I move it.

I toss the napkin on top of the cake and sigh. I love wedding cake. Usually I'd have eaten the whole piece by now, starting with the icing. The more I think about Kyle, the more my appetite dwindles. Even cake doesn't taste good right now.

Instead, I'm stuck between Bradley and a gang of old ladies like an Apple Cart club sandwich—gossip and bad advice being the main ingredients.

"Why are you still here?"

"I asked you to dance, but never got an answer." Bradley narrows his eyes and straightens his hat.

"I don't recall you asking. You just stuck your hand over my cake like a raccoon."

He snorts. "As sheriff of this fine county, I demand you dance. You need cheering up."

I fold my arms in protest, then unfold them when Bradley reaches toward me. He's clumsier than he thinks, and I don't want him to accidentally grab something besides my hand.

He smiles when I hold out my hand. I'll regret this, but he's clearly not going away.

We walk to the edge of the dance floor, far from our table. Bradley holds me at arm's length the way they dance in any ballroom movie scene. Fine by me, as nobody will suspect us for a couple. That's the last thing I need.

"I had to get you away from those old birds to talk. Ethel will run right to church tomorrow with whatever we say, clouding it as a prayer request."

I laugh loudly.

"She will. Trust me." Bradley glances around and lowers his voice. "Kyle likes you."

I roll my eyes. "How very junior high of you. Why didn't you write it on a napkin and have me check yes or no for him?"

"Because your napkin is soiled with icing."

I bop his head with the heel of my hand.

He rubs his forehead. "Geez, Daisy. You're gonna ruin my moneymaker."

"I don't think a handsome face is a requirement for sheriff."

"It'll help come reelection."

"You're running again?" That doesn't surprise me, but it does surprise me he hasn't already been campaigning.

"As much as I'd love to talk about me, this is about Kyle, and *you*. Don't go thinking he ditched you tonight. He's stuck at that tractor pull. Parts were flying all over the place like loose cannons—"

"Is he okay?" I've never attended a tractor pull, but Bradley makes it sound deadly.

"Yeah. But he's busy putting all that crap back together. The old men depend on him too much, and he's too nice to tell them no like the rest of us."

I nod. "I was hoping it was something like that and not that he didn't want to be seen with me."

Bradley's brow draws together. "Why would he not want to be seen with you?"

I shrug. "He's Kyle, and I'm Daisy."

"And . . ."

"I'm the weird goat lady who has unnatural hair half the time."

"Honey, this is Apple Cart County. You're far from the weirdest citizen."

I laugh. "Thanks."

"I mean it. Do you not remember me arresting Rufus for crashing his lawn mower into the Pig, while drunk?"

I nod and smile.

"Kyle likes you, and you need to know that. I didn't like seeing you all mopey while everyone else was enjoying the night."

My face softens as a warmth rushes through me. "Bradley, you try and act tough, but you're really sweet when you want to be."

Either Bradley doesn't like hearing compliments on sweetness, or he didn't hear me at all. He's glaring over my head, across the dance floor.

Without saying a word, he pulls me closer. We're now past the Renaissance era into junior high distance.

"What's wrong?"

His nostrils flare, and I follow his gaze to Ashley and Samuel.

"Bradley, you need to tell her how you feel."

"I can't."

My nerves tingle, as that's the first time—at least to my knowledge—he's admitted liking Ashley.

"She's with him, and I'm not one to break people apart. I tried that once with Lacie and bombed. And we had all this history. She's now happily married with a baby on the way. I almost ruined that for her. I had to kidnap Collins just to get them back together."

I sigh. "This is different. Samuel isn't good for her, and I'm pretty sure she likes you too."

He lets out a breath, his nostrils flaring once more. I glance back at the couple. Ashley doesn't look happy, and neither does Samuel. Bradley is smiling when I turn back to him.

"Don't worry about me tonight, Daisy Mae. Your knight in shining grease stains just arrived." He tilts his head toward the side of the lodge.

I turn to Kyle standing under a row of garden lights, smiling.

CHAPTER FIFTEEN

Kyle

The moonlight shines around Daisy, highlighting her hair and eyes. She's wearing a bright pink dress with flowers. Her sweet appearance instantly relaxes me.

I don't even care that her hands are on my best friend. The smile she's giving me, along with the goofy grin on Bradley's face, lets me know she's one hundred percent into me.

She steps away from Bradley, and I step forward. I'm dirty, grimy, caked with dirt and grease. I sympathize with that Pig Pen character walking into the school dance on Charlie Brown cartoons.

A few women snarl their noses at me. Either from my smell or appearance—maybe both.

Daisy rushes toward me, erasing any insecurities I have about showing up to the formal event of the week dressed for the ultimate old-man event of the year. She puts her hands on my arms and pulls me toward her.

My arms shock into submission, but I hesitate.

"Daisy, I'm nasty."

"I don't care." She presses against my gritty chest, and I hold her close.

Her floral scent sifts under my nose, beating out my own dusty aroma. We fall into a casual sway to the music.

"I'm glad you came." Her voice vibrates against my chest and warms my insides.

"I wanted to come earlier, but Wendall kept me busy."

"I'm sure."

"And I wanted to come this morning. My shoulder could really use your touch."

She leans back and stares into my eyes. "I'll give you a complimentary massage one day this week."

"That's the best news I've heard all day. Including the infamous words 'final pull.'"

She laughs. "Glad to know I can compete with that."

"It's not even a competition." I glance down, taking in her full appearance, from her tall heels to her bright dress. "You look beautiful, by the way."

"Thanks. Adrianne's magic."

"You don't require any magic to look beautiful."

Her cheeks blush. "Thanks, but it is her dress."

"No wonder you didn't mind hugging me."

We share a laugh. The music changes to something faster, and everyone does one of those dances we all know from prom. I didn't care much for doing it back then, and I don't care much for it now.

Bradley, however, is in the middle of the dance floor leading the way. We take a few steps back, and Daisy slants her eyes at me.

"Do you want something to eat?"

My stomach pings at the mention of food. I haven't eaten since a burger around noon.

"Sounds good to me."

"Come on. It's all set up inside since the weather warned about a pop-up summer storm."

She takes my hand and leads me inside. We greet a few people milling around the house, including Paul. He's circling the food tables with a to-go box like a buzzard at a dove hunt.

Daisy scrunches her nose at him. I laugh, then notice my hands as I reach for a plate. I pause and turn them over.

"I really need to wash my hands first."

"Okay. Do you know where the bathroom is?"

"Uh, I think I need dish soap."

She wrinkles her brow. "Okay . . . the kitchen, then."

I follow her to the kitchen, where Mary is rushing around, plating cookies. She lifts her eyes when we walk in and shakes her head.

"Carla outdone herself this time. These are some of the prettiest cookies I've seen." She holds up one shaped and decorated like the Auburn University logo. "And that's saying a lot, 'cause I'm a Bama fan."

She laughs, revealing the gap in her front teeth. Daisy laughs with her. Mary stops and glances at her, then back at me. She wags a finger in front of us.

"I knew there was something between you two."

I look at Daisy, who's blushing again.

"Mrs. Mary, do you know where I can get some dish soap?" I lift my grease-stained hands.

She holds up a finger, then ducks behind the counter. After she sets a bottle beside the sink, I go around to wash my hands.

"How was the tractor pull?" Mary asks.

"Same as always—hot, dirty, and loud."

"So a lot like this kitchen was twenty minutes ago." She smiles and fans her face with a nearby oven mitt.

At least, I think it's an oven mitt. It looks like a stuffed fish. I soap up and scrub my hands, then reach for what I know is a towel.

"Do you need any help, Mrs. Mary?" Daisy asks.

"No, sugar. You enjoy this evening with your handsome date." She drops the mitt and starts stacking more cookies.

Daisy nods. "The cake was wonderful. I'm going to make sure Kyle gets a piece before it's gone."

"You go do that." She winks.

We exit the kitchen and run smack into Paul. Three Styrofoam boxes hit the floor—all filled with cake. He hurriedly closes the two boxes that didn't flip, then places them on top of two more boxes in his arms.

"Sorry, y'all," he mutters as he ducks toward the front door.

Daisy sighs. "You go fix yourself some supper. I'll clean this up."

"No, let me help."

Mary is at our side with both a dry towel and wet towel before I can move.

"That crazy Paul. No wonder he's never been married." Mary grits her teeth and drops a cloth on the floor.

I bend before she can and wipe the crumbs. Mary gives me the wet rag in exchange for the one holding crumbs.

"Ms. Dot seems to like him a lot," Daisy comments.

Mary huffs. "She's lonely."

I stand, and Mary grabs the wet towel from me. She frowns.

"Royce could drop dead tonight and I wouldn't get that lonely."

Daisy cackles out, and I laugh too. Mary arches her

brows, then heads toward the kitchen. Daisy links her arm through mine and leads me to the cake.

I fill a plate full of deer poppers and crackers while she grabs some cake and punch. We go out the front door and sit on a porch swing. Voices and music echo from the back, but we're alone here.

I settle my food on my lap and wrap my left arm around Daisy. The stars twinkle through the trees above, and a slight warm breeze blows through the porch. I stare at Daisy as the wind blows her hair back from her face. My pulse speeds up at her long eyelashes and rosy cheeks highlighted by the shadows. She turns to me and half smiles.

I tilt my head down and kiss her lips gently. She kisses me back, and I hold the back of her head in my hand. Her soft curls brush against my calloused hands as our mouths melt together. She leans into me, and I kiss her deeper.

My lips tingle against Daisy's soft ones. I'm under her spell and barely hear a loud whistle from the other side of the porch.

"Man, look at y'all!"

Daisy jerks back and turns toward the voice. I open my eyes to Paul smiling at us. He has a toothpick in his mouth and Ms. Dot on his arm.

I sit back in the swing, almost spilling my food. Paul is really messing with my game tonight.

Daisy tightens her lips and blushes. She stares at her lap before looking at me.

"I best go help Adrianne anyway. We're supposed to clean up once the couple leaves."

I open my mouth to ask her to stay, but she's off the swing and opening the front door quicker than I can speak. My plate of cake slides off the swing and onto the porch.

Paul steps forward and picks it up. "If you don't want this, I'll take it off your hands. I didn't get a piece for Dot."

I stand and rake a hand through my dusty hair. "Take it. I'm no longer hungry."

Paul snatches my plate. I step around him and walk into the darkness toward my Jeep. He's interrupted my plans enough for one day.

Daisy

"Breathe in and arch your back, allowing your goat to cross your shoulders."

I give Adrianne side eye, as that last direction doesn't apply to her. Socks, one of my newest goats, has jumped on her twice. Each time, she flicked him off like a pest. Seriously, why come to goat yoga if you don't want to do yoga with goats?

Mullet marches across my shoulders like a seasoned pro. He should be. We practice yoga together often. One of my marketing slogans is that I never ask students to do something I haven't first tried myself.

Adrianne ignores my glare and presses into the movement without a goat. I turn toward my other students, biting my tongue. I'm not going to waste my breath explaining the benefits of how a goat can enhance your workout.

Hannah smiles back at me, so I focus on her. Aniston has scooted up a row beside her in Carolina's usual spot. Aniston doesn't have much balance, and I sometimes hear her curse quietly, but she's dedicated. And she allows the goats to work their magic—unlike someone I know.

I continue leading the room, choosing to ignore both

Adrianne and Skeeder, who claims he is here on doctor's orders. He's wearing jeans and is playing with the goats more than doing yoga, so who knows.

So tonight's class consists of women my age, one really fit middle-aged woman, and a guy who can't hold down a job and really needs a haircut. Typical Apple Cart County crowd. All we're missing is Paul.

I laugh to myself. Nope, we're not missing Paul. He can stay away from my house and my food. The last time he came for a massage, he took three tomatoes off my hanging plant on the porch. And they weren't even ripe!

Who steals green tomatoes from someone's porch plant?

Paul, that's who.

We transition to standing poses, which Adrianne always enjoys. Skeeder is slowest to stand and has trouble balancing on one leg. He falls against Donut, causing the goat to bleat.

"Are you okay?"

He raises a hand. "Yeah, I'm good."

My face heats, and I bite my tongue. I was asking Donut, not him. Donut stands and shuffles away from Skeeder, so I take it that he's okay.

I lead the remaining poses I have planned for this session, then ask everyone to take deep breaths in and out. My eyes are closed, but I open them at a squeal.

Ashley bounces on one leg. She shakes one foot and stares like it's a poisonous snake.

"Ashley, are you okay?"

I make sure to address her by name, since I am checking on a person this time.

"It peed on my foot!" She hops to balance so she can point to Socks a few feet from her.

Socks turns to me, and I swear he grins. I march to the back and notice a wet spot on Ashley's mat. Trying not to laugh, I grab Socks by the collar and take him toward my bedroom.

"We're done for today. Venmo me if you're a drop-in and not a monthly student," I call behind my back.

Once I'm in my room, I shut the door and sigh. "Socks, buddy, I thought you were ready."

He bleats as if trying to explain. I shake my head and open the closet in the attached master bathroom. I keep a pack of diapers for reasons like this. Not baby diapers, but the old-people kind. They slip on goats perfectly, and the material is easier for me to cut a tail hole.

The only downside is the looks I get when buying Depends at Dollar General. Hmm . . . maybe that's why I'm still single.

Socks doesn't put up much of a fight, but stands bowlegged once the diaper is in place.

I step back and put my hands on my hips. The little goat pleads at me with puppy-dog eyes.

"Don't even try that. You messed up, and these are the consequences. Now stay in here and play with Big Chick or something."

He bleats and retreats to the pink pile of plush in the corner of the room. Mullet might get jealous of that later, but I need something to occupy Socks.

I hurry out of my room to apologize to Ashley. She's wiping off her mat with the help of Adrianne. Everyone else is gone.

"I got some cleaning spray for her," Adrianne says.

"Thanks." I look at Ashley. "I'm so sorry, Ashley."

She shrugs. "It's fine. I was more scared than anything."

"I'm sorry. I know it's not an excuse, but he was possibly trying to mate with you."

Ashley's face contorts.

I laugh awkwardly. "Not actually mate, but trying to woo you by peeing on his face."

She snarls her nose. "Eww."

"Yeah, goats are weird. I thought he was ready for coming inside, but I guess not."

Adrianne shakes her head and rolls up Ashley's mat. "I'll never understand animals."

"I'll pay you back for this class, and your mat," I tell Ashley.

Her face softens. "No, it's fine, really. Animals are unpredictable. Samuel has this pet bunny that rubs its chin on everything."

"Samuel has a bunny?" Adrianne and I ask in unison.

Ashley's neck and face redden. "Yeah, he wanted a roommate, but doesn't really like people."

Adrianne arches a brow at me. Neither of us comments.

It's surprising that Samuel would have a bunny, but not at all surprising that he doesn't like people. He's not a likable person—at all.

"Anyway, thanks for the workout, Daisy."

"You bet." I smile tensely as Ashley slips into her sandals.

She still treats the pee foot like it's got a disease. When she opens the front door, Skeeder is on the porch, cuddling Hoss's face.

Adrianne shakes her head at me. I laugh at Ashley shuffling past him and closing the door.

Adrianne hands me several towels. "Here's the pee stash."

"Thanks." I take them to the laundry and listen for Socks on the way.

No sounds, so maybe he fell asleep.

I'm not even halfway in the living room when Adrianne starts grilling me.

"How'd it go last night with Kyle?"

"Good. I could tell he was tired, so I went ahead and started helping y'all."

She leans up from her spot on the couch. "Daisy, you could've stayed with him. We had plenty of help."

"Yeah, but I promised."

"So you just left him?"

My body tenses, and I shrug. *Was that the wrong thing to do?* I'm so inexperienced at this. How is it that I know the mating tendencies of goats so well, but I have no clue when it comes to men?

"Daisy, you've got to let him know you're interested if you are."

"I am. We kissed right before that."

Adrianne drops her head in her hands, then sighs. "So y'all kissed, and then you walked away?"

"Okay, so you're making it sound worse than it is. Paul came up and interrupted our kiss."

"Paul interrupts everything with everyone."

"True." My case for walking away is falling apart.

I'm now a ball of nerves, afraid Kyle thinks I don't want to be with him.

"Look, I'm not trying to make you feel bad." Adrianne smiles sympathetically. She can read me like a book.

"Thanks," I mutter.

"I can tell how much you like him and that he likes you. I just don't want you to ruin it."

"Ruin it?" My words come out hasty, with a hint of hurt and anger.

"I didn't mean it that way."

"How would I ruin it?"

Adrianne twists a lock of her hair. "I know you don't have a lot of experience dating is all, so I want to help."

More like zero experience.

All logic says I should listen to Adrianne. She's had guys

beating down her door since puberty. Still, I'm a little offended by her offer. My ego is soft as hot wax, and her coddling and pity has lit my candle.

"I've got some candles to make."

"Tonight? It's eight-thirty."

"Yeah, I like to work at night."

"No you don't."

I press my lips tightly. This is the problem with her knowing me so well.

"I just want to be alone for a while."

Adrianne's lips pout, then straighten. "Okay, but I'm here if you need me."

I nod. "Thanks."

She drops her head and goes to the door. I plop down on the couch and sigh.

The door creeps open behind me, and I hear Adrianne.

"OMG, go home, you weirdo!"

I jerk my head to her yelling at Skeeder. He's twisting the pool noodles on Hoss's horns like they're balloon animals. I stand and march toward the door.

"Please go home, Skeeder. You're messing up my horn blockers."

He gives me a dazed look, then trots down the porch toward his pickup. I slam the door and lock it so no other weirdness can creep in.

Then I retreat to my bedroom, where Mullet climbs on the bed, begging me to cuddle. I give in, as usual.

Mullet has a way of soothing me, but not tonight. All I can think about is how sad my life will be if I end up holding goats instead of Kyle.

CHAPTER SIXTEEN

Kyle

I haven't seen Daisy since the wedding, but we've texted a little each day. She's been working, and I've been busy working on tractors beat down from the pull. This morning she had an opening for a massage, and I gladly took it.

When her house comes into view, I get the same rush I did lining up against an opponent on the line. Let's just hope I don't get too excited and tackle Daisy.

I park close to the porch in case Hoss isn't in a pen. I don't want to be tackled either. Shutting the Jeep door carefully, I tiptoe up the steps and knock on the door.

Daisy answers after two knocks, and I slide inside unscathed. The familiar scent of bacon mixes with the floral smell of her hair. That has to be my favorite. She should turn it into a candle. Daisy & Bacon. Not the most creative name for the scent, but it would sell like hotcakes once people took a whiff.

"I smell bacon." Also not the most clever thing to say, but it beats tackling Daisy.

She smiles. "I lit a candle in here and one in the massage room." She hooks a thumb toward the hallway. "You can get ready for your massage."

I smile back and resist the urge to kiss her just now. One thing I've learned about Daisy is that she takes her job seriously. It's time for my massage, and she likely has another appointment after me. Best not mess that up.

The massage room is cool and quiet except for some soft music playing in the background. I undress and lie under the sheet with my head in the hole. My shoulder twitches when I shift to get comfortable.

Daisy should remedy that twitch soon.

But my bodily aches are secondary in concern to the ideas flooding my mind. I want to take Daisy on another date. One with a perfect ending in which I redeem all our kissing mishaps.

A strip of light appears, then disappears when Daisy closes the door. I hear her shifting a few things before she speaks.

"The way you described your shoulder pain, I think we should try a combo of hot rocks and then elbow kneading."

"Whatever you think," I mumble best I can with my face cheeks in the hole.

Spots on my shoulder and back heat as she places hot stones one at time. My muscles melt under the warmth, and I relax against the table. Ocean sounds come from the background music, making my mind wander.

I close my eyes and imagine I'm on a beach with the warm wind blowing across my back. Daisy is massaging me —while wearing a bikini.

Would it be too much to drive to the beach for a date?

Probably so, considering we live half a day's trip from the coast.

Maybe one day, us at the beach can become a reality. Until then, I'll settle for my face crammed in a table with bacon aromas.

Daisy starts removing one stone at a time, massaging the area under it. My shoulder pinches at first, then the knot breaks apart and mushes under her spell. My eyelids grow heavy, and I drift into dreams of Daisy and me walking on the beach.

It's such a vivid dream that I imagine her calling me in my mind before I realize she's actually wanting me to flip on my back.

My eyes pop open, and I raise up just enough to turn under the sheet. She smiles at my face, which I'm sure is smooshed from the hole in the table.

"Nice nap?"

I nod and close my eyes again. She laughs and drops a warm towel across my face. Her soft touch tickles across my chest and stomach, working its magic against my skin. I feel myself smiling as she works on my legs, but skips my ticklish feet.

The massage ends sooner than I'd want—as it always does. I curse myself for falling asleep and missing half of it, but my shoulder will still thank me later.

Daisy gently tucks the sheet below my arms and peels the towel from my face. I blink until my eyes adjust and focus on hers. Then I lift onto my elbows, putting my face close to hers.

She turns to walk out and let me change like she routinely does. Instead of watching her go, I grab her wrist. Her head turns, and our eyes meet. I watch her pupils dilate as I tug slightly, pulling her closer.

She inches toward me until she's standing against the

table. I lean closer and move my free hand to her face. Her eyelashes flutter until her eyes close, and she tilts her head toward me.

For the first time without interruption, I kiss Daisy.

My back is sweating, and I'm pretty sure I'm wearing another weird pair of underwear since I haven't had time to do laundry. But none of that matters, because the room smells like Daisy & Bacon, and she's in my arms.

Her hair tickles my face, which I shaved this morning for the first time in a few days. I loosen my grip on her wrist and slide my hand up her back, pulling her closer. She rests her hand on my chest and kisses me back.

I could stay like this all day, kissing Daisy. But I'm suddenly aware of the fact that nothing but a sheet shields her from me, and I don't want that temptation. I ease back and stare at her.

Daisy's eyes blink like a doe searching the forest. Her lips are pink and full from kissing me so much, her cheeks rosy.

"Would you like to go on a date this weekend?"

She nods. "Yes."

"Saturday night?"

She nods again. "Sounds good to me."

I smile and brush her hair behind her ear. Her face is hot and soft. She slides her hand from my chest and rests it on my hand.

We lock eyes in mutual silence for a moment. I shift against the table, clutching the sheet so it doesn't fall.

Daisy takes a step back. "I'll let you get dressed."

The side of my mouth quirks into a grin. I watch her leave the room before stepping off the table. Then I take longer than usual to get dressed, since I need a minute to come off the high of that kiss. My jeans and T-shirt feel like a hotbox after the stones and Daisy and all that beach daydreaming.

I leave the room to Angela sitting on Daisy's couch. My face flushes as if I'm a schoolboy caught in the locker room with a cheerleader. Angela isn't *that* much older than us, but she's a lawyer and a very proper person. Something tells me she would find Daisy unprofessional if she knew our massage ended in a heated make-out session.

Daisy half smiles at me in a way that looks natural but has an underlying layer of mischief. It makes me want her even more. I file that smirk for later when I can kiss her again. I reach for my wallet, but she stops me.

"This one's on the house."

I laugh. "No, I always pay you."

"It's a makeup appointment, remember?"

I hesitate, mainly to keep her hand on mine a second longer, then I replace my wallet. "I'll pay you back later."

Angela clears her throat. I hope it's to spur Daisy along with her own massage and not in disapproval of our exchange.

"Call or text me later." Daisy grins slightly.

"Okay, thanks." I resist the urge to kiss her on the cheek.

I pause at the door and glance back. Daisy is already rushing to the massage room. Angela glares for a second before dropping her gaze back to her phone.

Saturday. I've got to plan something fun, great, exciting. I want everything just right before I ask Daisy to officially be my girlfriend.

Daisy

A knock at the door causes me to drop my mascara wand. I set it on the dresser and screw on the top before marching to the front door. Maybe I don't resemble a raccoon. I've been mindlessly adding mascara to my lashes while I waited on Kyle to get here.

I open the door to him covering his backside and sliding against the edge of the house. Hoss stares at me from the top porch step and snorts.

"Down, boy," I tell him.

Hoss turns and trots off the steps. Kyle peels himself from the wall and drops his hands. I open the door wider.

"Why don't you wait in here while I grab my purse?"

He nods and smiles. I hurry toward my bedroom as he shuts the door behind us.

A quick glance in the mirror reveals that one eye is more mascaraed than the other. I take a few seconds to try and correct that. Maybe he didn't notice.

Then I grab my purse and blink to hopefully spread around the heavy globs on my top lashes. I pick at my right eye as I leave my room.

"Ready?" Kyle asks.

"Yeah."

He opens the door and motions for me to go first. He stands against the house when I lock it, then takes a death grip on my hand. I bite back a laugh, knowing the extra tension is from fear of Hoss.

Funny how a grown man is scared of a goat with pool noodles on its head.

He opens the passenger door for me, then hurries to his side. Hoss snorts at Kyle from the driveway as we leave. I burst out laughing.

"What?"

I laugh harder. "You and Hoss."

"He doesn't like me."

"That's because he thinks you don't like him."

Kyle frowns. "Well, I don't now. Thanks to the way he treats me."

I laugh so hard I snort. Kyle laughs at that, causing us both to laugh more. We settle down at last. He takes a sip of Mountain Dew and nods at his cupholders.

"I brought you a Gatorade."

"Thanks."

He's eaten with me enough to realize that's my go-to when I don't drink water. My entire insides perk at the thought of him bringing not only my drink of choice, but also my flavor of choice. Either guys are more observant than I think, or Kyle cares enough to notice little details about me.

As long as he doesn't notice my heavy eye makeup tonight, we'll be okay.

We chat on the way to Tuscaloosa about the past few days since we've seen one another. Although we've texted a lot, we haven't carried on any long conversations.

"I didn't get you in trouble with Angela, did I?"

I wince. "She seemed a bit frustrated that her room wasn't ready at exactly ten, but afterward she raved about how relaxed her neck felt. I think that made up for it, and she tipped me well."

"Good." Kyle smiles. "It's my fault. I shouldn't have kept you so long after my massage."

"That's perfectly fine by me." Heat rushes up my neck toward my face.

I've kissed Kyle several times now, so I should be getting used to it. Still, none of the other times involved him on my massage table, in his underwear, in the dark. Nothing else came close to happening, but the thought of it happening in the distant future scares me.

Like most women my age, I've fantasized about getting married to a handsome man one day. Having never dated until now, that dream seemed far-fetched and nearly impossible. It never materialized into the reality of things married people do. Things Kyle has likely already experienced before.

Even if we were to get into a relationship, then marry, how would I ever live up to other women?

"You still want to go to a movie, or had you rather eat someplace nice?"

I snap my head toward Kyle. His question brings me back to reality. He's on a date with *me*, so he has to like me. No sense in putting the cart before the horse and getting myself all worked up over something that may or may not happen one day.

"A movie's good." I unscrew the lid on my Gatorade and take a huge gulp.

"You sure?"

I meet his concerned gaze and nod. "Yeah."

After a minute of silence, I ask about the tractors he's working on. I don't care or know enough about tractors to carry on a conversation, but it beats the alternative—sitting in a sea of thoughts in which Kyle's comparing me to a sea of other women.

Women who don't have the body of a twelve-year-old and who probably know what to do with it. I've attended several lingerie showers in recent years and can confidently say I would not fill out even the skimpiest of lacy outfits. Even if I did, I'd likely freeze when wearing it.

Like a miniature poodle in a sweater.

Yep. That's me, a tiny dog. All the other women are golden doodles with long legs and poise.

We stop at a red light and Kyle turns to me.

"After I rebuild the front end of that International, things should slow down. We can go to the lake one day when we're both less busy."

"The lake?"

"Yeah, you can swim, right?"

I laugh nervously. "Of course I can swim."

"Good. Dad has a boat we can use if we want to ski or tube or just fish."

"Sounds fun." I smile at a relaxing day on the water.

My smile grows when I picture Kyle in swimming trunks. He must get outside a fair amount without a shirt, because he doesn't have as big of a farmer's tan as I would expect. My face straightens when I think of myself in a swimsuit. Would my lack of curves and cleavage turn him off?

I've never batted an eye at wearing a two-piece since I'm tiny. But I've never cared to impress a man with my looks —until now.

We arrive at the movie theater, and Kyle stops the Jeep. He opens my door and takes my hand. I lace my fingers through his and try not to overthink everything.

We're on a date. Enjoy it, Daisy.

"I've been wanting to try this place," I say.

"Yeah, I don't think it's been open long."

I scan a light-up sign with movies on one side and a menu on the other. A mid-grade restaurant in a theater isn't a new idea, but new to Tuscaloosa.

Kyle drops my hand to pay for our tickets. My arm tingles like it's going through withdrawals from his touch.

He hands me a ticket and reaches for my hand again. My heart picks up like he's gifted me an extra life on a video game. We find the theater for *Guardians of the Galaxy*. I got a little too excited when he threw out that suggestion. I'm a bit of an Avengers fan, and a lot of a Chris Pratt fan.

The room is starting to get crowded, but we find two seats in the center row. Each row is a long table with reclining, rolling chairs pulled up to it. Not unlike a nail salon setup.

Menus sit in front of each seat. There is a button on the

table between our menus. Kyle flips his menu to the back, then the front. "Huh, we push that when we want to order."

"Like Sonic."

He laughs. "Apparently."

We settle on a pizza and mozzarella sticks for an appetizer. Shortly after ordering, the lights dim and all the warnings and promos play before the movie.

Kyle scoots his chair close to mine and touches my arm. I relax against the tall seat and enjoy my two favorite guys—Kyle and Chris Pratt.

Both of whom I never thought attainable until recently.

Our food arrives not too far into the movie. We eat and laugh, and there's no place I'd rather be at the moment. I should pitch the idea of a restaurant/movie theater to Earl Ed next time he goes all entrepreneurial.

Pepperoni pizza and a band of space misfits is all I needed to get me out of my funk. Who knew?

The movie ends, and I start to stand. Kyle grabs my arm before I stretch.

"We've got to stay until the end."

I motion toward a black screen.

He shakes his head. "They always add in something else."

I stretch, then sit back in my chair. The sudden urge to pee hits me. "Actually, I need to run to the restroom."

"Okay, but you'll miss it."

I snort. "I think I'll live." I hurry down the aisle and toward the exit. About a fourth of the people are still in the theater, obviously waiting on whatever it is Kyle hopes to see.

"Excuse me." A tall woman slides past me as I enter the restroom.

I do my business, then double-check that my eye makeup hasn't morphed into Kiss mode during the movie. Then I wash my hands and hurry back in case Kyle is waiting on me.

Kyle is still in his seat, but my seat is now occupied. The

tall woman who passed me in the bathroom is sitting beside him, and they appear to be in deep conversation.

What in the world?

I stand, frozen at the theater door, watching them from afar like a nosy neighbor who has no business butting into their conversation. When I in fact have every right to march over and take *my* seat by *my* date. But my feet refuse to move.

Her mouth moves ninety to nothing as Kyle listens intently. Then he stands. She reaches toward him, but he pulls away and marches toward the exit.

I can't let him find me spying on him.

I may have a lot of insecurities, but he doesn't need to know that. With what little pride I have left, I manage to back out of the door and into the hallway. Whatever I do, I cannot cry. This mascara is not waterproof.

Kyle bolts out the door when I'm a few feet from it. He spots me and sighs, then smiles.

"You ready to go?"

"Yes." My answer comes out a little too enthusiastically, but I want to put distance between us and that woman.

They must know each other. May have even dated before. You don't go sit by someone and strike up a deep conversation when you've never met. Well, unless you're Misty. Or maybe Paul, or Skeeder, or Slim.

But this girl looked totally normal, and tall and hot.

Oh crud. I wrap my arms around my stomach. *Don't cry or barf.*

So much for an enjoyable date.

CHAPTER SEVENTEEN

Kyle

"Are you feeling okay?"

Daisy nods, but her face is pale. I wrap my arm around her shoulders and pull her close.

"Let's go home." I speed walk out of the theater.

Daisy sighs when I slow to a stroll in the parking lot. Her little legs must have taken three times the steps mine did to get out of the theater.

But when a random woman comes up, asks if you're Kyle Tolbert, then says she's your sister . . .

There's no way I could've prepared for that.

Considering I haven't seen or heard from my mom since I was six, there's a good chance the girl is lying. Why is beyond me. It's not like I have a ton of money to offer her. Maybe this is a sick prank by one of my old college buddies.

I unlock the Jeep and open Daisy's door. She climbs in, and I hurry to my side, then back out of the parking lot.

We're on the main road, headed toward home, before either of us speaks.

"You sure you're okay?"

"Yeah, you?" She gives me a concerned smile.

I nod. "Yeah. Did you want to stop anywhere in town before we head back to Apple Cart?"

She shakes her head. "I'm good."

I continue through town, thankful she agreed to going home. Whoever this woman is, I doubt she knows about Apple Cart. Or if she does, I doubt she will know how to get there or even try. In the few shocked minutes I listened to her, she spouted off that she grew up in Texas and is a student at The University of Alabama.

That makes her story even more unbelievable. My mom ended up in Texas? Highly unlikely since her family is from south Alabama and her parents died before I was born. What would she do in Texas?

I squint at the city lights and try to focus on the road. Daisy shifts in her seat, reminding me she's there.

Say something, so Daisy won't think you're mad.

"What did you think of the movie?"

"It was funny. A little weird, but aren't they all?"

I chuckle. "That's part of the appeal."

"True."

We make small talk about our favorite parts. I'm back at ease until she asks about the extra ending.

"It was good. A little anti-climactic, is all." I grit my teeth after lying to her.

I hate lying, especially to Daisy. What was I supposed to say? Admit that a strange young woman jumped in her seat and claimed to be my long lost half-sister?

She'd run for the hills, thinking I'm crazy after that. Heck, I think the woman is crazy. *Karson, she said her name was Karson.*

I grip the wheel so tightly my knuckles pale. The less I know, the better. I don't want to think of a secret sister running around, much less know her name. If it is true, who's to say Mom didn't have more kids?

Daisy talks about how much she hated the ending of *Avengers: Affinity War*. Good, that's a conversation I can carry.

We chat about all the ways they could've made it more upbeat and still set up for the *Endgame* movie. That leads to us agreeing on how much we miss Iron Man.

This makes me love Daisy even more.

Love?

I file that thought for later. Tonight I need to get through acting normal without burdening her about my family.

The Avengers save the night for me by supplying the conversation all the way to Daisy's house. On occasion, I even forget about the strange woman. That is, until Daisy comments that one of the biggest surprises in the franchise was Mantis being Peter's half-sister.

Just great.

I pull up to her house and turn off the Jeep. We sit in silence except for a few crickets chirping into the dark. The moon reflects on the gravel road, and her profile is visible when my eyes adjust. I turn toward her.

"I had fun tonight." I really did despite the huge bomb dropped on me while she escaped to the bathroom.

She half grins. "Me too."

But did she really? Her face is now solemn.

I unbuckle my seat belt and slide closer to her. I reach across the console and take her hand. She wraps her small fingers with mine and blinks at me. I lean closer and press my lips to hers. Her floral scent shoots up my nostrils as I pull her closer.

Kissing Daisy makes all my worries disappear. If I could

spend all day, every day, kissing Daisy, then life would be great.

And it is for several minutes. But all good kisses must come to an end.

We soon come up for air, and she rests her head on my chest. I wiggle to get comfortable in the awkward position I'm in, half across the console. She scoots toward me, which helps some.

"What's this?"

She pulls a bag from behind my seat. It's the pillow I bought her at Buc-ee's.

"Oh, I almost forgot. I bought you that."

She stares at the gas station bag. "More Gatorade?"

I laugh. "No, something more permanent."

"Like a gift?"

"Yeah." I flip on the interior light and pull out the pillow.

Daisy takes it and smirks. "Crazy Goat Lady." She looks at me. "The pillow we saw together."

"I may have snuck and bought it when you went to the restroom."

She twists her lips, then smiles and kisses my cheek. "Thanks."

"You're welcome." I smile back and settle more into my seat. "I can call you tomorrow or text after church."

"Sounds good."

"Check your schedule for a lake day." I raise my eyebrows playfully.

She blushes. I kiss the red of her cheeks, then open my door. She gets out and meets me in front of the Jeep.

We take a few steps and Hoss snorts. Lime green catches the moonlight, and bounces up and down.

"What's he doing?"

"Just butting his head."

I back up a step, and Daisy laughs. "It's fine. You don't have to walk me to the door."

"Are you sure?"

"Yes." She laughs and hugs me. "Thanks again for tonight, and for the gift."

"You're welcome." I kiss the top of her head and retreat to my Jeep like a coward.

She smiles back, then continues up her porch. I watch until she's safely inside. Then I crank the Jeep and drive away from that demon of a goat.

My phone dings several times on the way to my house. I glance down to make sure it isn't Daisy or my dad. When I notice Facebook, I continue driving.

It's not until I get in my own house that I check all the notifications. I have a friend request from Karson Knox. My stomach buckles when I stare at the profile photo of the same woman who ambushed me earlier.

Against my better judgment, I click on her profile. The background photo is one with her and a woman who looks an awful lot like an older version of my mom.

Feeling faint, I fall back in my recliner. I hit "delete" on the request, but she also sent me a message request.

She wants to meet and talk with me about "our" mother.

Why? What good could come from talking with her? And why, for the love of God, would she ruin my plans to have a perfect night with Daisy?

This was supposed to be the night I told her I was falling in love with her and wanted to be exclusive. Not the night I found out I had a secret sibling living an hour away.

Daisy

"You should feel special. JoJo wanted to come, but I told him this was our night."

I smile. "I've missed riding go-karts."

"Me too." Adrianne laughs, then pats her ponytail. "Although it's been good for my hair to skip a while."

A gang of little kids wheels into the parking deck at Earl Ed's command. He whistles loudly to get the attention of a kid who didn't stop. The little punk laughs and keeps driving.

Earl Ed waits for him to come around again, then leaps onto the track and falls across the hood. Adrianne and I gasp. The kid screams and stops.

Earl Ed rolls off the hood of the go-kart and stands clumsily. Then he dusts his jeans as if he didn't just jump onto a moving vehicle.

"Get out, go to your mama, and let me park it."

The kid hops out and races toward the exit gate. Misty comes from the parking lot, blowing vape smoke. She waves to Adrianne, who begrudgingly waves back.

"I thought you fired her," I say through clinched teeth.

"I tried. She's co-oping, so I have her at least one more semester as a favor to the JuCo dean."

I nod and bite back a laugh.

The kid races to Misty. He's dressed head to toe in baseball logos, with two gold chains around his neck. I don't know Misty's family well, but I'd bet that's one of the kids by her ex, Jeffrey. He runs a mobile-home repo place and thinks he knows everything when it comes to sports.

Earl Ed parks the go-kart behind the others. He steps out and pops his neck one way, then back. Adrianne and I enter the track after the last kid leaves.

"Are you okay?" I ask.

Earl Ed chuckles and slaps his belly. "Just peachy. Mackenzie always says I should get into stunt doubling."

"I can see why."

A few more people enter as we're selecting cars. Adrianne rushes to a red one, which is her favorite. Not because of speed, but because she likes the way it looks. I always get whichever one is in front to have a head-start advantage.

The other drivers are two teenage couples, Aniston and her two kids, and Morgan's four kids. Morgan waves to us from the sidelines, where she's eating a snow cone.

"Hey, ladies," Aniston calls. "If I beat y'all, I get to take a goat home for one night."

"Sure." I smirk at Adrianne. "She didn't specify which goat."

Adrianne laughs crazily before pulling onto the track. Earl Ed moves out of the way for the cars to whiz by, then crosses the track to the exit.

I squeeze between two kids and catch up to Adrianne. She bumps into my side, and I bump back. We lock up in the center of the track before going downhill.

"Turn your wheel, and I'll turn mine."

Adrianne does as I say, but nothing works. We plummet into the tires set up as buffers against the edge of the track. Earl Ed comes toward us, rolling his eyes.

"I've told y'all to quit this. These ain't bumper cars."

"Hey, there's an idea—or even bumper boats."

"Not the time, Daisy." He pulls my car off Adrianne's with one swift jerk.

I swerve around before she can catch up to me. Unfortunately, we're a loop behind everyone else. Aniston zooms past with an evil laugh.

By the time Earl Ed calls us in, I'm behind everyone except Adrianne and Morgan's youngest daughter. So basically two high-maintenance females.

Aniston waltzes over to me, her hair a tangled mess. "Guess I get a goat for a day."

"Sure. You can have Hoss since you have a pool. He comes with his own flotation device."

Her grin straightens and she stares at the sky. Any minute now she'll connect which goat is Hoss. I don't wait around for that.

Adrianne runs her fingers through her ponytail and catches up to me. We leave the track and head for my car.

"I need caffeine," Adrianne huffs.

I laugh since she usually prefers water. We go inside Double Drive and pass the arcade section. Mackenzie is behind the snack counter.

"Hey, Mackenzie."

She greets us and takes our order. I expect her and Earl Ed to get married at some point, but her career keeps her all over the place.

Talk about an oddball couple. She directs movies, and Earl Ed spent a decade in jail for stealing mail. Maybe there's hope for Kyle and me after all.

Adrianne must read my mind, because my butt's barely in a booth when she starts grilling me.

"You never told me how your date went Saturday."

"Good. We went to that new dinner-and-a-movie place, and he was super sweet."

"That's nice. Now tell me something juicy." Adrianne wiggles her eyebrows.

I press my lips together, praying she doesn't read my mind. How I've overanalyzed every text since that date and tried to read between the lines of his gift.

Crazy goat lady. Did he really buy that pillow because he thought I liked it, or because he thinks I'm crazy? Will Hoss eventually drive him away?

And that's just my thoughts on us. The mysterious woman is a whole other can of worms.

"Dais?"

I sigh and drop my head in my hands. My stomach rumbles and my head throbs. I have to talk to someone before I burst.

I lift my eyes to Adrianne giving me a stern look across the booth. "I went to the restroom at the movies. When I came back, there was a woman in my seat talking to Kyle."

Her brows thread together with concern. She doesn't speak, but nods for me to continue.

"They were in deep conversation, then he got up. I walked out and acted like I'd just come out from the restroom when he saw me."

Adrianne opens her mouth, then closes it. She leans back against the booth and sighs. Earl Ed comes by with our food.

We both thank him. Adrianne talks a long drag of her Coke and sighs louder. She waits until Earl Ed leaves to speak.

"Kyle is one of the sweetest guys I know. So sweet I thought he was boring." She laughs.

I'm a little offended but stay calm.

"Anyway, that doesn't mean he's not seeing someone else too. Y'all haven't gone on many dates." She taps a pink nail on her chin. "Have y'all had a DTR?"

"A what?"

"Define the relationship. You know, a talk to see where you both stand, what you both want."

I chew on the end of a fry and think back to all our conversations. Kyle keeps asking me out, and we keep kissing and saying that we both have a good time. That's all.

"No, we haven't had a DT, whatever you said."

She stabs her fork in the center of her salad, shaking the table. I flinch.

"He may still be dating other people. Kyle's a nice guy, so maybe that's why he hasn't had that talk with you yet."

I shove several fries in my mouth and chew. My cheeks

puff like a squirrel's and my head starts to spin. I reach for more fries, but Adrianne's hand lands on mine.

"Dais."

I slowly lift my eyes and swallow the wad of potatoes in my mouth.

"This is part of dating. You have to accept that. It's perfectly normal for him to date other people until he makes up his mind."

She moves her hand from mine and picks up her fork. "The problem is when they tell you they're only seeing you, but they're still dating others."

She takes a bite of salad, letting her teeth rake across the fork. A shiver rushes up my spine, and not just from the eerie fork-biting noise.

What Adrianne said makes a lot of sense. Why wouldn't Kyle date more people? I'm certain he has a lot of options. He's probably testing the waters to make sure he's sure about me—or even the other girl.

I swallow hard. *What if I'm the other woman?* That would explain why he was in such a hurry to leave the movies.

Oh boy, life sure was easier when all I did was sit at home with goats and chickens.

CHAPTER EIGHTEEN

Kyle

Everything in me screams "run," but I couldn't resist.

Seeing my mom in that Facebook photo clued me in that Karson wasn't totally full of bull. She at least knows my mom. And since I have no fame or fortune for her to gain, why else would she find me?

I wipe my sweaty hands down my jeans. My leg bounces with nerves. I grip my knee to try and steady the fidgeting. I'm on a park bench in Tuscaloosa, feeling a little lost like Forrest Gump.

Maybe I should've brought along a box of chocolates to stress eat?

Across the soccer field, a tall light-haired girl toting a tiny dog appears. When she gets closer, she smiles. It's Karson.

I lean forward and swallow. She picks up speed until she's standing in front of me.

"Can I sit?"

I scoot to one end of the bench and clutch both knees with my palms. She balances the dog on her lap. I don't know what breed it is, but it's ugly.

"Thanks for meeting me."

I nod, still unable to find my voice.

Karson raises her sunglasses to reveal the same dark blue eyes as mine. My stomach buckles. They're the same color as my mom's—rather *our* mom's. I couldn't tell in the movies. Partly because it was dark, and partly because I didn't want to look her in the eye.

"I know it's harder for you. You just found out about me, and I've always known about you."

"You have?"

She shrugs. "Since I was about eleven or twelve. Old enough to find some old photos of you and ask questions."

"And?"

"Mama sat me down and told me the truth."

My jaw unhinges and I lean back against the bench. I can't imagine my mom nonchalantly talking about me the way she left. Then again, I was six at the time, so I never knew much about her.

"Are you . . ." I clear my throat to try and dislodge the knot forming in it. "Are there more?"

She shakes her head. "I'm an only child." She pets the dog, then adds, "Except for you."

I nod. "And you're how old?"

"Eighteen. This is my first year of college."

"You said you were from Texas. What made you come to Alabama?"

She shrinks back to her side of the bench, acting shy for the first time.

"Mama thinks I came because they have a great marketing school. I did." She winces. "But I also hoped to run into you."

I blink. It's hard to believe someone would pick a college based on the chance of running into their half-brother who lived an hour away and had no idea they existed.

"Seriously?"

"It was more of a hopeful bonus, and it worked out." She smiles, then her face straightens after meeting my gaze. "At least, I hope so."

"Karson, what is it you want from me?"

She tucks the dog tighter under her arm. "I wanted to meet my brother, that's all."

"But you never knew me."

"Aren't you excited to know you have a sister?"

I hesitate. I don't want to crush this young girl's spirit. There's no nice way to say I prefer to keep my life the way it was, and that if it weren't for her bursting into the theater last weekend, I might have a girlfriend instead of more family drama.

"I'm sorry." Karson stands to leave.

"No." I'm not sure why I say that.

I actually want her to go, but something in me feels sorry for her. Maybe Mom wasn't that great of a mother to her either. Whatever the case, I have this big-brother instinct to protect her.

Karson meets my eyes and sits slowly. The dog whimpers until she pets it.

"What's your dog's name?"

"My dog's name?"

I shrug. Stupid question, but it's the best I could come up with for an ice breaker.

"Lamby."

I chuckle. "It does kind of look like a not-quite-right lamb."

Karson balks, then smiles. She pets the dog's coarse hair. "She's a Bedlington Terrier."

"Why are her ears like that?" I touch the tip of one that's a small puff of fur like a poodle's.

"It's the style."

"Okay."

She laughs louder. I hold my hand out for Lamby to sniff it.

"See, she likes you."

I lift then lower one shoulder. It twitches. My joints and muscles have gotten spoiled. They know when it's close to Daisy time.

I pet the weird little animal and even let it lick my hand. Even though in my opinion, dogs should be big and hyper and used for hunting. Not sitting in laps with cotton-ball ears.

"I shouldn't have ambushed you like I did."

I shake my head. "That's fine. I was shocked is all. I've been an only child for twenty-eight years, raised by my dad and grandparents."

"I get it. All I've known is Mama, so when I found out about you . . . " She smiles sadly. "I've always wanted a family."

"What about your dad?"

"I have no idea. I asked, even pressed her a few times. In all honesty, I don't think she knows."

My jaw clinches. I sympathize with Karson, while also thanking God for my dad. How lucky that I had a good parent to pick up the slack. Who knows how attentive Mom was to Karson, if at all?

I scan the girl in front of me coddling the ugly dog. She's attractive and friendly. There's a good chance she wanted to move across the country to keep her life together away from my mom.

"I'm sorry. That sucks."

"It's fine. That's just more reason why I wanted to meet you."

Her dark eyes meet mine, and she twists her lips.

"Well, I'm glad you did."

The corners of her lips turn into a smile. She twists toward me and scoops her legs underneath her. Lamby growls slightly at the sudden shift in position. Karson pets her.

"I had like this whole plan to find your number and call you or go by that Apple Sauce town."

I laugh. "You mean Apple Cart."

"Yeah." She wavers her hand. "Anyway, then I saw you at the theater and had to say something."

"It doesn't matter now."

Karson bites her lip and glances at the sky before looking at me. "Want to get some ice cream?"

"Uh, sure."

We stand. She has the same tall frame as me. My dad was the really tall one of my parents, which leads me to wonder what her dad looked like. She has Mom's light hair and blue eyes. The same eyes I have.

They've been both a blessing and a curse. Everyone goes on about the rare and handsome color of my eyes. But every time I look in a mirror, I'm reminded of looking into those same eyes and asking them not to leave me. It's good to see them on another happy face besides mine, even if it belongs to a long-lost sister.

She sets Lamby on the ground and unwraps a pink leash. We head toward an ice cream stand not far from the park. Lamby trots beside us at a decent speed.

A bald-headed man and brown-haired woman stand at the window ordering ice cream. There's something very familiar about them together. They remind me a lot of . . .

"Adrianne and JoJo." I try not to sound too surprised when they turn around.

Adrianne smiles, then glances at Karson. I want to introduce her, but I'm not ready to say who she is. If I tell Adrianne she's my sister, I may as well tell Daisy. I'd rather have time to plan that conversation and prepare for questions.

JoJo gives me a pleasant face—for him. I recall seeing him smile exactly twice. When he married Adrianne, and once during a paintball game when he hammered us all.

"Hey, Kyle." She cuts her eyes to Karson once more.

Karson smiles and holds out her hand. "Hi, I'm Kyle's friend, Karson."

I exhale, thankful she didn't drop the sister bomb just yet. Adrianne shakes her hand, and JoJo nods solemnly.

"Adrianne. This is my husband, JoJo." Adrianne's gaze drops to Lamby. She jerks her head, as if startled by its appearance—and rightfully so. "Oh, who's this?"

"Lamby." Karson holds Lamby toward her face and snuggles her close. "Want to pet her?"

"No thanks. I have my ice cream and all." Adrianne snarls her nose but somehow manages to make it look polite.

"It was nice meeting you." Karson beams.

"You too." Adrianne puts on a different kind of smile. The same kind she wore at halftime during football games. Her majorette smile.

I'm not sure what that means, but I'm relieved when they walk away. I can't keep Karson a secret forever, but I don't want anyone telling Daisy about her besides me.

Daisy

. . .

My hands graze across Kyle's back like I'm slipping on my most comfortable pair of sneakers.

We typically text once or twice a day and had lunch earlier this week at Mary's. But we haven't been alone since last weekend's date. He said he had something to do with family last night, and I used that time to make a new batch of soap.

Funny how making soap on Friday nights feels so *Little House on the Prairie* since I've started dating Kyle. If that's not evidence I needed to get out more . . .

A light glows on the table beside us, then my phone vibrates. That's the second time since I started Kyle's massage. This early on a Saturday, it has to be a telemarketer. I ignore it until it goes off again, then again, and again.

After a good five minutes of constant buzzing, I slide my hands from Kyle's shoulders and step toward the table.

A ton of missed calls and one text—all from Adrianne. Normally, I would turn my phone over and call her after my client. But Adrianne is not a morning person, and her text alarms me.

Call me. NOW.

"Kyle, I've got to get this. I'll be right back."

He mumbles something under the table as I slip into the hallway with my phone. I blink as my eyes adjust to the sun pouring in from the living room window.

Before I can call Adrianne, she calls me again. I answer, my fingers tingling with anticipation.

She's okay or she couldn't call. Unless it's JoJo on her phone.

"Hello?" My voice is shaky. Adrianne doesn't have family here. What if something happened and they need me?

"Hey, Dais."

I let out a long sigh at the sound of her voice. "You had me worried something happened."

"Something did happen, just not to me."

"Is it Grandpa Joe?"

JoJo's grandpa lives with them, and everyone in town loves him. Although it wouldn't be a total surprise for an eighty-year-old man to pass away, it would still leave a huge hole in Apple Cart County.

"No, no. We're all fine, but I saw something last night I need to tell you about. I tried calling once when we got in, but I guess you were asleep."

"Okay?"

"It's about Kyle."

I glance back at the massage room door, then step into the living room. My house is old and the walls are thin. If I can hear a goat scratching a stuffed animal through a closed door, Kyle can hear me on the phone.

"JoJo and I were in Tuscaloosa and stopped to get a waffle cone. We saw Kyle with a girl."

My throat tightens as the tall girl from the movies flashes through my mind.

"Some girl with blond hair."

"Was she tall?"

"Not really tall. Around my height."

That's tall.

"She introduced herself as Kyle's friend, but they looked a little closer than that to me."

My pulse beats so fast I can feel it in my ears. Fire floods my insides and a chill races down my limbs like a reverse sunburn.

"Dais?"

"Sounds like the girl from the movies," I manage to say when my ears stop ringing.

Adrianne breathes into the phone. I lower myself onto the couch and lean my head against the cushion. She takes another deep breath before talking.

"I'm not saying that they aren't just friends. I'm just saying to not fall too hard just yet. She looked at Kyle like she worshipped him, so my bet is she wants to be more than his friend if she isn't already."

I close my eyes, and immediately regret doing so. The image of those two at the movies plays in my mind like a horror film. They would make a beautiful couple, and he wouldn't have a hard time kissing her in flats. Even in four-inch heels, I'm still staring at his neck.

Good thing I'm a massage therapist. Kissing me forever would cause him neck pain.

"I didn't want to upset you, but I would want to know if it were me. I wanted to tell you before you saw Kyle again."

"Thanks." The word tingles on my tongue.

Everything in me wishes I'd have answered her sooner. She has no idea he's half naked on my massage table, right now. And to think I lit my last bacon-scented candle for him.

What a waste.

"I'll let you go. Call me or text again if you need me."

"I will. Thanks, Adrianne."

I drop my phone in my lap and run my hands over my face. I need some time alone. Nobody would fault me for getting in my car and driving away. But I can't.

I care too much about my business to let Kyle ruin it. I have to act professional. I have to give him a good massage.

My lips curl as I stand and tuck my phone into my pocket. Oh, I can give him a good massage.

I march to the massage room and slide in as calmly as I

left. Kyle lies still in the position I left him, facedown—and vulnerable.

An evil laugh plays in my head as I eye the hot stones warming on the table. I have them waiting for an athletic massage in a few hours. Might as well give them a test run.

I grab a stone so hot my fingers singe, but it will be worth it. I put one between Kyle's shoulder blades. His neck draws up and he groans.

"Too hot?"

"A little," he mumbles.

"Oh, let me move that." I lift the stone, then "accidentally" drop it on his butt.

Even with the sheet between the stone and his rear end, he draws up and seethes. I bite back a laugh.

"Sorry. I dropped it." I pick it up and return it to the table with a loud clank that startles him even more.

"Let's try something else."

I step onto the table and grab the bar above. I purposely turn my foot toward his ticklish side. Then I dig my toes in deep and mush them around.

He jerks and squirms. I hold tighter to the bar and dig in deeper. Just before he raises up, I lift my foot and go to the ground.

"Okay, flip over."

I turn to the table for the warm cloth so I don't have to face him. If our eyes meet, one of two things will happen. Either I'll fall under his handsome spell and abandon my torture tactics, or I'll throw a hot stone at his face. Neither is acceptable.

Instead, I wait until he's lying down to turn around. Then I drop a towel on his face before we can make eye contact.

It's harder to torture someone when they're face up. Especially someone twice my size with quick hands. I massage his chest and shoulders like usual, until I get close to his neck. My thumbs slip a few times and dig into that tender spot around his collarbone. Oops!

Once I'm satisfied with my work, I step back and open the door.

"Okay, you can get dressed."

I exit and close the door behind me, leaving Kyle to peel the towel off his face so I won't have to look at him. Last time we shared a very heated kiss when his massage ended.

I'm a different kind of heated right now and don't need a kiss to confuse me.

Mullet bleats from outside and stares at me through the living room window. I open the door and let him in. I swear, he can probably sense my hurt and frustration.

New goal: find a man who understands me like my goat.

I pet Mullet's head, and he licks my hand. For a brief moment, I forget Kyle's in the other room. I have to face him in a minute no matter what. My chest tightens, and I pace the living room floor. Mullet follows me on the short path I've created in front of the couch.

We make a few rounds before the door closes. I pause and stare at Kyle walking toward me, hands in his pockets.

He stops in front of me and hands me cash as always. I take it and silently scold myself for enjoying the brush of his hand against mine. I have to stand firm. I cannot succumb to his charm.

If guys have taken advantage of Adrianne, they will definitely prey on someone as weak and inexperienced as me.

Kyle smiles at me like I didn't just dump hot rocks on his bare skin and mutilate his neck with my thumbnails. What is wrong with this guy?

I have to stand firm, no matter how handsome he is.

"I've got Dad's boat today. You want to go out on the lake?"

A shirtless Kyle, skin glistening with lake water and teeth shining in the sunlight, pops into my head. *No, I will be strong.*

"Today's not that good. I have another massage."

"I thought that wasn't until this evening? It's only like ten now."

Ugh. Why did I mention my schedule earlier?

"Yeah, but the Baptist Women's Group may come by and pick up some soap for their service project."

"Can't you just set it out somewhere?"

I huff. "With Hoss?" Perfect excuse. Kyle is scared of Hoss.

"Good point." He twists his mouth and glances at the floor. "Wait, I can drop it off for you. Where's it going? To Dot, the church?"

Crud. That's what I get for lying about church.

I tighten my hands into fists, pressing my nails into my skin. Mullet steps beside me and nudges my side as if offering his support. I rest one hand on his head.

"Kyle, I think I need some time alone."

"Okay." He runs a hand through his hair.

That dark, silky hair that would look great slung back at the lake. *No, stop it, Daisy. You've waited this long for the right guy, what's twenty-eight more years?*

I swallow, hoping it doesn't take that long again. But I can't let him use me.

"Maybe tomorrow after church?"

Be strong.

I take a deep breath and exhale. "Kyle, I mean that I need to be alone for more than today."

His mouth opens, then his eyes widen. "Oh."

His voice is so sad, it breaks a piece of my heart. Still, if I keep on seeing him while he's seeing the other woman, he will shatter my heart. Right now it's only a tiny break, like a crack in a windshield. I'll forever see the damage he's done as I try and move forward, but I'm not undriveable. Not yet. But I know Kyle has the power to total me if I don't stomp the brakes on this ASAP.

"Can I text you later?"

I shrug. I want to say yes, but need to say no.

He nods, as if getting the hint that I'm trying to end whatever I thought we had.

"I'll see you around, Daisy." He leans in and kisses my cheek gently.

I close my eyes and commit his lips to memory. If I can't have him, I can have this moment.

My eyes are still closed when I hear the front door shut. I peek one open to his Jeep driving past the window.

And just like that I stand alone, with a goat, and watch what could've been the love of my life drive away.

CHAPTER NINETEEN

Kyle

I park in my driveway and stare at Dad's boat. He's not home and said to take it out all day. Wherever he went, it must be important to lend out his fishing boat that long. He's very particular about it and fishes most days.

I could go fishing by myself, but that sounds super depressing. I can't ski by myself, and I don't want to deal with Bradley today.

His idea of cheering me up would involve a gun or a girl, maybe both. You never know with him.

The boat catches the sunlight and glistens as if calling me to it. I hesitate. Relaxing on the water wouldn't be so bad. Except that I'd have plenty of time to think.

Nah. I'll pass.

I turn and go in the house, slamming the door behind me. The air-conditioning welcomes me as I plop down in my recliner. I'll lie here a while, then start working when my thoughts get carried away.

I kick off my boots and raise the recliner legs. My shoulder numbs where Daisy stuck a hot stone. That was by far the oddest massage she's given me. It's almost like she was trying to keep me from coming back.

Then she all but told me not to come back.

What a rotten day. I lost my supposed girlfriend and masseuse at the same time. Now I'm stuck with a broken heart and a hurt shoulder.

I stare at the ceiling and replay our last conversation. I should've fought against her brushing me off.

But that's not me.

I'm not a "take whatever I want" guy like Bradley, or obnoxiously flirty like Tanner, or even demanding like JoJo. I'm Kyle, "the nice guy."

I don't have it in me to try and talk her into being with me, because deep down, I want her to be happy more than me.

Maybe after all this Karson craziness dies down, I can try asking Daisy out again. That will hopefully give her time to miss me while I sort out my family situation.

I never came up with a way to tell her about Karson, much less tell my dad.

My plan was to take her out on the lake, play on the water, have a picnic, then ask her to be my girlfriend. Maybe that last part sounds a little junior high, but I wanted to make it official.

I have trouble reading Daisy sometimes. And this morning proves I misread her a lot. One more reason not to press her to go with me today.

If she already feels like we're moving too fast, convincing her to spend more time with me might pressure her. I shouldn't have kissed her on the massage table last week. Or maybe buying her a gift was too much.

I close my eyes and sigh. Most girls love gifts and attention . . . and kisses. What did I do wrong?

My skin itches as the cliché excuse of "it's not me, it's her" comes to mind. In this case, it may be true.

Daisy simply might not like me the way I like her. The way I *love* her.

If that's true, then there's nothing I can do to change her mind. Either way, I'm better off focusing on the problem at hand—what to do with Karson.

She asked tons of questions about my dad and Apple Cart. Who's to say she wouldn't show up at my house randomly like she did the movies?

Of course, she was already at the movies with friends.

Still, I don't want to chance it. I kept my answers vague. It's only a matter of time before she presses me further. It was hard enough trying to explain why we don't need to be Facebook friends.

I'm not a big social media presence, but I can promise if someone like Karson shows up on my friends list, someone like Adrianne will do some digging.

The woman I want to spend time with pushed me away, while the one I want to keep at arm's length wants to meet my grandparents. That's the last thing I need. Granny would welcome Karson in and make her an honorary grandchild. Not that it's a bad thing.

Just a not-yet thing.

I've got a lot of junk to sort out. I sigh and open my eyes. All I did was go about life as usual. Somehow I've upset two women I care about in very different ways.

I kick the footrest into my recliner and stand. I may not can fix things with the woman I love or the sister I just met, but there's a tractor in front of my kitchen that I can fix tonight.

Daisy

Mullet hops down as I arch my back.

After Donut's debacle, I've limited goat yoga to only goats that are for sure potty-trained and for sure not in heat. My goat-whispering skills can only go so far.

Ashley entered hesitantly and didn't bring her own mat this week. I can't say that I blame her. But she did sigh and smile at the advanced selection of goats.

I'm sure Adrianne is glad too, since the three goats joining us today know not to mess with her. They've been around long enough to pick up on her unwelcoming vibe.

The door opens behind me, and for a split second my spirits lift. *Is it Kyle?* Of course it's not. Kyle hasn't entered my property since two days ago when I told him I needed alone time, and he likely won't again.

I might as well condition myself to quit perking up at an open door like a dog anticipating its owner.

Carolina peeks her head through the door and winces.

"Sorry, I'm late."

"Come on in. We're just now finishing the warmup." I motion for her to join us.

She tiptoes to her spot up front. Hannah saved it for her in case she made it back from her honeymoon in time.

Personally, I'd skip goat yoga if I'd spent a week on a

tropical island and it was my first night at home with my new husband. But I'm happy for her business.

All eyes are on Carolina as she unrolls her mat. Her face is glowing, her skin is tan, and her wedding band is shimmering in the dim light of my living room.

"You look great," Ashley comments.

Aniston crawls toward the front for a better look at her ring, while Bianca compliments her tan. Even Skeeder shows interest.

"Y'all have good weather?" he asks from the back.

"We did." Carolina beams.

I wait a few more seconds to let the gossip die down. Then I lie on my back and clear my throat to get their attention.

"Welcome back, Carolina. We're going to transition into abs now."

A few people groan, either from ending the questions or working their abs. Still, everyone follows my lead.

I take a little satisfaction in having control over something in my life. I can't always control my animals, or how many candles and soaps I sell, or even if a massage client heals the way I anticipated. However, I can get people to follow my lead in yoga.

Good thing, because you can't get Kyle to date just you.

Ugh. If my mind would listen, I'd be in good shape. I shake my head so furiously that Skeeder mimics me like it's part of the next move.

Heat rises up my neck. I must look crazy about now. *Focus. Teach the class.*

Mullet bleats at me and tilts his head as if encouraging me to press on. I pet the long fur on his neck that earned him his name and continue teaching my class. I get in the groove of things and incorporate a few new moves that Mullet and I practiced this past week.

I point to Adrianne as my example of how to do them without a goat—for obvious reasons.

The next forty minutes pass calmly as I get in the zone. We bend, stretch, and breathe out our stresses. Or at least I do. A few seconds after I direct everyone to breathe in once more, they start chatting again.

That's perfectly fine, except that everyone wants to hear about Carolina's honeymoon. I would too, any other day. Just not two days after kicking Kyle out for fear he already has his eyes elsewhere.

Why isn't there a book on how to date for the first time in your late twenties? I'd write one myself, except I'm the one needing it!

Carolina reaches beside me and grabs a towel. She wipes her face and neck, then smiles at me.

"I was hoping you'd be in line to catch the bouquet at our reception."

I grab a towel too, but twist it in my hands to try and not scream. I force a smile.

"I was busy inside cleaning up."

"So sweet." Carolina touches my arm, then nods at Adrianne. "You two did so much to keep me from lifting a hand."

I laugh and watch Adrianne from the corner of my eye. "Well, you do for everyone else."

Adrianne gives me an apologetic smile and walks toward us. She holds her hand out to Carolina.

"I'll take your towel." She turns to me. "I can stay and help you with laundry tonight, Daisy."

That's code for "we need to talk."

I swallow and squeak out a weird noise. Carolina hands the sweaty towel to Adrianne. She pinches it with her fingernails and drops it on a dirty mat.

"I better get home. See all y'all next week?"

The ones who are left answer Carolina. I smile and nod,

my throat now the Sahara Desert. Hannah whispers something to Carolina, and she giggles. They head for the door, leaving only Skeeder.

Adrianne stacks my mats that have been cleaned and rolled up, while I gather towels. Skeeder gazes around the room and bends in front of Mullet.

"You're a cute little thang."

"Skeeder, can you bring us your towel?"

He continues petting Mullet and making baby sounds. Adrianne steps in front of Mullet.

"Skeeder, class is over."

"All right. And you wonder why I cut my own hair instead of coming to you." He shoves the towel at her.

Adrianne scrunches her nose and lets it hit the ground instead of taking it. Skeeder lifts his chin and struts out the door, slamming it behind him.

Adrianne narrows her eyes at me. "For the record, I do *not* wonder why Skeeder isn't my client. I'm sure you wish he wasn't yours too."

I shrug. "I'd rather have him for yoga than a massage."

"Yeah . . ." Adrianne kicks the towel at her feet toward the pile I made. "Let's talk."

My hands tense, and I drop the towel I'm holding.

"Have you talked to Kyle?" She crosses her arms and stares at me for an answer.

"Saturday."

Her eyes widen. "After I called you?"

"Yeah." More like while she called me, but I keep that to myself.

She sits on the edge of my couch, arms still crossed. "And?"

"I told him I needed time alone." My voice chokes on the final word. Saying it out loud reminds me that I created my loneliness.

"Dais." Adrianne pouts sadly. "I know it's hard, but if you're not okay with him dating other people, you did what you should have."

I draw in a deep breath, then exhale. When I stay silent, Adrianne crosses the room and hugs me. I close my eyes and grip her arms. She holds me for a few seconds before talking into my hair.

"It will get easier." She pulls back and gives me a smile so sad, it doesn't quite qualify as one.

I sigh deeply. "I really liked him, you know. But I couldn't keep liking him and get to liking him even more if he likes someone else while he likes me. Know what I mean?"

She lifts a brow. "I think."

I laugh. "Better now than when I think I'm in love. Definitely."

"If it helps, I don't know of anyone who married the first person they dated. Except for maybe my grandma." She wavers her head. "But that was a long time ago, when people married much younger."

"And they probably only dated one person at a time."

Adrianne shrugs. "Or it was easier to hide it back then."

I close my eyes and shake my head. "How do you ever trust anyone?"

"Good question. At the risk of sounding cliché, I can say you know when you've found the one you can trust to love only you." Adrianne twists her wedding band and smiles.

I try and take this as solid advice, even though she and JoJo are still in the honeymoon phase themselves. They had a whirlwind romance, and married after pretending to be married first.

Adrianne squeezes my shoulder. "It'll all work out, Dais. You'll find the right one at the right time."

"Yeah . . ." I muster a flattened smile and wear it until she walks to the door.

Any other time, I'd joke that she promised to stay and help with laundry. But I'm not exactly in the joking mood.

Although she's right, I wish with all my heart the right guy is Kyle and the right time is now.

CHAPTER TWENTY

Kyle

I climb the ramp and knock on the screen door. Replacing the front steps with a ramp is about the only thing that's changed in my grandparents' house during my lifetime.

Unless you count the extra spoons Granny has added from their travels. For some reason, she collects tiny spoons with various names and logos. She has one for every state, which is how I knew all my states in alphabetical order long before we learned it in school.

Before she and Gramps required a ramp, they did a lot of RVing. Every stop required a spoon. I even bought her a *Gone with the Wind* spoon off eBay.

The wooden door opens and Granny squints at me, then smiles. She straightens her thick glasses and opens the screen door.

"Kyle." She hugs me soon as I step across the threshold.

"Hey, Granny. What did you need?"

"It's the sink again. Your dad took Hubert fishing, and I'm afraid it can't wait."

"Okay." I press my mouth shut before I say what I'm really thinking.

The sink may not be as much of an emergency as she lets on. Granny has a track record of fixating on one thing and won't let it go until we fix it. So far this year, that's included a loose toilet seat, a squirrel eating from her bird feeder, and the screen door not latching properly.

Gramps said she wouldn't let him sleep until he tightened the door. She was afraid a snake might sneak inside.

"Do you want some lemonade? Or maybe sweet tea? I made both this morning."

"Granny, what's wrong with the sink?"

She pauses at the refrigerator. "It's leaking."

I turn it on and look for a leak. I don't see anything wrong, and the faucet has plenty of pressure.

"Granny, come stand by the faucet while I go under the sink."

"Sure thing, honey." She shuffles toward me, toting a pitcher of tea.

Her house slippers come into view as I crane my neck to get a better look at the plumbing. Everything is tight and where it should be.

"Turn the water off, then back on."

She does as I ask. No change.

"Granny, I don't see—"

She steps closer, pinning my legs against the cabinet door.

"Why haven't you brought Daisy by here yet?"

"What?"

"Daisy. That little girl you've been seeing with the goat

exercises. We have Sunday dinner every week. I want to meet her."

I wiggle, but Granny has me crammed against the door. She knows I won't force her away with her bad hip. That's when I realize the sink was a ruse to trap me in an interrogation.

"I'm waiting for an answer."

I lay my head on the floor and sigh. She's not going to let me up until I talk. I might as well come clean since she'll relay whatever I say to half the town by her next hair appointment.

"We're not seeing one another right now."

"Oh? Why not?"

"Her choice." I wipe a hand down my face.

I'm starting to sweat from the humidity under the sink and from Granny's questioning.

"What did you do?"

"Why do you always assume it's my fault?" I huff.

"Because you're the guy. It's usually the guy who screws it up."

I attempt to raise up and hit my forehead on the pipe. "Ugh!"

"Are you okay?" Her voice goes from scolding to soothing in a millisecond.

"Yes, ma'am . . . Maybe. Can I please come out if I promise to talk?"

"Sure, sure."

She shuffles to the side enough for me to slide out safely. I stand and rotate my shoulders, then rub my forehead.

"Sorry about that."

"For lying about the sink or me hitting my head?"

Granny stares at the floor, then busies herself making two glasses of tea. She ignores my question completely.

"Sit at the table. I've got you a drink."

I pull out a chair and rest my elbows on the table. It's that vinyl material that makes my sweaty arms stick. I stare at a picture of praying hands on the opposite wall while I wait on Granny to join me. She sets a glass in front of me and takes the seat beside me with her own tea.

"Now, tell me what happened?"

I chug my tea and wipe my mouth with the back of my hand before answering. Liquid courage is much needed before I have this conversation. I've asked myself this same question a million times and come up blank.

"I wish I knew. Like two weeks ago, I asked her to go to the lake, and she said she needed to be alone."

"Maybe she doesn't like the lake. Lots of young women won't swim where they can't see the bottom. This generation of girls is scared of everything."

Says the woman who lives in fear of a snake crawling through a crack in her door.

Granny sips her tea and stares at me over the glass.

"No, that's not it. She said she likes the lake, and the being alone part extended beyond that day."

"Oh." Granny stares at the tablecloth and sighs.

When she raises her head, she smiles at me sadly. It's the silent "bless your heart" kind of smile. The kind that makes me feel like a puppy at a pound.

"Well, at least you tried."

Geez, could she make me feel any more like a loser?

"Some men never try. I suppose your dad gave up after Cindy."

I cough on my tea and clear my throat. I'm not used to hearing Mom's name out loud. Dad never says it anymore, and I haven't heard Granny mention her in years. She's become the Bruno of our family.

We don't talk about Cindy.

Granny puts her hand on mine. I find it as comforting as

I did in childhood. Back when she would brush my hair out of my eyes, then pat me on the head.

"Don't you give up, Kyle."

I stare into her eyes and swallow. Her gaze is sincere and caring. No longer filled with pity.

"You have a lot to offer a young woman. You just have to wait on the Lord to bring you the right one."

I chuckle. That's what I thought I was doing when Daisy came along. I wasn't looking, just working and going about life as usual. Then a local girl I barely knew from growing up came along and charmed the pants off me—literally.

Just for massage purposes.

Still, I had grown to love Daisy and could picture a future with her. But if she doesn't feel the same about me, then we're better off splitting ways.

The last thing I want is to turn out like my dad. Giving my all to someone who leaves me nonchalantly like its the fourth quarter of a blowout game.

I want a woman who will stick it out for every play, no matter what.

"Thanks, Granny."

She pats my hand and gives it a squeeze before letting go. Then she stands and brings the pitcher of tea to the table.

"More?"

I slide my glass toward her for a refill. She pours the tea from that old orange-and-white pitcher, and memories from childhood race through my mind. I'm surprised that thing hasn't dry rotted by now as many times as she's ran it through the 1980s dishwasher.

"So the sink is fine?"

She smirks, and I roll my eyes.

"I had to get you to listen without rolling your eyes at me. I see it almost worked."

"Granny . . ."

She lifts a finger. "Oh, but while I've got you here, there's a spot on the bedroom wall where the wallpaper is peeling. Hubert can't reach it without a stepladder."

I slap my hand to my face, and immediately regret doing so as it aggravates the sore spot where I banged my head.

"Can I finish my tea first?"

"Yes, of course." Granny grins mischievously and raises her own glass.

It's times like these I wish I had cousins.

Daisy

Instead of Kyle's slick, muscular back, I'm staring at Paul's graying back hair.

Not the best way to start work on the weekend. But he was the first to ask about a Saturday slot after Kyle's opened up.

Since I haven't heard from Kyle, I assumed that meant he wouldn't be back for a massage. Who could blame him? I told him I needed time alone right after his last massage.

Note to self: Never date a client—no matter what.

I'll only make an exception if Chris Pratt waltzes through my door wanting a deep-tissue massage. And the chances of that happening are zip!

Lucky for me, Paul is the furthest thing from temptation.

I finish his back and ask him to flip over. A shiny belt buckle catches the candlelight when he turns. He'd asked if he could keep his pants on this time since he didn't need any work done on his legs. I gladly agreed that would be acceptable. Somehow I assumed he'd take off his belt.

Maybe he won't blame me for the discomfort of lying on a huge buckle half of his massage.

"This side right here is most sore in the front." Paul pats his right rib cage. "I think I pulled a muscle moving a coffin."

"A coffin?"

"Yeah, in the store. Someone bought the one I had in the back and wanted it brought to the front."

"You probably shouldn't move coffins by yourself." Add that to the list of things I never thought I'd say.

Of course, it's not too surprising coming from the man who runs the General Store with a slogan on his sign that reads, "Everything from a cradle to a coffin."

"I had it on rollers. All was fine until I had to maneuver it past a sack of fertilizer in the aisle."

"Well, promise me next time you move a coffin, you'll get some help."

"Okay." He closes his eyes before I drop a warm towel over his face.

In a few minutes, he's snoring loudly.

It's like I've unlocked a secret all of Apple Cart needs to know—how to make Paul shut up. Now if I could figure out how to get him to stop freeloading off everyone and everywhere, I'd be a genius.

I knead the spot he said was sore and stare at the candle across from us. It's a classic lavender scent, my default for any client who doesn't request something different.

Funny how I now associate the scent of bacon with Kyle. I haven't lit a bacon-scented candle since him, or eaten a piece of bacon. The other morning I ordered a bacon, egg, and cheese biscuit from Jack's, then teared up when I smelled the bacon.

I had to feed it to Mullet.

When I pushed Kyle away, I expected heartache and loneliness, but not the inability to eat bacon.

The rhythm of Paul's snoring changes, jolting my attention. I flinch, then look down at him. The towel sucks in and blows up as he snores. That's a good sign I didn't hurt him, at least. I'm always more cautious with my older clients.

Really the only time I wasn't cautious with a client was when I dug my toes into Kyle and dropped a too-hot stone on his butt. Bless his heart, he toughed it out.

Bless his heart, nothing. He was with another woman!

There's the other side to the coin. My internal monologue is a constant battle between calling him to apologize for the rough massage and flaky brush off, and making every move to avoid him at all costs. The latter might be easier said than done living in Apple Cart.

He might not have noticed me much before coming in for a massage, then dating me, but I certainly noticed him. No other guy can look equally sexy in church clothes and a greasy mechanic jumpsuit.

I work on Paul's shoulders some more to complete his massage. He's still snoring, which reminds me of the time Kyle fell asleep during his massage. I let him sleep and made him lunch.

That was the day he burned his hand. I flex my own hand and remember rubbing ointment on his. If I could bottle the way his dark blue eyes followed my every move while doing so, I'm sure I could sell it.

I sigh and peel the towel from Paul's face. He snorts and snores, catching me off guard again. I jump back and take the towel to the table. I'm now a safe distance to wake him.

"Paul, you're done," I say rather loudly.

He snores again. I speak in a whisper yell like preschool teachers use to scold during nap time.

"Paul!"

He jerks his head toward me and opens one eye.

"Your massage is over."

He blinks both eyes open and sits on the edge of the table. Then he grabs the sheet and uses it to wipe drool from his mouth. He drops the sheet on the floor, making me more thankful he chose to keep on pants.

"I'll give you a few minutes to get dressed."

He nods and yawns as I leave the room.

I shut the door behind me and take a seat in the living room. Sunlight beams through the window, announcing another hot summer day. Would Kyle be on the lake today or working? Part of me argues that I shouldn't care, but I do.

My Saturday plans involve another massage, followed by milking goats and maybe painting my toenails. Any of which I'd gladly toss aside for Kyle.

That is, if he weren't with someone else. *What if he's at the lake with her?*

I shake that thought from my brain before it has time to materialize. The door opens behind me, offering a small distraction. Paul walks out, offering a much larger distraction.

He has chosen to leave his pearl-snap shirt halfway unbuttoned and rolled up the sleeves to his elbows. He pulls a fat wallet from his back pocket and grabs a wad of cash.

"It's all here, but you can count it."

I take the stack of bills and wrinkle my nose. They're wet, and I'm not sure why. Every one is a two-dollar bill. I can't say that I've ever been paid in those, but it does total to the exact amount.

"Thanks."

He nods, then glances around my living room. "You got any complimentary snacks or anything?"

I shake my head. "No."

He frowns. "That's a shame. You just lost a star on Yelp."

I open my mouth to respond but can't think of anything appropriate. Paul struts past me and out the front door. I sit back on the couch with my wad of moist two-dollar bills. I can't wait to see the look on Ashley's face when I take these by the bank.

CHAPTER TWENTY-ONE

Kyle

I'm upside down, holding an engine with motor oil dripping down my arm, when Dad's phone rings.

"I need to get that."

I groan. "Well, please help me set this down first."

He takes longer than I'd like reaching for a rag before gripping one side of the engine. Once it's on the ground, he hurries out the door with his phone to his ear.

I slide out from under the hood and wonder what the heck just happened. When did Dad worry about his hands staying clean or care so much about answering his phone?

And that ringtone. When did he change the usual ringing sound to a Conway Twitty song? He's so secretive too. He used to always answer the phone in front of me and talk way too loudly.

I pray he hasn't fallen into something illegal, or worse, fallen for a pyramid scheme.

I wipe my own hands and walk toward the door. He's laughing on the phone like a middle school girl. I shake my head. If he doesn't tell me what's up, I'll have to get Bradley to follow him for a while.

Good idea. I'll threaten him with that.

"Okay, I look forward to it too." Dad's face is all smiles when he hangs up the phone.

I lean against the door frame and stare at this resemblance of my father. He's tall, bulky, and wearing a worn-out jumpsuit. But his hands aren't grease stained and his usual serious scowl is replaced with a huge grin. Is that a dimple? He's so solemn most of the time, I've never noticed it before.

He turns to me after tucking the phone in his pocket. "Sorry about that. We can go back to work."

I push off the door and raise my eyebrows. When he comes to the door, I stop him with my hand.

"Hold up. What was that about?"

"What was what?" He wrinkles his forehead like he didn't just undergo a personality transplant.

"That phone call," I clarify.

Dad's confusion morphs into a dreamy grin and his eyes glaze over a minute. He pats the pocket holding his phone and laughs.

"That was Sue."

"Who?"

"Sue."

"Sue who?"

"Sue from Mississippi."

Like that clarifies it. I cross my arms and stare at him for more details.

"This woman I met."

My eyes bug. "Like as in a woman you're interested in?"

"Yep."

His grin goes goofy—a sign my dad has it bad. He's a lot of things, but never goofy. This is strange.

"How did you meet a woman from Mississippi when all you do is fish with Gramps, drink coffee at the gas station, and hang around here?"

"We met on Farmer's Only."

"But you're not a farmer."

"I have a tomato garden."

I drop my head and sigh. What kind of warped universe is this?

"They let me build a profile with that."

I lift my head. "Why after all these years did you decide to date again?"

My mom left twenty-two years ago, and this is the first time I've heard of him even attempting another relationship.

Dad clasps his hand on my shoulder and walks me inside. We sit in my living room, and he runs a hand over his balding head.

"For a long time I was still in love with your mother. After I got over her, I spent many years afraid."

"Afraid of what?"

"Getting hurt again. You were still at home, and I didn't want to bring someone into the family and confuse you if it didn't work out. Or worse, it would work out for a season, then she'd leave us like your mom."

I nod. "I appreciate that."

He gives me his usual solemn smile of approval.

"But I also want you to be happy. I hate knowing you stayed lonely because you didn't want to risk hurting me."

"Don't flatter yourself." He chuckles. "I didn't want to hurt myself either. And I wasn't lonely. I had you, my parents, plenty of friends, and work."

"I know what you mean. It's hard to be lonely when you're involved in so much and work all the time."

"You don't miss Daisy?"

I lean back in my recliner and rock slowly. Dad gave me "the talk" about girls and random advice along the way. But he's never asked specifically about a certain girl. This must be a new feature in his personality transplant.

"I do," I whisper after a few minutes of silence.

"Have you talked to her?"

"Not since she said she wanted to be alone."

"I saw her at the Pig a few days back."

I perk up. "You did?"

"Yeah, she didn't look that happy either."

"That doesn't mean it's because of us. Is anyone really that happy about grocery shopping?"

"It's up to you if you decide to call her, but one day you'll find someone, whether Daisy or someone else. You're a good man, and you deserve someone good. Don't let what your mom did to us scare you from living your life."

Dad runs a hand over his head. "Find someone before you start losing your hair like me."

I laugh. "Isn't baldness a trait from the mother's side?"

"Maybe. Who even knows about your mother's family?"

My chest tightens. All this talk about Daisy and whoever Sue from Mississippi is has pushed Karson to the back burner.

"Dad, since we're talking about women and Mom some, I met someone in her family a few weeks ago."

"Really? She was an only child with dead parents when we met." He rubs his jaw. "Or so she said."

"I'm pretty sure that's all true, but she had another kid after me. A girl who's grown now and attending UA. She found out about me and approached me in Tuscaloosa. We've been talking some."

"Really?"

I nod. "I wanted to tell you, but wasn't sure how. It took

me a while to get used to the idea of having a half-sister and, to be honest, I was a little jealous at first that Mom never left her."

"That's nothing to feel bad about, son. I suppose I'd react the same way."

"She's asked stuff about you, Granny, and Gramps. She doesn't know her own dad, so she seems desperate for any sort of family. I feel sorry for her, but I haven't told too much. It's all so new."

"If and when you want, you can bring her to meet us. I'm sure Granny and Gramps would love that too."

"Thanks." I rock a few times, then look at Dad. "You know you can bring Sue to meet us too, right?"

"We've only met a few times so far, always at the Cracker Barrel in between us." He grins. "But I've mentioned you to her."

My insides warm. For all the love my mom didn't give me, my dad and grandparents made up for it ten times over. No matter what, they've always stood by me and supported me. Even after the incident that kicked me out of college, they were nothing but helpful and encouraging.

"You think we can work on that engine now, or do you expect another call from Sue?"

"I'm good to work. I told her I'd call later tonight."

"All right." I stand and try not to laugh at this man in his fifties acting like a teenager in love.

And I try even harder not to be jealous of my dad's love life.

Daisy

. . .

"There." I angle the box fan so it will blow more on Mom.

"Thanks." She clips her hair up and fans her face. "I didn't think it would be so hot today."

"It's the end of summer in Alabama."

"Yeah, but the weather said mild."

I laugh. "Maybe compared to yesterday."

"There's still a good crowd."

"Yep." I shade my eyes and survey the crowd.

Anytime there's a festival named after an animal or produce a lot of people show up.

I take my seat beside Mom and straighten the row of candles in front of me. I have candles and soaps, along with a few bath bombs I made as a test. The one upside to having so much time to myself is coming up with new products.

Mom watches as I stand to find more soap from the boxes behind us.

"Where's your helper?"

"Helper?"

"Kyle, right?"

I pause from collecting soaps. "How did you know he helped me?"

"Toby mentioned running into him whenever he'd make a delivery."

I nod. "Yeah, he was there for a massage."

"Uh-huh."

I straighten and roll my eyes. "Really, Mom?"

She giggles. "I know you two went on dates."

"Just a few." I don't recall mentioning this to her, but she has enough friends still in Apple Cart to find out.

Since I've never dated, I knew Mom would make a big deal out of me going out with Kyle. Kind of like she's doing right now.

I busy myself with the soaps and try to ignore her laughter. A couple walks toward our table, saving me from more taunting.

"Hi." I greet them as the woman unscrews a jar and sniffs the candle inside.

The guy steps forward and reads the labels. He moves the candles around so he can read each one. Then he stares at me.

"Are you the girl who did the bacon candle?"

"Yes."

He scans the table and frowns. "You still do that?"

"They're out of stock right now."

He groans and looks at his wife. She holds a jar toward him.

"This one is nice, smell."

He takes a big whiff. "Too girly."

She shakes her head and smiles at me. "I'll take two of these." She pats his chest. "For the living room."

He bites his nails, then spits to the side. While she's paying, he picks up soaps, disturbing my cute little display.

"You got any bacon soap?"

"No, sir."

"Are you gonna bring the bacon back anytime soon?"

The woman swats his arm. "Henry, stop."

"What? I like the bacon stuff."

"I apologize for him." She presses her lips together.

"It's fine." I drop a card in her bag. "My number and website are on this card. You can order candles from there. Check back in a bit, and I may have some bacon."

Henry grins. "Thanks."

"Thank you." The woman smiles and nods.

They walk away, and I work on restocking the soaps. Of all the candles and all the scents, he had to bring up bacon. Truth is, I'd love to bring bacon back—in the form of Kyle.

But if that never happens, and it likely won't, I don't see me basking in the heavy scent of bacon just to make candles.

"So this Kyle and you?"

From the corner of my eye, I see Mom turn toward me and stare. I stack a few more bars of soap, my hands shaking. I adjust one bar and they tumble like a leaning tower of Jenga blocks. I sigh and face her.

"What?"

She shrugs. "Are you seeing him or not?"

"Not."

"That's a shame. He has a cute butt."

"Mom!"

"What, he does." She huffs and focuses on a group of women approaching our table.

Mom greets them while I line up the soap in a row. My nerves can't handle intricate displays right now.

I show one woman my lavender soaps and bath bombs, while Mom talks herbs and oils with her friends. We both make sales, and the women show interest in our websites. Mom doesn't have one, and makes sure to mention that she doesn't trust the internet.

I fight off rolling my eyes. It took me years to convince her to upgrade to a smartphone, only for her to go back to a flip phone once they became available again.

Mom plops down in front of the fan and closes her eyes. "All butts aside, I hate that it didn't work out with you two."

I narrow my eyes as she opens hers and laughs. She thinks she's so clever with her puns.

"Seriously though, opposites attract. Take your dad and me, for example. He was Southern, military, very salt of the earth." She fans her hands down her colored kimono and wiggles her thin eyebrows.

I sigh. It didn't work so well for me.

"Or you could always try dating someone opposite of the opposite you dated."

"Do what?"

Mom pouts her lips. "I don't know, say Toby, maybe?"

"Toby?"

"He's a very intelligent man."

"Yeah, but he kind of reminds me of a younger Paul."

Mom scoffs. "Daisy Mae. He doesn't steal food, and to my knowledge, he's never worn a belt buckle."

"Eh."

"He thinks you're pretty."

I glare at her. "How would you know that?"

"Because he said so, the first time he was working when you stopped by the house."

I shake my head.

"What, you don't find him attractive?"

I shrug. "To be completely honest, I've never looked at him that way, so it's hard to say."

"Maybe because you were so fixated on Kyle and his butt."

I toss a bath bomb at her, and she curls up in her lawn chair. It grazes the side of her skirt and bounces in the grass.

"Daisy? What has gotten into you?"

"Sorry, Mom." I drop my head in my hands. "I shouldn't have done that. I've been stressed and not sleeping well, but it's no excuse."

Mom's arms are around my shoulders as they start to shake. "Oh, baby. It's okay. I'll send you home with some lavender oils."

I hug her back as she squeezes me. I suck down a tear and force myself to keep it together. By the time Mom lets go, I'm a rock . . . at least on the outside.

No matter how much I care about Kyle, she and Adrianne are right. He isn't the only guy in the world. It's time I quit acting like he is, because he sure didn't act like I was the only girl in the world.

CHAPTER TWENTY-TWO

Kyle

My front door swings open to Bradley holding up handcuffs.

I stand from my recliner and sigh. What is he up to now?

He comes toward me, leaving the door open. Blue lights flash from the yard, which would definitely draw attention if I didn't live way off the main road. Unfortunately, I do live beside Dad.

"What are you doing with handcuffs and your lights flashing?"

Bradley cuffs me before I can move and narrows his eyes. "You're under arrest."

I shake my head. "Very funny, Officer."

"You are."

"For what?"

"For moping around here."

"I'm not moping around." I sling my arm toward the TV, and Bradley's arm jerks with it since he refuses to let go.

He huffs as I pull him with me, and I smile. He can lift dumbbells all he wants, but I'll always be stronger.

"I've been watching TV after a hard day's work."

"Well, you're wanted at the lodge."

"First arrested, then wanted? Wow, Officer."

Bradley jerks my arm and attempts to tug me toward the door. "Come on, Ronald and Macon are in town, and we're having a massive poker match. There's lots of deer poppers and desserts."

I drop my head as he tugs again. Bradley grunts when I don't move.

"Can I at least shower first? And can you please turn off those blue lights before my dad thinks something is wrong?"

"Yes, and yes." He uncuffs me and stares. "But I'm watching you."

"Please don't. I'm getting in the shower."

Bradley growls and heads for the door. I chuckle and go to the bathroom. Good food and poker with my friends don't sound so bad. I wasn't moping, but it might've turned into that.

Standing under a hot shower helps some too, though hot water is a poor excuse for a massage. I've debated calling around Tuscaloosa for a massage place, but don't want to give up on Daisy. Not just yet.

If my shoulder can hold out a little longer, maybe I can muster the courage to call and book another appointment with her. She didn't say I couldn't be her client. But I didn't want to make it awkward for her, or hard on me.

The shower at least energizes me enough to enter society. Aside from the few times I've met Karson, I haven't gone anywhere but church and the grocery store since that last day at Daisy's house. I guess Bradley has a point.

He's waiting by the door when I walk out clean and fully

dressed. He tips his hat back and lets out a long, deep whistle. "Don't you clean up nice."

I grit my teeth at him. He laughs while I turn off the TV and head toward the door. When I stop in front of him, he takes my arm. "Ready for our date?"

I sling his arm off mine and shake my head. He laughs louder. I lock the door and follow him to the cop car.

"Are you on duty?"

"Yeah, but what better place to stake out than a poker game?"

"Whatever."

"Hey, play nice, or I'll make you ride in the back."

"Yeah, whatever." I get in the passenger seat and watch Bradley adjust some radio controls before driving.

We sit back and listen to the radio on the way to Gamer's Paradise. And by radio, I mean the police scanner. It's full of public safety announcements and crazy call-ins to the fire department. Granny sometimes listens to one, so I feel like I'm right at home. Half of her prayer requests in her Bible study come from what she hears on the scanner.

By the time we reach the lodge, I'm caught up on summer storm warnings and a woman calling the fire department to remove an armadillo from her kitchen. Bradley takes that opportunity to joke that it's the Apple Cart Armadillo mascot.

I jump out as soon as he parks, happy to hear conversation of substance, no matter what the topic may be.

Bradley joins me and leads me to the game room in the lodge. He wasn't joking about a massive poker match. Ronald and Macon sit in the center of the room at a table with Jack, Jonah, and Tanner. They show up several times a year and stay at Gamer's Paradise to check in on the outdoors store they built on the back of Jack's property that faces the interstate.

Ronald is always kidding around, and Macon is more reserved and serious. Jonah once joked that they were an older version of Bradley and me.

Everyone greets us, and we stop at a long table of food and fix plates. Then I follow Bradley to a table with JoJo and his grandpa. JoJo gives me a scowl. Coming from anyone else, I might take it personally, but that's just his normal face.

Grandpa Joe shuffles a deck of cards like a card shark. I admire his skills and pop a deer popper in my mouth. JoJo frowns at the table and slowly slides the cards he's dealt toward him. As much as I like to win, I don't want to beat him. He's the kind of guy you need on your good side.

Earl Ed and his cousins sit at the table behind us, and some of the older men in town sit at a fourth table. They're all dressed head to toe in camo even though it isn't any kind of hunting season. Come to think of it, I've never seen Roy in anything but camo. He must wear it as a marketing ploy for his taxidermy business.

Jack stands and reminds everyone of a few rules. We're to play so many hands among our table before moving into brackets based on our winnings. He points to a chart he drew that resembles something you'd see on the wall at a Little League tournament.

"And most importantly, no pairs. Every man for himself." Jack grins and takes his seat again.

JoJo stacks his cards, then fans them in his hands. He lifts his eyes and grimaces my way. I lean back in my seat, intimidated by his hooded lids and thin lips.

If his goal is to scare me into playing scared, it's working.

Bradley talks about anything and everything, clueless to the tense vibe at our table. I'm clueless as to *why* there's a tense vibe. JoJo isn't staring down Bradley or his grandpa. Is it because I'm seated directly opposite of him? Or maybe he chose to pick on the guy who isn't his elder or county sheriff.

I concentrate on my cards and food. A few hands, then I can move to a different table—one I hope doesn't include JoJo. Grandpa Joe wins the first hand and cheers. We congratulate him, and even JoJo smiles slightly.

"Kyle, you better step it up," Bradley jokes.

I don't play cards as often as them, which gives him one more thing to jab at me.

"Kyle." Grandpa Joe slurs my name and stares at me.

"Yes, sir?"

He pokes out his lip, then turns to JoJo. "Is this the man Adrianne was talking about?"

"Maybe," JoJo huffs.

"The one who liked her friend. Petunia."

JoJo shakes his head. "Daisy."

"Well, I was close. I knew she was a flower name."

Heat travels up and down my spine like an overactive barbed-wire fence. I squirm in my chair. This was the one place in Apple Cart County I expected not to hear about Daisy.

I may as well have gone to the beauty shop with Granny.

Grandpa Joe points at me. "But Adrianne said he was at the Waffle House."

JoJo wipes his hand over his beard and sighs. "No, Grandpa, that was another guy."

"Another Kyle?"

"No, he doesn't like Daisy now. She went to Waffle House with the other guy."

Doesn't like her now? OTHER GUY?

Bradley makes eye contact with me. He turns his cards upside down and folds. I do the same, leaving the two Culp men in the game. JoJo wins that round, putting Bradley and me in a lower bracket than him and his grandpa.

"I think I'm gonna need more cookies before we try and claw our way out of this slump. How about you, Kyle?"

Bradley stands, and so do I. We walk to the refreshments. "Where are the cookies?"

"In the kitchen." He passes the table, and I follow him again.

Bradley stops by the kitchen counter and puts his hands on his hips.

"What's going on?" I ask.

"I threw the game."

"Yeah, I know. You never fold, even when you have a crappy hand."

He shrugs. "I could tell you wanted out of there. Sorry I forced you to come tonight."

"It's fine. How could I know Daisy would be out with another guy?"

Bradley grabs my shoulder. "Don't worry. I'll gets the deets before we leave." He starts walking toward the game room, then comes back.

He grabs a cookie from the counter and holds it up. "You get one too, so we don't look suspicious."

I snatch a chocolate cookie and groan. For better or worse, I just gave Bradley the green light to gossip with a group of men about my love life.

Daisy

I'm usually not one to feel overdressed, but I'm on a first date at Waffle House.

That's about what I would expect from someone like Toby. So much for keeping an open mind and giving him the benefit of the doubt. He said we were going someplace nice to eat, so I recruited Adrianne to help me get ready.

I guess nice is a relative term.

Toby hops out and slams his door, catching me off guard. I get out and walk beside him. We're in an old station wagon he converted to run off vegetable oil. Considering that, it's a good thing we stayed local.

The last thing I need is to be stranded far from home in a sketchy station wagon with a guy I barely know.

Prissy greets us at the door and leads us to a booth.

"You're looking right pretty tonight, Daisy." She flashes her fake pearly smile.

"Thanks, Prissy."

I smooth my hand over the stomach of Adrianne's satin shirt. If I get syrup on this, she'll kill me.

Toby slides in across from me and smiles. I study his features. He's not handsome in a strikingly obvious way like Kyle, but he's not bad to look at either. He has a kind face and trusting smile.

If I had to compare him to someone, it would be a clean-shaven, real-life version of Shaggy off *Scooby Doo*.

He drops his eyes to the menu and lets out a breath. "What are you getting?" he asks without looking up.

"Probably some waffles." That is, if I can trust myself to eat syrup in this blouse.

"Me too, even though I don't really care for waffles."

I scrunch my brow. "You don't have to eat them because I am."

He lifts his eyes. "Oh, it's not because of you, it's because we're at the house of waffles. It would be like going to Chick-fil-A and getting a burger instead of chicken."

I open my mouth to argue that Chick-fil-A only serves chicken, but decide to let it go.

Prissy stops by to get our drink orders. Toby gets black

coffee and chocolate milk. I find it a little strange that he ordered two drinks, and even stranger that he ordered the preferred drinks of old men and toddlers.

I order water, and Prissy leaves us to look over the menus longer. Toby glances between me and the menu, then smiles.

"Thanks for going out with me."

"You're welcome." I try and hold back a laugh, but a tiny one escapes.

"You look pretty tonight."

"Thanks." I straighten my giggles and smile.

Toby's really trying, and he obviously likes me. I need to try and take this date seriously.

That's easier said than done when Prissy comes back—on roller skates! My eyes widen at her wobbly legs. She windmills her arms and bends forward, rolling up to our table.

"Prissy, why are you on skates?"

"Oh, my cousin who works at a Sonic does this and gets an extra buck an hour. I talked the boss lady into me trying it out."

I lift my chin and put on a fake smile. Good thing they keep syrup on the table. She'd for sure spill that on us.

"Y'all ready to order?"

"Yes." Toby smiles.

Prissy flashes her pearly teeth, and they lock eyes. She stares at his lips as he orders the All-Star Special and specifies the options within that meal. His eyes are on her bone-thin, wrinkled fingers writing the order.

They're oblivious to me as I look on like I'm watching a movie.

When it's clear she's completely forgotten about me, I clear my throat. Prissy continues to ignore me. "I haven't seen you before. You must not be from around here," she says to Toby.

"I live in Tuscaloosa right now."

I clear my throat louder. Prissy finally turns to me.

"I'd like pecan waffles with a side of bac—just waffles."

Prissy jots down my waffles. "Got it. I'll get that in for y'all."

She winks at Toby before pushing off our table and sliding behind the counter.

"That was interesting," I say.

"Yeah, she's great." Toby has a goofy, smitten look plastered on his face as he watches Prissy across the room.

I may not like Toby in that way, but how rude to gawk at another woman while he's with me. This date has not been the easy confidence boost I thought I'd get.

"So what made you want to study botany?"

Toby turns toward me at last. "I'm fascinated with all things plants. It started when I was a kid and got into some poison ivy."

He drones on about the powers of plants. I glaze over until something hits the window outside. I jolt to attention and scan the parking lot. All I see is someone in full camo, running into the darkness.

Probably a drunken deer hunter. No, it's not deer season, but the deer hunters in Apple Cart County wear their camo year-round.

I glance back at Toby, who never broke his story about botany. He doesn't stop speaking until Prissy rolls our way with a tray of food.

My nerves tense as she wobbles over. I slide the syrup to the back of the table and cross my arms over Adrianne's blouse. Prissy sways back and forth before gaining enough momentum to roll toward us.

She hits the table, and the tray slides. Luckily, Toby grabs it before everything goes everywhere.

"My hero." Prissy beams.

"My pleasure." Toby grins.

I slide my plate of waffles in front of me and pour syrup on them. Those two can have their little moment. At this point, I'm just here for the food.

Toby starts eating as well, with Prissy still at our table. They talk for a few minutes, then he asks if she'd like to sit with us. There are no other customers, so she sits.

I'm officially the third wheel at Waffle House.

Prissy and Toby start bonding over their love for aloe vera plants. She uses them frequently for her sunburns. As much as she tans, that's saying something.

I run a big bite of waffle through my syrup and lean over my plate to make sure I don't stain Adrianne's clothes. I try and look on the bright side: I'm getting to eat waffles and I wasn't into Toby anyway.

That outlook keeps me happy until Prissy rolls away to get the check, then rolls back with her number scrolled across the back in red ink. First the movies, now Waffle House?

What is it with women hitting on my men in front of me?

Toby eyes the check, then frowns. He glances at me. "Think you could spot me a twenty? I spent my last paycheck on vegetable oil."

"This one's on me."

I sigh and grab the check from him, then walk to the register. Toby follows and chats with Prissy as I pay the bill. They say their goodbyes while I walk out the door.

Toby comes out a minute later, tucking the check in his front shirt pocket. God forbid he lose Prissy's number.

I try not to laugh as I climb in the station wagon. It smells like fried okra from Mary's Diner when he cranks it.

We ride in silence to my house, and I almost doze off. But Toby says something to catch my attention.

"Looks like the sheriff's out here."

I open my eyes and glance out the window. "That's where Bradley lives now."

It's Adrianne's old house, on the way to mine. I start to close my eyes again, then do a double take when I notice Kyle's red Jeep in the yard. It's not unusual since they're best friends.

However, seeing the Jeep floods my mind with memories and my heart with feelings I'd be better off if I could erase.

CHAPTER TWENTY-THREE

Kyle

Bradley's front door swings open to Earl Ed. He's dressed in head-to-toe camo with his face painted like he's on a safari.

We stare at him, then look at each other. He slams the door behind him and rushes toward us. Bradley puts his hands on his hips and narrows his gaze. "Any info?"

I look at Earl Ed, then back at Bradley. "What's going on?"

He nods toward Earl Ed. "He owed me for helping him get Mackenzie, so I called in a favor."

Earl Ed grins and holds up his phone. "I got him."

I scrunch my brow as his sticks the phone in my face. It's so close, all I can make out is a Waffle House sign. I grab the phone and hold it back.

"It's a picture of Daisy." I pinch the screen to zoom in. "And looks like Toby."

"Toby? Who's Toby?" Bradley asks.

"This odd guy who helps her mom."

"They were eating supper, and she was dressed real nice. Like she was going to Red Lobster or something."

"Red Lobster? We don't have a Red Lobster here," Bradley comments.

"Yeah, but if we did, y'all would all go there thinking it's nice. This town has no culinary sense," Earl Ed argues.

I roll my eyes and hand him the phone. "Who cares where they were. She was on a date with him."

"Maybe you should bring that blond chick around here. Take her to Double Drive," Bradley says.

"I can give you some two-for-one milkshake coupons." Earl Ed smiles.

I shake my head. "What are y'all talking about?"

"The blond girl you've been seeing in Tuscaloosa," Bradley clarifies.

"I haven't been seeing a blond girl in Tuscaloosa."

"JoJo said he seen you with a blond woman and an ugly dog in yoga pants," Earl Ed adds.

"An ugly dog had on yoga pants?" Bradley's face wrinkles with confusion.

"No, the woman did," Earl Ed says.

"Then you should've said yoga pants after the woman. That's a misplaced modifier. It's confusing," Bradley corrects.

"Thanks, I didn't pay much attention in English class, I—"

"Stop." I hold up my hands, and Earl Ed pauses with his mouth hung open. "That woman is my sister."

Earl Ed's jaw drops even lower and his eyes bug. "You're dating your sister?"

"No, you dumb butt. I'm not dating my sister."

Bradley scowls. "You apologize. Earl Ed is not dumb. He just doesn't remember the parts of speech."

"Look, I'm sorry, Earl Ed."

"Wait, you have a sister?" Bradley cocks his head, giving me his criminal-questioning stare.

"Yes, a half-sister, and I didn't know about her until about a month ago. She bombarded me at the movies when Daisy went to the bathroom."

Bradley snaps his fingers. "So the girl who Daisy told Adrianne about who Adrianne and JoJo then saw you with is your half-sister?"

"Yes."

"Are you sure y'all aren't dating?" Bradley cocks his head further.

I shove him against the wall. "Oh my gosh, yes, I'm sure. Why would you think that?"

He shrugs. "They said y'all looked mighty friendly buying ice cream, and she is your half-sister."

"What is wrong with you banjo-playing people?"

"I only play the guitar, and you know that," Bradley quips.

I rub my temple. "Look, she was happy to have found me. I'm the only family she has besides our deadbeat mother. Can I not look happy spending time with an attractive female and not like her that way?"

"Maybe you can, but I can't." Bradley straightens against the wall and his cocky grin returns.

"Well, I can. And since y'all know everything I don't, tell me how Daisy knows about her?"

"She told Adrianne that she came back in the theater and saw the girl in her seat. Then Adrianne told her about the ice cream in the park. Daisy thinks you're dating her too."

I fist my hand and bite my knuckles. Is this why she wanted to be alone? Because going to Waffle House with Toby isn't exactly being alone.

"So Daisy thought you were dating someone else, but you weren't. Then she goes and dates someone else."

"Thank you, Captain Obvious," I say to Bradley.

He straightens his lips.

"Why don't you just go to her house and explain?" Earl Ed suggests.

"That's a good idea, but what if the guy's still there?"

"Then kick his tail." Bradley makes a punching motion and smiles.

He's way too excited about a potential fight. That means he's been binge watching either *Cops* or *The Bachelor* again. Probably the latter. I'll never let him live down the time he applied for the leading role.

They never contacted him back, and he blamed it on his demanding role in law enforcement. Although most of those guys don't have real jobs, I doubt that was their deciding factor on Bradley.

"I'm not going to beat up some guy. If Daisy wants to date him, then that's her choice."

Bradley pouts. "Why don't none of y'all want to fight for love?"

"Don't you think it's a little rude to bust up someone's date, Bradley?" Earl Ed gives him a scolding stare.

"Not if it's Kyle busting up that guy's date." He points toward Earl Ed's phone and wrinkles his nose.

"Earl Ed's right. That's not how adults should act. I'll talk to Daisy, just not tonight. Let her have a nice date."

Bradley kicks the side of my wall in frustration, and Earl Ed shakes his head. He glances at Bradley, then me.

"Since we're all here, y'all wanna try a new dish I made?"

Bradley perks up. "What is it?"

"A lemon-glazed salmon with orzo pasta."

"Sounds delicious." Bradley grins.

"Y'all go eat, I'm staying here."

"Oh, I've got it in the truck." Earl Ed hooks a thumb behind him.

"Why?"

"In case I got hungry during the stakeout at Waffle House."

"Who packs salmon and rice for a snack?" I scratch my head.

"Someone watching their carbs. I've been eating lots of small meals a day, but I packed enough for all of us since I didn't know how long this might take. I just lucked out and got a picture sooner than later."

I shrug. "What the heck. I'll pour us all a drink."

I'll eat salmon with them, but if this night gets any weirder, I'm going to bed.

Daisy

Hoss stands beside me as I shine a flashlight for Toby. He made the mistake of killing the station wagon when he walked me to my door. Now he can't get it to crank.

I insisted he not walk me to my door, but he wanted to "end our date like a gentleman." A gentleman wouldn't have pocketed our waitress's phone number.

But we're beyond that mattering, and my current concern is how to get Toby off my property ASAP. It doesn't help that the only tow truck in town belongs to Kyle.

Life sure was easier before I decided to date.

Toby tinkers with something under the hood, then raises his head and sighs. He turns to me. "Maybe I need more oil. You got any?"

"Olive oil in the kitchen. Essential oils in the candle room."

"Nah, I need vegetable oil."

"Sorry, I don't use that."

He beats the side of his vehicle with his fist, then bows over and whines.

"Are you okay?"

He nods. "I will be. I forget these old vehicles are made from real metal."

I give him a sympathetic smile. Hoss snorts at me, then walks away. Toby shakes out his hand and stares at the engine. "Maybe we should call someone? You know a mechanic?"

My hand goes numb and I drop the flashlight. I fumble to pick it up.

"Or maybe even a tow truck."

Please shut up.

I snatch the flashlight and stand. "It's a little late for those. How about we call the sheriff?"

"Don't tow trucks work all the time?"

I shrug. I honestly don't know the answer to that, and I'd prefer not to find out tonight.

"What's wrong with the sheriff? He'll know what to do, and he's less than a mile down the road."

Toby's throat bobs. "Uh, he wouldn't drug test me, would he?"

I arch my eyebrow.

Toby raises his hands. "I wasn't driving you under the influence, but I have had some medical marijuana in the last few weeks."

I slap my hand to my head. Could this night get any worse?

"Here." I hand Toby the flashlight. "I'm going inside

where I have better cell service. I'm calling the sheriff. It will be fine."

His jaw drops as he takes the flashlight. I maneuver around the chickens to the house. Toby's sat at the edge of my yard for at least an hour. If I can't call Kyle, Bradley is the next best choice to escort him away.

Bradley can drive him home safely and arrange to have Kyle move the station wagon while I'm not home.

I reach for my phone and pull up Bradley's contact. My hands hover over the screen as I contemplate what to text. I can't say anything about car trouble, or he'll bring Kyle. I'll keep it brief and vague.

Hey, I need your help with something. Not life or death, but kind of urgent. I'm at home.

Be there in five.

I barely have time to put away my phone when blue lights and sirens take over my front lawn. I rush out the front door to Toby lifting his hands high and Bradley coming toward him.

"Bradley, stop."

Bradley lifts his head to me as I hop off the porch. He cuts his eyes to Toby and snarls.

"Did this guy hurt you, Daisy?"

"No, his car broke down in my yard."

"Is that all?"

"Yeah."

"Then why didn't you call Kyle?"

I exhale, my nostrils flaring.

Bradley holds up a finger. "We'll discuss that in a minute. First, let me see what's going on over here."

"Kyle?" Toby drops his hands. "I thought y'all were over."

"He's a mechanic . . . and has a tow truck," I offer.

Toby grins. "Then I appreciate you calling the sheriff instead of that motor-oil head."

Bradley steps toward Toby, who has a good six inches on his decently tall stature. He puts his hands on his hips and stares up at Toby, not the least bit intimidated.

"I'll have you know, mister, that motor-oil head is a good man." Bradley sniffs. "And I wouldn't be calling people out for motor oil when you smell like a dumpster behind Waffle House."

Toby crosses his arms. "No need to bring Waffle House into this."

"You're the one who did that by taking Daisy out."

"Do people in this county need your permission to date?"

Bradley grits his teeth, and they lock eyes. If I had time, I'd run in the house and make popcorn for the show. This is getting good.

"No, but if y'all had never gone out, this wouldn't have happened." He fans his arm toward the car. "Now, if you'll get in the car, I can drive you home."

"I'm not riding home with you."

"I think you are. Now, we can do it peacefully or by force." Bradley tips his hat.

Toby squirms. "No disrespect, but I have a ride on the way."

Bradley turns to me. I shrug. Both guys stare at me as if silently asking what to do next. *I can't call Kyle.* Since that's not an option, I go into Southern belle mode and say the first hospitable thing that comes to mind.

"Would anyone like some popcorn?"

"I'd love some," Toby answers.

"Thanks, but I'm good." Bradley pats his stomach. "I just ate a salmon and orzo medley. It was awesome."

"Okay . . ." That was rather specific. "Be right back."

I hurry in the house away from the circus outside. Mullet follows me in this time. I pet him while I wait for the popcorn to pop. The microwave dings, and I divide the bag into three bowls. I put one bowl at the table for Mullet and take the other two outside.

Bradley is smiling and laughing when I return. Strange, but at least there's no more tension between these two.

"What's so funny?"

"You'll see in a minute." Bradley winks at me.

He asks Toby about the car and vegetable-oil engines while we snack on popcorn. I'm halfway through my bowl when headlights shine down my drive.

My stomach clenches. Could that be Kyle? Surely Bradley wouldn't call him to come here. That's a little low—even for our honorable sheriff.

Nope. It's an old Toyota car. It stops beside Toby's vehicle, and Prissy climbs out. She's still in her Waffle House uniform, minus the skates. A wide grin crosses her face when Toby looks at her. "Ready to go, Toby Woby?"

Toby Woby? They've known each other an hour, and she already has a pet name for him?

Bradley glances at me, then cackles out. He bends, clutching his knees to try and catch his breath.

"Are you okay?" Toby puts a hand on Bradley's shoulder.

He coughs, then regains his voice. His face is red from laughing. "It's all good, big dog." He brushes Toby's hand off his shoulder. "I don't need veg oil on my uniform. Dry cleaning is expensive in a small town."

"We don't have a dry cleaner."

Bradley turns to me. "I know, and it's expensive to take it out of town."

I shake my head.

Toby shuts the hood of the station wagon. "Y'all will make sure this gets back to me soon as possible?"

"Yes," Bradley and I say in unison.

I guess he's as ready as I am to see these two leave. Prissy motions for Toby to get in her car. He moves the seat back far as it will go, ducks his tall frame, and climbs in. She gets in the driver's seat and cranes her neck to see us around the furry pink dice hanging from the mirror.

She flashes her teeth and waves. Toby gives us a goofy wave too. Bradley and I both lift a hand as Prissy backs out of my drive and leaves.

"That was . . ."

"Hilarious!" Bradley laughs harder than before.

"I was going for super weird, but it was kind of funny."

"Kind of?" He chuckles. "That's the best thing I've seen all week, and I busted a group of old ladies swapping prescription pills and stopped a guy from soliciting home-cut steaks in front of the Pig."

I pop a piece of popcorn in my mouth and chew. And I thought my life was crazy. I swallow and smile at Bradley. "Thanks again for your help tonight."

"No problem, though I'm sure you could've handled it." He taps my shoulder with his fist.

I gaze at the broken-down station wagon. "I know this will probably require Kyle's help. If you can just give me a heads up before he comes, so I can be out?"

Bradley shakes his head. "No, ma'am. Y'all need to talk."

I narrow my eyes at him. "That's none of your business. You don't know what happened."

"Actually, I do. You don't know what really happened."

"Then tell me, Mr. Sheriff."

"It will mean more coming from him. Just trust me on this."

I press my lips together and exhale through my nose. Do I really want to trust a guy who has to get a haircut every two weeks but wears a hat 24/7?

Not really, but if it gives me another chance with Kyle, I'll risk it.

CHAPTER TWENTY-FOUR

Kyle

I flip on my opposite side and ball my pillow under my head. In the past two hours, I've adjusted the air, pulled off my extra sheet, and covered a light on my bathroom outlet. Nothing has worked to help me sleep.

I throw back the covers and stand. Maybe something to drink will make me sleepy. Granny swears by drinking warm milk before bed. I'm not sure why it needs to be warm, unless waiting on the milk to warm makes you sleepy.

But it's worth a try.

I grab a glass from the cabinet and pour it full of milk. The white glass glistens in the moonlight as my eyes adjust from completely dark to refrigerator light to dark with minimum light. I wrap my hands around the glass, hoping that will help warm the milk quicker.

Most people talk about hitting rock bottom by going to jail, losing a spouse, or having some big financial crisis. For me, it might just be sitting in my underwear, waiting for milk to warm.

Pathetic as that sounds, I have a quiet moment to contemplate my life. No family or friends giving me advice, no clients on me about the status of their motors. Just me and a glass of lukewarm milk.

The conversation I had with Bradley and Earl Ed plays in my mind. Daisy thought I was seeing someone else. I'm not surprised Adrianne mentioned seeing me with a girl or that she didn't believe Karson was just my friend. But I had no idea Daisy saw her with me at the movies.

I've got to set this straight. First thing tomorrow.

If this dad-blamed milk would hurry up and warm so I can drink it, then I can sleep and get rest to go see Daisy. She's for sure asleep by now, like I should be.

I clutch the glass so tightly I fear it might break. This isn't working. Not the milk or the waiting.

I've got to talk to Daisy—now.

I move my hands from the glass to the counter, and push myself to standing. In a few minutes, I'm wearing jeans, boots, and a T-shirt, rushing out the door.

My keys jingle in my hand as I nervously lock my house. Then I hurry to the Jeep and start down the route I could drive with my eyes closed. And good thing too, because I'm finally feeling sleepy.

Too bad. I roll the windows down to keep me awake. If I don't do this now, I'll regret it forever.

Daisy may not want me back or even to hear me out, but I have to at least try. For all my faults, I'm not one to give up easily.

Aside from a few people outside of the Quick Stop, there's no sign of life this late in Apple Cart. I drive through town toward Daisy's road. I pass the house Bradley's renting.

His pickup and patrol car are both in the drive, so he's likely asleep too.

I creep down Daisy's driveway, careful not to stir any animals. The few chickens running free pay me no mind. I assume the goats are in their pens. That is, until green flashes in front of me. Hoss's eyes glow in my headlights and he snorts.

I dim my lights and pull to the side, getting as close to the porch as I can without hitting it. Before I put it in park, I notice a strange vehicle at the edge of her yard. It's a brown station wagon.

What in the world?

A light bulb comes on in my head as I recall Earl Ed mentioning a station wagon at Waffle House. Every inch of my body tingles. Could it be?

I didn't take Daisy for the type to have a date overnight, especially someone like Toby. Not that I'd take advantage of her, but I'm a little hurt she'd proposition someone like that over me. I put my Jeep in reverse and start to back up.

A loud growl bellows behind me. I glance in the mirror at Hoss standing firmly behind me. I put it back in park and kill the engine.

Hoss snorts, and I get out.

I shut my door gently to not wake anyone. "Hoss, could you please move so I can leave?"

He snorts again and prances toward me. I get in football-ready stance, prepared to take him out if needed.

Instead of attacking me, he nudges me forward. I straighten and walk backward at his leading. He pushes me all the way up the porch, then grunts. I turn and stare at the front door.

Like something you'd see from a magical reindeer in a Christmas movie, he nods.

"For real?"

I swear, he nods again. It's probably him trying to dislodge the pool noodles from his horns, but I take it as a sign to continue my mission.

My arm weighs a ton as I lift it to knock on the door. I don't want to wake Daisy up, but I really hope she's asleep. If they're still awake, I've got more problems than I thought.

I force my fist against the door and knock. I wait a few seconds, then knock again. Nothing. I shove my hands in my pockets and change my mind several times about leaving. Then Hoss makes the most annoying, frightful sound I've heard from any animal. As someone who lives in rural Alabama and has gone hunting a good bit, that's saying a lot.

His head rears back, and I half think he's preparing to charge me. Just in case, I back into the door. Except there is no door.

I stumble, then turn around to find that Daisy has opened it. She blinks, then lifts her brows when she sees it's me.

"Kyle?"

"Sorry to interrupt."

She cranes her head around me. "Hush, Hoss. Go to bed."

He whines and trots off into the darkness. I stare at the yard, impressed by her command.

"Come in." She moves to the side for me to enter.

My eyes gravitate to her shorts and matching shirt. I try not to stare at the daisy-print pajamas. Then heat rises up my neck when I imagine Toby staring at them—or worse, what's under them.

I ball my hands into fists, ready to punch his lights out. How dare that hippie take advantage of her.

"Where is he?"

"Probably the pen. He sneaks out all the time and can get back in."

I shake my head. "I'm not talking about Hoss."

Daisy waves her hand dismissively. "Oh, he's in the bed."

My blood boils under my skin until I'm itching all over. I tighten my fists until my knuckles whiten. That's it. I can't stay calm any longer. I march past Daisy toward her room.

I've never been in there because, obviously, I'm a gentleman unlike others. But I know where it is. I sling open the cracked door and scan the room.

No sign of Toby or anything of a man's to indicate he's been here.

"That punk better hide."

"Punk?"

I spin around to Daisy behind me.

"Yeah, where is he?"

She laughs as if this is funny. "In the bed."

I rush toward the bed and throw back the covers with one hand, the other still in a fist. I draw back my hand to punch, then drop it when I see a goat, in a onesie, snoring.

"Mullet?"

"Yes. I told you he sleeps in the bed."

I blink, both confused and embarrassed. I was within seconds of punching a pet goat to defend her honor.

"Where's Toby?"

"Toby?"

I flare my nostrils, a little tired of Daisy playing innocent.

"Yes, Toby. I know y'all went out, and I'm pretty sure that's his ride out front."

She crosses her arms. "We did go out, but he left hours ago."

"Why is the station wagon here?"

"He rode home with Prissy."

"Prissy? From Waffle House?"

Daisy nods. "His car broke down and she took him

home. Bradley was going to call you tomorrow to come fix it or tow it, or whatever it needs."

I sigh and re-cover Mullet. He snores lightly, not having a clue we're even in here.

"I'm sorry, Daisy." I run a hand through my hair and contemplate the best way to start this conversation. "Bradley said you thought I was seeing someone else, and I'm not."

She frowns. "Yeah, the woman at the movies. I suspect she's the same woman Adrianne saw you with in the park."

"She's my sister."

Her eyes widen. "You went out with your sister?"

"No." I wrinkle my face. "What is wrong with you people?"

Daisy shrugs. "We're in Alabama, so you never know."

I shake my head. "I found out at the movies I have a half-sister. She walked up and dropped that bomb on me. She has no other family but my mom, and you know what she's like."

Daisy presses her lips together and her features soften.

"She wanted to get to know me, so we've met up a few times in Tuscaloosa. She's in college there, and I didn't want everyone here seeing us and asking who she was. Having a sister isn't something I expected or want announced in town until I get used to it myself."

Daisy steps toward me, and my heart picks up a beat with every inch she comes closer. She stops a few inches away and grazes her hand down my arm. My veins light up with the voltage of a hundred Mustang engines at her fingertips. I've missed her touch so much.

"I'm sorry too. I'm insecure from never having dated. Adrianne's had so many crappy guys, she convinced me to be cautious."

I nod. "Understood. I'm sorry for accusing you of Toby staying over."

Daisy laughs. "That was pretty low of you."

I frown as she continues.

"I mean, I wouldn't do that, but if I did, Toby?"

I chuckle. "My thoughts exactly. That's why I was ready to punch his brains out."

We both glance at the bed. The covers move up and down slightly with Mullet's soft snores. Daisy snorts, and we both laugh.

After a minute, her face straightens. She stares at the ground and fumbles with the hem of her shirt. Then she lifts her eyes to me. "I thought you didn't like me because I'm quirky."

"What? I love how you are."

"You don't think I have too many goats?"

I shake my head, then stop. "Well, maybe one too many."

"I told you, Hoss is a rescue. Any day now, he can be rehomed."

"Good."

She swats at my arm. This time, I catch her hand and hold it. I pull her closer, closing the few painful inches separating us.

She lifts her head and smiles. As much as I adore her smile, I abandon the view to draw her in for a kiss. She loops her hands around the back of my neck and kisses me back.

We stand there for several minutes of pure bliss until something nudges the back of my leg. I break away just enough to glance behind me.

Mullet head butts my thigh and bleats. I ruffle his head, and he wags his tail.

"Yes, I missed you too."

Daisy laughs. "Mullet, you'll have to wait your turn."

"Yes, not yet, boy. Daisy is the GOAT to me."

Daisy giggles more as I dip her and kiss her again. We

stay like this until we're both out of breath. Then I smile at her and kiss her on the forehead. "See you tomorrow when I take a look at that piece of crap outside?"

She nods. "You can expect a complimentary massage as payment."

I grin. "Best deal I've ever made."

I back away, letting our hands linger until I can no longer hold hers without pulling her. Then I let go, content knowing I'll hold her again tomorrow.

Something tells me I'll have no trouble sleeping soundly when I get home.

Daisy

Kyle and I stare at the station wagon. He messes with something else under the hood, then palms the back of his neck and sighs.

"I can't work on an engine run from vegetable oil without possibly blowing it up, and myself in the process."

I twist my lips. "So take it back?"

He closes the hood and nods. "Do you know where Toby lives?"

"Yeah, he's at a campground in Tuscaloosa."

"Okay, give me about an hour to go get the wrecker. If you've got his number or something, let him know we're bringing it."

"Gotcha." I smile at Kyle, then head in the house.

I have Toby's number on my phone from when he called me about the details of our date. I snort. Some date that was.

In the end, it worked out as it should. I got Kyle back, and I didn't like Toby anyway. I just took a little bruise to the ego on the way there. Here I was preparing how to let Toby down easy, then he passed over me for Prissy.

Ah, who cares? Kyle and I are back together.

I hear his Jeep pull away and find my phone. I go to the recent calls for Toby's number since I didn't bother to save it in my phone. Shows how much faith I had in us having a thing.

It rings three times, then a woman answers. By the raspiness of her voice, I know it's Prissy.

"Hey, uh, Prissy?"

"Yes, who's this?"

"Daisy."

"Oh, sweet Daisy. I meant to apologize to you for stealing your man. We had this weird instant-love vibe."

"No hard feelings."

"Thanks, hon. But I hate to be the man stealer. It always seems to happen like that for me."

It does? What kind of men is she stealing?

"No, seriously, Prissy, it was our first date, and I'm back with Kyle, so . . ."

"Well, that's just great."

"Yeah, um, I called to let Toby know we're going to bring back the station wagon."

"Okay. Kyle fixed it?"

"Not exactly. He doesn't have any experience with vegetable-oil motors. He's more of a gas-only mechanic."

"Oh, I see."

"If one of you will be around, we can bring it back in a few hours."

Prissy mumbles something away from the phone before answering me. "Yeah, we'll be home."

I raise my brows. She's already calling Toby's place home. After one night? It takes a minute for me to find my voice.

"Sounds good. See you soon." I hang up and shake my head.

This intel should help me prove to Mom why Toby is wrong for me. Although she loves him, I'm certain she'll be happy I'm back with Kyle. If for no other reason than she likes his butt.

I try and dislodge the thought of Mom ogling Kyle's butt from my brain as I get ready to leave. The chickens and goats need fed before we head to Tuscaloosa.

I start with the chickens and finish in the house with Mullet. He's the only one I can trust to eat in here. I fix him a bowl of cereal with minimal milk per his liking—one-half Cheerios and one-half Fruit Loops.

Kyle comes in when I'm pouring the milk.

"We can eat in Tuscaloosa."

"Oh, this is for Mullet."

His eyes widen as Mullet takes his seat at the table and bleats when I push the bowl in front of him.

"You're welcome." I pet Mullet's head.

He laps up the cereal without spilling a drop. I comb my fingers over his mullet and ruffle his fur.

"Be good. I left the doggy door unlocked for you."

Kyle is still mesmerized by Mullet eating like a proper human when we walk out the door. He has to help me into the wrecker, which isn't short-people friendly.

He checks the station wagon one more time to make sure it's secure before we drive away.

We chat and listen to the radio on the drive. I relax against the seat, soaking in our conversation. I've missed Kyle in every way, not just romantically. We had an easy friendship long before our first kiss.

"It's at the state park. We need to turn right on the next main road."

"Okay." He leans forward and watches the road signs.

We drive down a winding road by a lake that leads to a park entrance. Kyle rolls down his window when we stop to pay.

"Hello, how many?"

"Two adults," Kyle answers.

He pays the woman taking admission.

I slide closer to the open window. "Hi, could you direct us to the campground where Toby Cobblestone is staying?"

"Just a moment."

She steps inside the hut and returns with a folder. After flipping a few pages, she looks up. "His spot is in the back. Very last campsite." She points ahead of us. "Follow this main road toward the end. You'll find an area of tents. His name should be on the lot."

"Thanks." I smile again.

"Uh-huh. Enjoy your visit."

"Thanks," Kyle replies. He waves a hand, then turns to me. "He's in a tent?"

"Are you surprised?"

Kyle shakes his head and hangs his arm out the open window. I roll down my window and survey the park as we pass playgrounds, grilling areas, RVs, and a small beach area. The water is filled with people swimming near the sand and others fishing and canoeing in deeper parts.

Right past a curve in the road is an area full of tents. The road dead-ends into a cul-de-sac. I turn to Kyle. "This has to be it."

He turns into the smaller road leading to a row of tents. I crane my head out the window and watch for a name I recognize.

"This must be it on my side."

I twist toward Kyle. "Do you see his name?"

"I don't have to." He widens his eyes at me, then cocks his head toward the left.

Prissy is in a bikini hanging sheets on a clothesline. Toby sits nearby picking a ukulele.

"Now that's something you don't see every day," I observe.

"Thank God," Kyle adds.

We laugh a little, then he works on parking the wrecker where he can easily dismount the station wagon in their yard. To Toby's credit, he has a big lot. Large enough for a firepit area, clothesline, and cornhole boards set at regulation distance. Pretty impressive for someone living in a tent.

"Hey, y'all." Prissy waves her arm when we get out.

"Hi."

She's so thin and tan that from a long distance, someone might mistake her for a strip of leather.

"If I'd known y'all were coming around lunchtime, I'd have thrown extra Spam on the grill."

"Thanks for the offer, but we're headed to eat after this." Kyle says that with a straighter face than I ever could.

He gets to work unloading the station wagon and suggests a few places around Tuscaloosa that might could fix it. "Worst case, I can come put a new motor in it and you can go back to using gas."

Toby shakes his head. "I appreciate it, but you know what they say."

He stares at us until Kyle finally speaks up. "I'm afraid I don't know what they say."

"Once you go vegetarian, you never go back."

Kyle strokes his jawline. "Never heard that one."

"I have." Prissy beams. "It's on a commercial for food."

"Yeah, okay." Kyle turns to me. "Ready?"

"Yes," I say a little too enthusiastically.

Toby stretches out his hand and Kyle shakes it. "We need to all hang sometime, let me return the favor."

Kyle shakes his head. "Nah, this one's on me. Take care."

We climb in the wrecker and head out of the park. Kyle peers at the picnic tables as we leave. "I would say it's a nice day for a picnic, but I'm afraid they'd join us."

I laugh. "Let's don't chance it."

"There is someone I'd like you to meet while we're in town." He takes his phone and scrolls. He holds it where I can see the contact. It reads "Karson (sister)." I raise my brows.

"Is that okay?" He pulls the phone toward him. "She hasn't met anyone in my family yet. I wanted her to meet you first."

"Really?"

He nods. "Yeah, and I already know she doesn't have class right now."

My heart flutters. I'm honored he wants her to meet me before his dad. "Sure."

Kyle smiles and presses the phone to dial her number. I listen to his end of the conversation as they pick a place to eat. They decide on Mexican, which is perfect to me. I like Mexican, but avoid Enchilada like the plague. It's nice to eat at a place that doesn't double as a laxative.

We leave the park and drive a few miles to the restaurant and park up front. The woman I once envied and semi-hated at the same time stands at the door smiling. I hop down from the wrecker and join Kyle.

"Daisy?" We're within maybe ten feet when she greets us.

"Hi, you must be Karson."

She leaps forward and wraps me in a hug. I raise my arms and hug her back, sensing this is a genuine hug. She pulls back and smiles.

I study her face for the first time and notice she has the

same eyes as Kyle. A dark blue color I haven't seen on anyone else. That alone convinces me they are siblings.

We go inside and get a table. Karson pulls a menu from the condiment stand and smiles widely at the two of us. "I'm so happy things worked out. Last time I ate lunch with Kyle, he mentioned you wanted to take a break. He was so sulky." She giggles.

"You, sulky?" I glance at Kyle, who is the most even-tempered, easygoing guy.

"What can I say? You have that effect on me."

He grins, and I narrow my eyes. Karson laughs more. I turn my head forward and a sudden wave of fear washes through me as I watch her.

Does she know she's the reason I told Kyle I wanted a break? Not that it matters now, but I have this itching desire to come clean just in case.

"Uh, Karson?"

"Yeah?" She smiles, anticipating what I have to say like Mullet anticipating cereal.

"Hi, do you know what you'd like to drink?"

I jerk my head toward the waitress, happy for the interruption. We give her our drink orders, then she leaves. I drop my gaze to the menu, as I have no idea what this place serves.

Well, they serve Mexican, but I'm optimistic for something cooler than the Enchilada special.

"Karson?" I keep my eyes on the menu. It's easier to say this without looking her in the eye.

"Yeah?"

"I have a confession." I swallow.

The waitress pops back in and slides drinks on the table. I take a huge gulp of my water, not bothering to stick a straw in first.

Kyle and Karson order, then everyone stares at me

gulping my water. I set my glass down and sigh. "Hot day." I laugh nervously, then stare at the waitress. "Fish tacos."

I went with something I would never get at Enchilada. They would use catfish at best, but most likely sardines.

"I'll get that right in." She leaves again.

I force myself to look at Karson.

"Karson, I thought Kyle was seeing you. That's why I told him we needed a break."

Kyle gets silent. Karson's face falls. Gosh, I'm a horrible person.

"But you're okay with us hanging out now, right?"

I bite back a laugh. "Absolutely. This was before I knew he had a sister."

Her face deadpans for a split second, then her mouth opens. "Ohhhh." She laughs so loud, the couple in the booth across from us stares.

"If you only knew how he talks about you, Daisy, you'd have nothing to worry about. Kyle is so in love with you."

I clutch my glass, and my eyes widen.

Karson covers her mouth and winces at Kyle. "Whoops."

I turn to him. "Love?"

He squirms in his chair like he's nervous. "I wanted to tell you several times before, especially last night, but I wanted the timing to be perfect."

I laugh. "You do realize where we live and the kind of things we deal with every day? I mean, we just delivered a broken-down station wagon to a guy in a tent."

Kyle laughs. "You make a good point."

He smiles at me and takes my hand. I stare into his dark eyes and melt like a bucket of cheese dip. He wraps his other hand around our interlocked fingers.

"Daisy Mae Duncan, I love you."

Out of impulse, I pull him to me with my free hand. I full-on kiss him smack in the middle of the Mexican place.

Is this inappropriate behavior for a proper Southern woman? Yes. But the man I've always admired from afar is staring at me, saying he loves me. Who could blame me?

I soon forget where we are and get lost in kissing Kyle. It's a hot kiss too. So hot that steam hits my face.

"Hot plate!"

I flinch and Kyle pulls away. That was steam . . . from his fajitas. I press my lips together and give an apologetic look to the mom next table over who's covering her toddler's eyes.

Karson has a dreamy look on her face and smiles at me and Kyle. "I can't wait to be an aunt."

We all laugh for a minute, before I say, "You already are, to a bunch of goats and chickens."

Kyle wraps an arm around my shoulder and kisses my cheek. That's all the reassurance I need that this man loves me in spite of all my goats.

EPILOGUE

A Few Months Later

Kyle

I set chairs around the tables in my yard. Good thing the weather is cooling down and fair, since I have more room outside than in. It doesn't help that I often have a truck broken apart behind my couch.

Daisy and I really need to work on our use of space if we ever plan to marry. I have vehicles in my living room, and she uses two rooms of a three-bedroom house for her business.

I don't want to put the cart before the horse, but I have toyed with the idea of one day building a house beside my shopdominium and converting this place to hold her businesses too.

Only thing is we need to figure out where to put all the animals.

Daisy comes from inside with a covered platter. I move some plates down so she can set it on the long table by the house.

"All the burgers are ready," she says.

"Good, does Granny need anything else?"

She shakes her head. "She's finishing up the cake now."

"Perfect."

I wrap my arms around her waist and rest my chin on her head. She hugs her arms around mine. I give her a quick squeeze before stepping back. "Thanks for all your help."

"Of course." She smiles. "And Karson is still clueless. She texted me about an hour ago asking if she could bring anything."

"Good to know."

When Daisy found out Karson's birthday was coming up, she wanted to surprise her with a party. Karson's only extended family is mine, which isn't her real family. Although Granny told her she was officially adopted by the Tolberts the first time they met.

She will love this surprise, and I love Daisy even more for coming up with the idea. That is, if I could love her more. I may or may not google "best engagement rings for women who work with farm animals" when I have trouble sleeping.

I set up the last of the chairs, then follow Daisy into the house. She busies herself pouring chips in bowls and getting dips out of my refrigerator. Granny finishes drawing Karson's name on the cake.

"That looks great, Mrs. Maudy."

Granny swats at Daisy. "Thank you, but please, call me Granny."

Daisy blushes. "Yes, ma'am, Granny."

Granny pats her arm and laughs. "Do you want to leave it in here, Kyle?"

"For now."

A car pulls up outside, and we all turn to the window. Except for Dad and Gramps, who are busy holding down my couch and recliner.

Daisy hurries toward the door. "It's Adrianne and JoJo with Grandpa Joe."

"Good, we've got a little time." I want everything in place before Karson gets here.

Daisy opens the door and welcomes them. Then she returns to the kitchen with Adrianne. They gather the chips and dips, and take them outside. JoJo leads Grandpa Joe to the living room. They sit beside Gramps.

"Hey, Joe. How's the weather been at your place?"

I laugh at the old men talking about the weather. They live maybe half an hour apart at best.

The women return for napkins and silverware as Granny counts out nineteen candles from the pack of twenty-four she bought at Dollar General this afternoon.

Gravel slings against the side of my house, calling my attention. The side door swings open to Bradley, out of breath.

"The birthday girl is on her way. She will be here in five."

"Okay?" I raise my brows, and everyone stares like he's insane.

"What did he say?" Grandpa Joe yells at JoJo. He quietly explains what's going on.

"We can all go outside, then, I guess."

Both old men mumble complaints of how they're not getting up until it's time to eat.

"I'll bring her in here, then. Everyone pay attention for when the door opens." I go outside to meet Karson.

An old pickup pulls into the driveway, and Paul hops out. I run a hand over my head. Bradley can't be that off.

"Hey there, Kyle. I hear there's a party here."

There's no time to get rid of Paul, so I have no choice but to send him inside.

I sigh. "Come on in."

He marches toward the porch, hands on his hips. When he gets to the door, I open it.

"Surprise!" everyone yells.

Paul jumps in front of me and claps. "For me?"

He laughs as everyone shares confused glances. Granny stands in the center with Karson's cake, candles lit.

Paul struts toward her and blows out the candles. Granny gives him a stern look and huffs. He reaches toward the cake, but she turns away and shuffles toward the kitchen.

"What happened?"

I turn around to my sister standing in the door.

Daisy's face falls like a lost puppy. She joins me beside Karson, while Bradley jerks Paul toward the back of the room.

"We planned you a birthday party. Sorry, the surprise got ruined." Daisy frowns.

Tears well up in Karson's eyes. Daisy's shoulders drop, and she hugs my sister. "We have a cake, but the candles might not light again. I apologize."

Karson pulls back and laughs through her tears. "I'm not upset."

Daisy wrinkles her forehead. "You're not?"

"Not at all. I'm happy. Nobody's ever cared enough to throw me a surprise party."

Daisy smiles at her, then me.

"We care." I touch Karson's arm. "Want to see your cake?"

She nods and laughs, then follows me to the kitchen. Granny hugs her. Out of nowhere, Grandpa Joe starts belting out "Happy Birthday." One by one, everyone joins.

Karson waves and blows kisses when we finish. Granny takes the cake slicer and cuts her the first piece. Paul wiggles his way over for the next piece. Bradley is quick on his heels, making sure he doesn't get more than his fair share.

Everyone else files in line, and Daisy announces that burgers and all the fixings are set up outside. She hurries toward the refrigerator to get the tea and lemonade we kept cool until the last minute. I touch her elbow before she opens the refrigerator door.

"Come with me a minute."

I lead her to my room and hand her a gift bag.

"Thanks, I'll put it with the others." She starts toward the door.

I grab her hand. "No, it's not for Karson. It's for you."

She turns and grins. "Me? Why?"

I shrug. "I wanted to get you something to show how much I appreciate all you did for this party, and all you do for me all the time."

She smiles wider and takes the tissue from the top, then pulls out a throw pillow. She drops the bag and laughs. The pillow is similar to the first I bought her, but with a different message: "You're the GOAT."

I draw her toward me. "No matter what, I want you to know you'll always be the greatest of all time to me."

I wrap my arms around her. The pillow squishes between us until I jerk it out of the way and toss it on my bed. Then I close the few inches separating us and kiss her in a way that I hope says I want to kiss her, and only her, for the rest of my life.

ACKNOWLEDGMENTS

First, I'd like to thank God for giving me creative ideas and placing the right people in my path to help see them to fruition.

My husband, Blake, gets credit next for always supporting my writing endeavors, even if he finds my stories a little too "girly."

Thanks to my friend, Brittany, for allowing me to put a spin on one of her famous stories. IYKYK!

I also want to thank my readers and ARC team for their support. You. Are. Awesome! I could not do what I do without my readers and support team. I love y'all!

Of course, I'd like to thank my editor, Joanne. She's always a pleasure to work with and polishes my books to help them shine.

ABOUT THE AUTHOR

Kaci Lane is a journalist turned fiction writer who believes all stories should have a happy ending. While unsuccessfully trying to learn Spanish for a decade, she has become fluent in sarcasm, Southern belle and movie quotes. She is married to a Southern Gentleman and has two young children who help keep her humility in check. Connect with her on kacilane.com or Facebook.

BOOKS BY KACI LANE

Bama Boys Series*

Hunting for Love

Chicken about Love

Hammered by Love

Cutting out Love

Geared for Love

Apple Cart County Christmas

Christmas in Dixie

Crazy Rich Rednecks

Schooled on Love Series

Taco Truck Takedown

Side Hustle

Buggy List

Off-Season

Books in Shared Series with Other Authors

No Time for Traditions

A Perfect Match in Silver Leaf Falls

*If you enjoyed the Bama Boys books, revisit Apple Cart County with the Christmas in Applecart series, starting with *Christmas in Dixie*. Set in Apple Cart, Alabama, it includes secondary characters from the Bama Boys series.

www.ingramcontent.com/pod-product-compliance
Lightning Source LLC
LaVergne TN
LVHW091717070526
838199LV00050B/2434